The Hollows Insider

contents

Chapter 1

Chapter 2

Chapter 5

Chapter 6

Chapter 6

(continued)

Chapter 7

Chapter 8

Chapter 9

Acknowledgments

I would like to thank first my editor, Diana Gill, who set me this daunting task and then stoically took what I gave her, seeing what I was trying to convey in my messy, scattered presentation done in a program never meant to do more than simple text. I'd also like to thank the production crew at Harper Voyager—especially associate editor Will Hinton, production editor Rachel Meyers, production manager Nyamekye Waliyaya, designers Paula Szafranski and Timothy Shaner, and copy editor Laurie McGee—who then took my messy scrawl and made my vision look like I always saw it in my mind. And I'd like to thank my agent, Richard Curtis, who told me it looked good when I needed to hear that the most.

I'd also like to thank Mark Rude, who did most of the pencil artwork you see here in the pages.

And, finally, I'd like to thank the readers at my Drama Box blog, who came forth enthusiastically and submitted photos for the newspaper articles. You will always continue to amaze me.

Dear Reader,

When my editor first came to me with the idea of a world book to help explain the Hollows, I was enthusiastic, but clueless.

Having no idea what she was looking for, I went to others in my genre to see how they condensed their worlds down to one volume. Spells, descriptions, an explanation of the two branches of magic, and maybe a little information in the form of maps and such. Sure! I could do that! Then I started to worry. How was I going to do that? Where do I even start?

Anyone who has tried to explain the Hollows knows what I mean. Yes, it is about a witch living with a vampire and a pixy solving paranormal crimes, but it's more than that. The Hollows is a web of cultures interwoven with each other, having the same pains, the same joys that we are familiar with, but that stem from a slightly different point of view. Trying to pull it all together threw me into a mild panic. Everything I was putting on the page was stale and dry. The Hollows was alive, and I was failing to capture it — until one morning when I slipped into my storytelling voice, and it all fell into place as if by, well, magic.

So here is the Hollows, taken from the viewpoint of someone who has lived within it, never really understanding it — yet trying to make sense of it. I invite you now to live two years with blogger and columnist Devin Crossman as he investigates the Hollows with an insider's eye.

I hope that you enjoy this deeper look into the Hollows. Bringing it all together for you was a tremendously fun endeavor, even if I couldn't fit everything in. And if you spot any mistakes, I'm blaming Devin. He's an unreliable narrator.

Kim Harrison

The Hollows Insider

Chapter 1

Kalamack Industries, Inc

Jonathan Davaros
Chief Personnel Officer
Kalamack Industries, Inc
Building A
15 Rolling Acres
Cincinnati, OH 45239

INTEROFFICE MEMO

To: Trenton Kalamack
From: Jonathan Davaros
cc:
Date: 4/6/06
Re: Contact Flag on Rachel Morgan

Sa'han,

The contact flag that you put on Rachel Morgan has been tripped by a Mr. Devin Crossman. He currently works for a local paper in the Hollows called the *Hollows Gazette* (circulation 7,000) and has shown interest in Ms. Morgan inasmuch as he has tried to gain information about her from both her employer at Inderland Security (I.S.) and the Federal Inderland Bureau (FIB). He has also attempted to file a complaint with the I.S. for a misfired charm that Ms. Morgan invoked in his vicinity. Apparently the man now has no hair.

It's my belief that this matter will be quickly dropped, despite the man's contacts with the *Hollows Gazette*. He's not on staff, but a popular blogger of some note that the *Gazette* has contracted to help boost their circulation. Please advise as to how you would like to proceed.

Yours,

Jonathan

Devin's
Journal
Entry

April 6, 2006

I got hit with a misfired spell on the bus two days ago on my way home from the mall. I wasn't paying any attention when a Were got on with a TV tucked under his arm, and I didn't duck fast enough when the witch chasing him invoked a charm that was apparently supposed to tangle his feet. Instead, it took his hair off. Mine too. And the woman sitting behind me. My God, that woman could scream. I don't blame her. The sensation of your hair falling off is one I don't want to repeat.

The next thing I know, the witch is shouting that she's an I.S. runner and for the Were to freeze. The driver is yelling at her, the woman behind me is screaming, and I can't see the paper I was reading because it's covered with my hair.

The Were laughed and dove out the window, leaving his hair and the TV behind, the witch in hot pursuit. I know he was a Were because he had tattoos all over him. I have never felt so violated in my entire life, and I can do nothing.

I tried filing a complaint with Inderland Security and got nowhere, spending thirty minutes on the phone with the I.S. attempting to find out who this woman was. It wasn't until I dropped my "Gazette Reporter" status that the complaint person directed me to the runner division. After an hour of phone tag, the head of the runner division informed me that he couldn't tell me which employee had accidentally spelled me unless I filed an official complaint. When I told him the woman in the complaint department sent me to him, he dropped my call while transferring me to his superior.

I'd let this go, except that I think there might be a story here, either in the mismanagement of the I.S. putting badly trained runners on the street, or corruption in the I.S. with them hiding their mistakes. I can't be the only person who has suffered from a misfired charm or bad spell. Interestingly enough, when I made the incident the focus of my column yesterday, I got about 30 angry e-mails.

I didn't have any luck at City Hall finding out who this red-haired woman is, even in the employment records. I had to go to the FIB to get her name. According to the records they keep on I.S. personnel, the woman who spelled me goes by the name Rachel Morgan. I'm not surprised that the Federal Inderland Bureau has better—or more accessible, perhaps—records than the I.S. The human-run FIB has to have some way to compete with Inderlanders, and gathering data doesn't take magic.

I did, however, have some success at the I.S. when I got a hold of a bag of files scheduled to be shredded. It was full of outdated species descriptions that might come in handy now that I'm writing for a mostly Inderlander audience after taking the job at the Gazette. I had to bribe a pixy for the documents, if you can believe it. They were paying him a jar of honey to watch them until the shredding company came. All it took was two jars to go dumpster-diving without his raising the alarm. The best part is that I can get reimbursed for the honey. Cha-ching! I'm sort of liking this part about working for the man. I put the itch cream on my expense report, too. Apparently pixy dust is an irritant. We'll see if it gets through. That stuff was expensive.

The I.S. species descriptions are outdated, but way better than anything I've ever seen. I didn't realize that there were two kinds of magic. The one that hit me was apparently a potion, which means my hair will grow back, thank God.

Trying to find out more about this woman is turning out to be harder than I thought, which could be a problem if I can't move faster on this. The paper is a stickler about having my column in by a certain time every day. I miss being able to post when I feel like it, but the steady paycheck is nice.

The woman I ran into at the <u>Gazette</u> is nice, too, a Ms. Winnie Gradenko. I might ask her out if she doesn't have a boyfriend. Apparently she just started at the paper. Moved in from a farm somewhere.

Hallows Gazette
EXPENSE REPORT

Employee:	Devin Crossman
Employee ID:	84-1698
Phone:	
Fax:	
E-Mail:	dcrossman@hollowsgazette.com

Invoice No.:	0416200649
Month/Year:	April/2006

Description	Date	Amount	Approved	
jar of honey / pixy bribe	4/5	2.37	Yes	2.37
anti-itch cream	4/5	15.95	No	
Total:		18.32	Total:	2.37

Review:			
Reviewed by:	Print		Sign
Approved:	Sandra Stamford		Sandra Stamford
	Yes with adjustments		
Comments:	Next time, don't piss off the pixies.		

Failure to attach original receipts will result in decline of reimbursement. Do not fill in shaded areas.

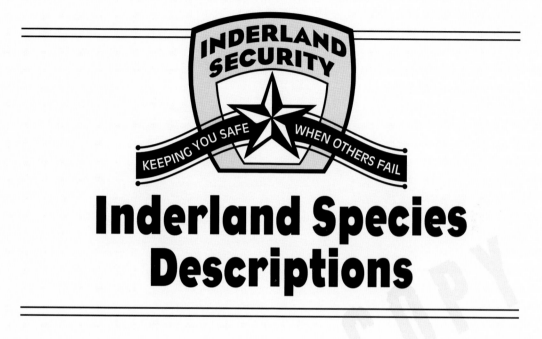

Inderland Species Descriptions

INTERNAL DOCUMENT

SHRED
AUTHORIZED _DIH_
DATE _4/3/06_

BANSHEE

CREATED: October 27, 1967

LATEST REVISION: February 9, 2001

557082-3499-01

DOCUMENT SHEPHERD: Travis B. Weston

Officer of Internal Documents

555-6979 (ext 720)

ORIGINAL PRESENTER: Jerry Ledbetter

BANSHEE

OVERVIEW: Body type is indistinguish-
able from human in cursory look.

INTEGRATION: High

DISRUPTION POTENTIAL: High

POPULATION: Less than 1000

OLFACTORY: Slight elevation over
human standard

AUDITORY: Within human standard

ENDURANCE: Low

LIFE SPAN: Estimated up to 400 years

DIET: See below

CULTURE: Solitary

T4 SENSITIVITY: Negative

Diet

- Auravore. Banshees exist entirely on the energy pulled from other species: in essence, they consume auras. In small amounts, spread over time, aura loss is replaced with only minor damage to the victim. Most donors are unaware that they're being fed upon, and the one-sided relationship can span years or decades. However, in large amounts or in quick succession, aura loss can cause death to the donor.

- Banshees can store emotional energy in crystalline "tears" that they produce themselves. These tears are black when holding energy, clear when not. Empty tears are often left illegally in emotionally charged areas with the intent to return and collect the stored energy at a later date. This can cause serious harm as it indiscriminately siphons aura energy with no regard to safe levels. This practice has been illegal since the Turn.

- Banshees can passively find enough substance in a walk through a busy mall to sustain themselves, but they're constantly applying pressure to the I.S. to allow

more aggressive feeding levels. To do so would be a serious error as it would allow more banshee children to be engendered. As banshees are apex predators, their numbers need to be closely monitored and regulated.

Sleep Patterns

- Diurnal to better support their feeding habits.

Reproduction

- Modified human reproduction, resulting in haploid children nearly genetically identical to their mother. Entire species is female.
- Banshees possess exactly half the genetic information of a normal human. Children are engendered with both a physical exchange of sperm and an energy draw of an aura from a human male. This usually kills the father outright. (See Dox:SS.7898.460.1.) Through a means not fully investigated, the male's genetic information is gradually lost during the first week of gestation, leaving very little of the father's genetic code incorporated. This makes banshee family lines all but unchanging through the centuries.
- Banshee infants require huge amounts of emotional energy. Most banshees are able to support only one or two children their entire long lives.
- Banshee children feed indiscriminately their first five years, often killing their playmates or care providers if not closely supervised.

Species Origin

- Unknown, but banshees claim to be older than vampires. Anderson texts support this, but it can't be verified with any certainty.
- It was once thought that vampires and banshees were closely related, as both banshees and the undead vampires require the energy naturally extruded from living souls. This theory is currently out of favor, but banshees still contend that vampires are the Neanderthals of their species, needing the visual clues of blood loss to know when to cease feeding on the aura.

BANSHEE

Interaction with Other Species

- Surprisingly meek for an apex predator, banshees are the most feared Inderlander species by those who know their potential threat. Banshees are perpetually balanced on extinction, keeping to the fringes of society where they can feed without notice.
- This species prefers to feed from humans, who are generally unaware of them. Banshees will often take a menial job at a low wage to surround themselves with unhappy people, then create unrest between coworkers in order to feed more richly. They have been called psychic vampires, a definition that fits surprisingly well.
- Banshees have no natural enemies, but they don't get along well with pixies, the only Inderland species who can naturally see auras.

Political Strengths

- Not political outside of their own species.
- Banshees have a history of policing themselves long before the Turn, and continue to do so to this day, eliminating members who feed heavily, and carelessly, enough to be noticed.

Species Assets

- Can outright kill individuals much stronger than themselves by stripping the victim's soul's energy in a quick burst.
- Banshees are unable to kill undead vampires outright, but stripping their borrowed aura will send the undead into the sun.
- Live a long time and have numerous resources, stockpiled over the centuries.
- Average intelligence, but appear smarter given long life span and accumulated knowledge.

BANSHEE

Species Vulnerabilities

- Physically, banshees are frail and lack extended senses.
- Have a tendency to look down on all other species, underestimating them.
- It takes several unnatural deaths in quick succession to engender a child.
- Because of their needs, they're highly territorial and will not leave an area they have claimed.
- Banshees are required to have a tear on file at the I.S. for individual identification.
- Pupils dilate during active feeding, giving their intentions away.

Overall Assessment

- The I.S. has no policy on banshees. Due to their "toxic" nature, even the undead are vulnerable. If a banshee steps out of line, the only recourse, saving allowing the transgression, is assassination. Knowing this, banshees are reticent in their illegal takes.
- Banshees do not represent a significant addition to the tax base.
- This is a highly dangerous species and should be handled only by highly experienced I.S. agents, and never alone.

Notes: _____

_____

_____

Reviewed by _____

          Print   Date   **No**
FFHC

_____

          Signature   PIC   **Green**
Level

DEMON

CREATED: October 27, 1967
LATEST REVISION: April 29, 2005

755920-4991-22

DOCUMENT SHEPHERD: Alex Stanton
Officer of Internal Documents
555-6979 (ext 43)
ORIGINAL PRESENTER: Marty Johanason

DEMON

OVERVIEW: Usual appearance is standard human form, but can vary.
INTEGRATION: Low
DISRUPTION POTENTIAL: High
POPULATION: Unknown
OLFACTORY: Within human standard
AUDITORY: Higher than human norm

ENDURANCE: Unknown
LIFE SPAN: Unknown
DIET: Unknown
CULTURE: Gregarious
T4 SENSITIVITY: Unknown, presumed negative

Sleep Patterns

■ Unknown, presumed to be attuned to a similar schedule as witches or vampires.

Reproduction

■ Unable to reproduce due to nearly all female demons having been assassinated by elves before they migrated to reality. Last demon born was five thousand years ago.

Species Origin

■ Until recently, it was believed demons evolved in the ever-after. Recent interviews with an anonymous, questionable source claims demons began in reality and were trapped in the ever-after by a misspoken curse when they tried to exile elves nearly six thousand years ago. (See DOX: D.975.3.)

ELF

CREATED: November 13, 1967
LATEST REVISION: February 6, 2001

390100-9750-30

DOCUMENT SHEPHERD: Shanny M. Michaels
Officer of Internal Documents
555-6979 (ext 772)

ORIGINAL PRESENTER: Susan Leans

ELF

OVERVIEW: Body type is standard human.
Hid well before the Turn.
Currently playing extinct.
INTEGRATION: High
DISRUPTION POTENTIAL: High
POPULATION: Estimated between 30,000 and 40,000

OLFACTORY: Slightly higher than human
AUDITORY: Slightly higher than human
ENDURANCE: Markedly high
LIFE SPAN: Average 160 years after infancy
DIET: Omnivore
CULTURE: Gregarious
T4 SENSITIVITY: See below

Sleep Patterns
■ Crepuscular, preferring to sleep four hours at noon and at midnight.

Reproduction
■ Difficult due to decaying genetic issues, but able to hybridize with humans with minimal difficulty.

Species Origin
■ Very little is known about this fiercely secretive species. Once thought to have originated in the ever-after, it's now believed that elves began in reality and were exiled to the ever-after by the demons sometime around five thousand years ago. It's well documented that, however they got there, elves migrated back into reality two thousand years ago. (See DOX: 990.3.)
■ It's difficult in present day to find an elf with a pure genome given the elven history of hybridizing with humans in an effort to save their species. Their

genome was thrown into a cascading failure an estimated six thousand years ago by a demon curse.

Interaction with Other Species

- Elves committed "self-genocide" on paper during the Turn, preferring to become a seemingly extinct species than to risk actual genocide by humans upset by the ancient elven practice of abducting children and leaving their own failing infants (cf. changelings). In truth, many marginal elves did perish during the Turn before the link between the Angel tomato and the virus was discovered. Pure-blooded elves were not affected by the Angel T4 virus, whereas those who carried too much human DNA died, which might be the source of the false rumor that elves engineered the virus.
- Elves have a highly complex social structure aligned more closely to pixies than any other species, but they adapt well to human society and can function invisibly within it.
- Elves are rare prey food for the undead, even though the undead enjoy their blood, which is said to taste of cinnamon and wine.
- Elves are unique among Inderlanders in that they have a distinct, ancient language. Much of it has been lost, leaving only a few salutations and honorifics.

Political Strengths

- This species is naturally highly political, and elves are quietly running most of the farming and drug industry through personal holdings, and much beyond that through blackmail. Internal political structure is based on the family unit.
- Though few in number, elves constitute a large threat to potentially unbalancing the current social structure. Their difficulty in reproducing has been a natural block to possible upsets. This species needs close observation to prevent further disruption.

Species Assets

- Can tolerate extremely low temperatures.
- Able to tap into the ever-after to change reality by using ley line magic, much

ELF

as witches do, but their use of "wild magic" makes the outcome of their spells and charms extremely volatile and unpredictable.

Species Vulnerabilities

◼ The elven species would be extinct without constant and ever-increasing genetic intervention to repair the damage wrought by the species-wide demon curse. This flagrant use of illegal genetic intervention is ignored by the few officials in the know as long as it remains unnoticed, seeing as it is a last-ditch effort to save their vanishing species.

Overall Assessment

◼ Elves are one of the most wily Inderlanders due to their ability to charm others through their highly developed ability to read a person and appear to be what they most desire.

◼ This species was on its way out until the Kalamack family single-handedly developed the genetic research needed to first save them, and then repair their genome one individual at a time. Any hint of threat to bringing their illegal genetic tinkering to the public's awareness is quashed by the incredible web of blackmail this species has on others.

◼ Once fierce warriors who fought demons spell-to-spell, elves now fight battles via economics, making them one of the most dangerous Inderlander species despite their few numbers.

Notes: _____

_____

Reviewed by _____

| Print | Date | **No** |
| | | FFHC |

_____

| Signature | PIC | **Green** |
| | | Level |

FAIRY

CREATED: November 15, 1967

LATEST REVISION: February 12, 2001

199472-3681-43

DOCUMENT SHEPHERD: Shanny Michaels
Officer of Internal Documents
555-6979 (ext 772)

ORIGINAL PRESENTER: Susan Leans

FAIRY

OVERVIEW: Body type is modified human, significantly reduced in size. Most outstanding feature is large, butterfly-like wings. Adult stands 6" tall.

INTEGRATION: Moderate

DISRUPTION POTENTIAL: Moderate

POPULATION: See below

OLFACTORY: Significantly better than human

AUDITORY: Significantly higher than human

ENDURANCE: Unknown

LIFE SPAN: 15–20 years

DIET: Strict insectivore

CULTURE: Gregarious

T4 SENSITIVITY: Negative

Description

■ Fairies have a generalized human body shape with long faces and thin limbs, hollow, lightweight bones for better air travel. Their mothlike wings can be any color and vary within the family unit. They are pale skinned with white hair, and they fashion clothes out of spiderwebs. Thin and gaunt, their appearance is much like a miniature grim reaper with butterfly wings. They speak English with a lisping accent due to their long teeth, which are needed to tear apart insects. Females are shorter than males, but have the same rights and responsibilities as their masculine counterparts. A passive, species-specific magic elevates their voices into the human audible range.

■ Population estimates at their wintering grounds put this species in the several million.

FAIRY

Sleep Patterns

■ Diurnal and nocturnal. Series of short naps in a 24-hour period. Schedule varies widely depending upon the season. Young will sleep significantly more.

Reproduction

■ Method unknown. Suspected that the young are produced in seasonal batches timed to local insect hatchings to give the young the best possible chance of surviving the yearly migration to Mexico.

Species Origin

■ Unknown, but fairies claim to have crossed to reality with the elves two thousand years ago.

Interaction with Other Species

■ Does not associate well with any other species and maintains a militant disregard for pixies.

■ Fairies are responsible for more nuisance calls to the I.S. than any other species. Their habit of destroying a garden to harvest insects puts them at odds with both witches and humans, but their biggest adversaries are pixies vying for the same space, though not the same resources.

■ Pixy/fairy wars are ongoing as soon as the fairies migrate back into a region looking for food. Skirmishes are generally ignored even if property damage results. Young city-fairies will often take the odd job in security to make a name for themselves before seeking a mate.

■ Fairies are not sought out as prey by the undead, probably due to their size.

Political Strengths

■ Not political outside of their own species, fairies are ignored as noncitizens with no rights or responsibilities. Internal political structure seems to be based on military leadership and crosses gender lines. Fairies live in large groups of

unrelated families, taking up residence in abandoned squirrel nests, large bird boxes, or in attics that have access holes. They will often destroy pixy homes to drive them out and take over their garden.

Species Assets

- Able to fly long distances to avoid cold season. Fairies can cause havoc if inclined to, but they will generally ignore people in their search for food if they are ignored in turn.

Species Vulnerabilities

- Small size is an issue.

Overall Assessment

- Not much is known about fairies apart from their migration route. They gather in Mexico for the winter orgy, where alliances are made anew for the next season, and return in late June and July to establish territories and raise young.
- When employed, fairies make reasonable backups; hard to get along with and sticklers with their union rules, but worth the effort as their senses far outstrip even the undead. Interesting note: fairies don't need the food they get in exchange for hours they put in, and seem to take the job to prove to potential mates that they can survive working with people.
- Predation or harassment by animals, humans, or Inderlanders is curtailed at the street level by the fairies themselves by mobbing the offender with poison-ivy-tipped arrows.
- Fairies don't seek revenge for individual, accidental killings, and there's no record of a fairy ever being involved in a homicide or crime.
- Fairy complaints are referred to the Runner Division at the I.S., which functions as more of a stockpile of information than a source of restitution.

FAIRY

■ Fairies do not contribute to the tax structure unless it is within the insurance field. Though destructive and potentially threatening, fairies are best ignored until they leave an area and repairs can be made.

Notes: _____

_____

_____

_____

Reviewed by _____

Print   Date   No

                                          FFHC

_____

Signature   PIC   Green

                                          Level

GARGOYLE

CREATED: October 20, 1967

LATEST REVISION: February 16, 2001

850528-2870-51

DOCUMENT SHEPHERD: Tavis B. Weston
Officer of Internal Documents
555-6979 (ext 720)

ORIGINAL PRESENTER: Jerry Ledbetter

GARGOYLE

OVERVIEW: Biped. See description below. Hid within pre-Turn society on church roofs where they still live today.

INTEGRATION: Low

DISRUPTION POTENTIAL: Low

POPULATION: US population estimated at several hundred thousand.

OLFACTORY: Higher than human baseline

AUDITORY: Higher than human baseline

ENDURANCE: Extremely high

LIFE SPAN: Up to 200 years

DIET: Carnivore

CULTURE: Gregarious

T4 SENSITIVITY: Negative

Description

■ Described as a cross between a rottweiler, a mythical dragon, and a squid.

■ Adults weigh in at 200 pounds and are correspondingly strong. Young are born weighing about 10 pounds, exhibiting little physical growth until nearly 50 years of age. Often referred to as goyles before puberty.

■ Males have red eyes, females have yellow. Few other external differences exist between sexes.

■ Gray, pebbly, rough skin, able to change color and texture to blend in and become almost invisible, much like chameleons. Adults have goatlike horns.

■ Big supple ears edged in white or black fur help direct sound to ears.

■ Long, hairless tail for balance. Tuft of fur on tip. Big eyes and thick canines, black flat teeth, forked tongue. Leathery, surprisingly big bat wings sprouting from middle of back, not connected to forearms or hands.

■ Pre-Turn sightings are thought to be the source of demons in human literature.

GARGOYLE

Sleep Patterns

■ Nocturnal. Adults are able to remain awake after sunrise with practice, but adolescents and young cannot.

Reproduction

■ Live bearer. Young are born singly, with ten years between children not uncommon.

Species Origin

■ Unknown, but gargoyles can be found on both sides of the ley lines, and they are thought to have migrated across with either witches or elves.

■ There's been some attempt to genetically link gargoyles with trolls because of their shared ability to increase their size with water intake. Neither species is cooperative, and the study was shelved in the 1990s.

■ Oldest record of gargoyles is a fragment of what is thought to be an original Anderson poem stating: "Pixies are to elves, as gargoyles are to witches." Meaning is unclear.

Interaction with Other Species

■ Though keeping to the high places, gargoyles get along well with most other species when necessary. Most individuals know how to read and write.

■ Young can be mischievous and will often spit unbelievable amounts of water on unsuspecting pedestrians.

■ Gargoyles are not considered appropriate prey by the undead due to their displeasing flavor.

■ Despite their literacy, gargoyles exist on the fringes of society, needing nothing we can give them, nor offering anything we need.

Political Strengths

■ Not political outside of their own species, gargoyles are ignored as noncitizens with no rights or responsibilities. Internal political structure is based on the family unit.

GARGOYLE

Species Assets

- ■ Able to ignore extreme heat and cold, and rarely venture into shelter.
- ■ Able to "see" or "hear" ley lines, though unable to tap into them and alter reality.
- ■ Able to fly.
- ■ Can quadruple size and mass with water intake.
- ■ Able to increase body temperature to give off large quantities of heat.
- ■ Able to shift skin color and texture much like a chameleon to appear invisible.
- ■ Can squeeze through cracks almost miraculously.
- ■ Physical needs are few, enabling them to survive on the surface in the ever-after.

Species Vulnerabilities

- ■ Are vulnerable while sleeping, especially the young.

Overall Assessment

- ■ A calm and sensible race needing little in the way of watching other than to be sure they're not taken advantage of.
- ■ Gargoyles are considered to be one of the more intelligent of the Inderland fringe species.
- ■ Like most fringe species, gargoyles add nothing to the tax base. Unlike most fringe species, gargoyles are not flourishing in the open spaces left after the Turn, preferring to live in the city. Much of their family life is unknown and will likely stay that way.

Notes: _____

_____

		No
Reviewed by _____		_____
Print	Date	FFHC
		Green
_____		_____
Signature	PIC	Level

G H O U L

CREATED: October 25, 1967
LATEST REVISION: February 15, 2001

200473-3977-11

DOCUMENT SHEPHERD: Shanny M. Michaels
Officer of Internal Documents
555-6979 (ext 772)
ORIGINAL PRESENTER: Jennifer Cormel

GHOUL

OVERVIEW: Modified human. Easily assimilated into pre-Turn society.
INTEGRATION: High
DISRUPTION POTENTIAL: Low
POPULATION: Insignificant
OLFACTORY: Slightly higher than human

AUDITORY: Slightly higher than human
ENDURANCE: Slightly higher than human
LIFE SPAN: Less than human average
DIET: Omnivore
CULTURE: Gregarious
T4 SENSITIVITY: Negative if enough vampire virus present

Sleep Patterns

■ Varies according to amount of toxins, graduating to living vampire preferences.

Reproduction

■ Human reproduction. Offspring will be human if ghoul is a male. Offspring will be a living vampire if the ghoul is female and enough vampire toxins are present. This is the primary way the undead begin new, high-blood vampire bloodlines.

Species Origin

■ Created at need by undead vampires by slowly and intentionally building up the levels of the vampire virus within an individual through frequent blood exchanges. Living vampires cannot make ghouls as they lack high enough levels of the virus necessary to begin the metabolic change from human to vampire.

GHOUL

Interaction with Other Species

- Ghouls are looked down upon by most of Inderland. Ignorant humans fear ghouls as ghouls are generally insecure bullies. This trait is fear based, as they may be forgotten at any time by their undead sponsor and allowed to die unturned.
- Ghouls have a marginal increase in senses and strength and must work hard to survive their undead sponsor's attentions.
- Ghouls are almost exclusively employed in the lower echelon of the I.S. where they can be watched and evaluated for possible inclusion into the undead.
- Most ghouls end up milked for their blood, and usually die from blood loss when their sponsor tires of them. It's the rare ghoul that survives his or her death, and even more rare that he or she lives past the tricky 40-year ceiling if they are turned. Most ghouls are made as entertainment for the undead.

Political Strengths

- None. Ghouls are used, abused, and abandoned.

Species Assets

- Ghouls have slightly elevated senses and strength, less than a high-blood, living vampire.
- If favored and feeding on the undead, ghouls can bespell the living, but this is rare.

Species Vulnerabilities

- Possessing human teeth and endurance, and a vampire's bloodlust, ghouls are disadvantaged.
- Easily forgotten by their masters, most ghouls become shadows of lower vampires and die within months of being abandoned. They're easily manipulated, and trust beyond what's prudent as they strive for immortality.
- Ghouls can be extremely vindictive as they try to impress their undead masters, which usually results in a near lethal correction.

GHOUL

Overall Assessment

■ Ghouls serve an important function in serving the blood needs of the undead, giving a much needed break to natural-born living vampires. They also provide the occasional new bloodline necessary in master vampires' breeding programs.

Notes: _____

_____

_____

_____

Reviewed by _____   No

Print   Date   FFHC

_____   Green

Signature   PIC   Level

LEPRECHAUN

CREATED: December 19, 1967

LATEST REVISION: March 30, 2001

481464-3901-00

DOCUMENT SHEPHERD: Travis B. Weston
Officer of Internal Documents
555-6979 (ext 720)

ORIGINAL PRESENTER: Jerry Ledbetter

LEPRECHAUN

OVERVIEW: Body type is modified human. Able to seamlessly integrate into pre- and post-Turn society using "size-up" charms.

INTEGRATION: High

DISRUPTION POTENTIAL: Low

POPULATION: Undetermined

OLFACTORY: Within human norms

AUDITORY: Slightly higher than norm

ENDURANCE: Average

LIFE SPAN: Claims greater than 150 years but is unproven

DIET: Omnivore

CULTURE: Gregarious

T4 SENSITIVITY: Negative

Description

■ Adult stands under four feet.

Sleep Patterns

■ Diurnal, preferring ten to twelve hours of sleep.

Reproduction

■ Live bearer, similar to human. Capacity to recover numbers is within normal parameters.

Species Origin

■ Believed to have evolved alongside of humanity and within our reality.

LEPRECHAUN

Interaction with Other Species

- Leprechauns work alongside other species well, but prefer to live in small ghettos at the outskirts of large cities.
- Came out of the closet in the Turn and slowly migrated to the edges of cities as humans and Inderlanders preying on humans moved into the center.
- Leprechauns are not a prey species of the undead, who are rightly concerned about a magical backlash.
- The largest concentration of leprechauns still resides in the UK, where their numbers have nearly doubled since the Turn.

Political Strengths

- Not political outside of their own species, but able to successfully lobby for political change when deemed necessary.
- Internal political structure is based on the family unit.
- Very political within their own species, their society runs on favors and kickbacks instead of money.

Species Assets

- Able to access the ley lines to effect change. This is the source of their "good luck."
- Uses ley line abilities to trade unspecified favors or wishes for goods and services. Though leprechaun magic is tightly licensed and regulated, it's difficult to catch illegal magic usage due to the subtle forces involved in its creation.
- Using their internal society structure, leprechauns can grant wishes to one person and fulfill another's wish to call the debt clear. This commerce-by-favor makes leprechaun society the closest to demons of any other Inderland species.
- Average intelligence. Though often considered lazy, leprechauns are simply self-sufficient, not needing the products of another society for their own.

LEPRECHAUN

Species Vulnerabilities

■ Their smaller size made it difficult for them to integrate into human society before the Turn, which is likely why they prefer to remain on the outskirts even today.

■ Tend to gamble far beyond what is prudent, relying on luck.

■ Have a distinctive odor of clover.

Overall Assessment

■ As a species, leprechauns are law-abiding, peace-loving people. As individuals, they have the potential for untold mischief leading to serious political or commercial unrest.

■ With their ability to perform magic, they have the potential to be a disruptive influence, but because of their stingy nature and strong distrust for anyone outside of their species, they will likely remain a marginal species despite their slowly growing numbers.

■ Leprechauns don't add to the tax base significantly, employing themselves in local cottage industries to supply their own needs, preferring an internal system of barter than to use money and perhaps have to pay taxes on their gains.

Notes:

Reviewed by _____

		No
Print	Date	FFHC
		Green
Signature	PIC	Level

PIXY

CREATED: August 10, 1967
LATEST REVISION: June 1, 2001

184420-4871-85

DOCUMENT SHEPHERD: Shanny M. Michaels
Officer of Internal Documents
555-6979 (ext 772)
ORIGINAL PRESENTER: Susan Leans

PIXY

OVERVIEW: Body type is modified human with significant size reduction and possessing wings.

INTEGRATION: Low

DISRUPTION POTENTIAL: Low

POPULATION: Undetermined, presumed several million in US

OLFACTORY: Highest in Inderland

AUDITORY: Highest in Inderland

ENDURANCE: Low

LIFE SPAN: Up to 20 years

DIET: Primarily nectarvores

CULTURE: Gregarious

T4 SENSITIVITY: Negative

Description

■ Small, well proportioned to their size. Usually fair-skinned and fair-haired. Adults stand four inches tall and possess dragonfly-like wings.

■ Passive, species-specific magic elevates voice into human audible range.

Sleep Patterns

■ Crepuscular, preferring to sleep four hours at noon and midnight, like elves. Young will sleep significantly more.

Reproduction

■ Live bearer. Healthy adults can bear up to a dozen "newlings" at a time, though five to six is the norm. Able to give birth all year, but spring newlings have a significantly higher survival rate. Families can have two to four dozen individuals in established groups.

Species Origin

- Unknown, but both witch and pixy oral histories say pixies originated in the ever-after and crossed several times until the last crossing about six thousand years ago.
- Recent findings indicate that though pixies can travel to the ever-after, they're flung back to reality upon sunup, paralleling the demonic inability to remain on this side of the ley lines after sunrise. (See DOX: P31.)

Interaction with Other Species

- Pixies get along well with most species apart from banshees and fairies.
- Upon occasion, a pixy will work within a human system, either in security, construction, and occasionally messenger service. They make excellent backup for the I.S. runner, but due to their fiercely independent nature and their intake needs, these interactions are rare.
- Pixy/fairy wars are ongoing as soon as the fairies migrate back into a region looking for food. Skirmishes are generally ignored even if property damage results.
- Pixies are not sought out as prey food by the undead due to their size.

Political Strengths

- Not political outside of their own species, pixies are ignored as noncitizens with no rights or responsibilities. Internal political structure is based on the family unit.
- Unlike fairies, pixies will not attack other pixy clans for resources but will poach from their pixy neighbors if they think they can get away with it. Trespassers are killed without remorse, and the death is not avenged due to pixy pragmatics that a smart pixy wouldn't have gotten caught.
- Though appearing a threat on paper, pixies are peaceful and will suffer great indignities rather than fight a pixy clan, human, or Inderlander species. This seems to stem from their wish to remain noncitizens so they can kill fairies without reprisal.

PIXY

Species Assets

- Able to hibernate to avoid the cold, thereby increasing their range.
- Excellent senses enable them to survive in a much larger world. Able to see auras.
- Dragonfly-like wing structure makes them incredibly fast, maneuverable fliers.
- Fierce warriors, trained for individual and group combat from birth.
- Able to modify their dust for a variety of effects including fire retardation, skin irritant, blood clotting, and illumination. Pixy dust is not an explosive, but it has been found in the residue of several unexplained detonation areas and on damaged hard drives.
- Can communicate simple meanings with whistles produced by their wings.
- One of the more intelligent Inderland species, but due to their size and need for natural spaces, they are mostly ignored.

Species Vulnerabilities

- Sudden temperature drops below 45°F can cause death.
- Infant mortality is high. Hibernation is the largest cause of death after the first year.
- The entire family unit dissolves upon the death of one parent, dispersing the young. Most orphaned children die from starvation or are killed by rival pixy clans for trespassing.
- Sensitive to changes in pressure or altitude, and allergic to most metals except copper and stainless steel.
- Known to become drunk on honey.
- Needs to eat every forty minutes when active.

Overall Assessment

- As individuals, pixies are fierce warriors, loyal to their family unit. Complex and still mostly a mystery to other species, they will vigorously defend their territory from birds, cats, and fairies, and yet stand by and do nothing as a bulldozer destroys their home and garden.

PIXY

- Pixies are one of the most widespread Inderland species both in number and range, living on almost every continent. Their numbers have grown substantially since the Turn, and though they keep mostly to the outskirts and badlands between cities, urban pixies are becoming more and more prevalent as humans design green spaces, both public and private, to attract them, as charmed by their spunky dexterity now as they were at the beginning of the Turn.
- Pixies seldom learn how to read.
- Predation or harassment by animals, humans, or Inderlanders is curtailed at the street level by the pixies themselves, relying on passive determent such as "pixing" and wiping hard drives.
- Like fairies, pixies forgive accidental killings by larger people, and there's no record of a pixy ever being involved in a FIB- or I.S.-investigated homicide or crime.
- Pixies are highly intelligent and have a complex social structure commensurate with our own. They have much to offer Inderland if they'd become full citizens, unsurpassed in areas of surveillance, but their fiercely independent nature keeps them at the outskirts.

Notes

- A pixy named Orchid sat on Rynn Cormel's shoulder at the original broadcast that heralded the beginning of the Turn.

Reviewed by _____

	No
Print	FFHC

	Green
Signature	Level

Date

PIC

CREATED: December 11, 1967
LATEST REVISION: February 8, 2001

005681-3385-28

DOCUMENT SHEPHERD: Travis B. Weston
Officer of Internal Documents
555-6979 (ext 720)
ORIGINAL PRESENTER: Samantha Wilds

TROLL

OVERVIEW: Modified human body type. See below. Almost unknown before Turn.

INTEGRATION: Low

DISRUPTION POTENTIAL: Low

POPULATION: Undetermined

OLFACTORY: Significantly less than human

AUDITORY: Significantly greater than human

ENDURANCE: Unknown

LIFE SPAN: Unknown

DIET: Modified omnivore

CULTURE: Solitary

T4 SENSITIVITY: Negative

Description

■ Though having a general biped form, trolls can regulate their size and mass by absorbing or excreting water. They generally shun clothing and are seldom seen out of the water due to a high sensitivity to UV rays and a reduced capacity to remain hydrated. Their skin is very porous. Depending upon water retention, trolls can range in size from thirty to three hundred pounds.

■ Trolls possess a dripping skin and pale complexion. Algae often grows in their sparse hair.

Sleep Patterns

■ Sixteen-hour sleep schedule. Strictly nocturnal, but can be awoken in daylight.

Reproduction

■ Hermaphrodites. Population has risen dramatically since the Turn. This is

credited to the near abandonment of small towns, leaving concrete bridges and culverts open to colonization. Young stay with parent for twenty to thirty years before striking out on their own.

Species Origin

■ Fossil records indicate trolls are more closely related to squid than humans.

Interaction with Other Species

■ There is very little pre-Turn interaction with either humans or Inderlanders, and beyond the fossil record (which there is very little of) there is only the Anderson brothers' sketchy prehistory, dubious at best since they cast trolls as aggressive, goat-eating barbarians when they're actually mild mannered and eat only the barest amount of protein.

■ Trolls do not pose any threat to humans or Inderland species and coexist with little friction apart from their habit of slowly eating bridges and the city infrastructure.

■ Trolls are not hunted by living vampires because they lack mammalian blood.

Political Strengths

■ None whatsoever. Trolls don't seek out any rights and exist on the fringes of society, harming none and asking for nothing. They are one of the few Inderland species that retain their own language based on body language and small changes in finger movement and size.

Species Assets

■ Trolls can change their size dramatically, from that of a domestic feline to that of a large bear. This is not magical in origin, but was, in fact, the first clue to their "squid" background and is due to a massive intake of water. Trolls will enlarge themselves to fight off rivals and defend their bridges from other trolls, but they are usually very meek when asked to move by even the weakest I.S. officer.

TROLL

- They are tolerant of extreme temperature highs and lows, becoming almost dormant during below-zero temperatures.
- Able to breathe through their skin while underwater, much like amphibians.
- Able to survive on water-borne plankton, snails, and the occasional invertebrate. They supplement their diet with concrete when shellfish are not present.

Species Vulnerabilities

- Fights over territory between trolls can be fierce, leading to death. They do not consider themselves citizens of the post-Turn world, and do not seek help when injured.
- Very sensitive to bright light and loud noise, which are often used to drive them out from under bridges.

Overall Assessment

- Trolls are meek apart from defending their territory from other trolls. Most don't know English, even in the city. This is a species that could be introduced into society, but likely won't because trolls need nothing we have, and have nothing we need.
- Tax base is nil.

Notes: _____

_____

_____

Reviewed by _____

	No
Print Date	FFHC
	Green
Signature PIC	Level

LIVING VAMPIRE

CREATED: September 7, 1967
LATEST REVISION: February 14, 2001

200473-8729-61

DOCUMENT SHEPHERD: Shanny M. Michaels
Officer of Internal Documents
555-6979 (ext 772)
ORIGINAL PRESENTER: Jennifer Cormel

LIVING VAMPIRE

OVERVIEW: Body type is human. Easily assimilated into pre-Turn society.

INTEGRATION: High

DISRUPTION POTENTIAL: High

POPULATION: Encompasses one fourth of all Inderland.

OLFACTORY: Significantly higher than human

AUDITORY: Significantly higher than human

ENDURANCE: Significantly higher than human

LIFE SPAN: Less than human average

DIET: Omnivore, leaning to Sanguinivore

CULTURE: Gregarious

T4 SENSITIVITY: See below

Angel T4 Tolerance

■ Tolerance is high in living vampires and is the reason behind the ghoul boomers of the late '60s and '70s.

Sleep Patterns

■ Prefer a more nocturnal lifestyle, rising near noon and ending their day before sunrise.

Reproduction

■ Primary reproduction: Identical to standard human in established, high-blood family lines.

■ Secondary reproduction: Humans can become ghouls if exposed to enough blood toxin from an undead. Offspring from female ghouls are technically living

vampires, and this is how new, high-blood vampire bloodlines are created. (See DOX: V.83.2.)

Species Origin

■ Created as an offshoot from undead vampires. Offspring from a ghoul/ghoul pairing or female ghoul/human male pairing will often result in a living vampire of moderate strength. Most of today's living vampires have been produced from living vampire pairings and are correspondingly stronger.

Interaction with Other Species

■ Living vampires get along extremely well with almost every faction of human and Inderland. Possessing much of their undead brethren's skills and few of their liabilities, living vampires have an almost tragic place in society as beloved children of the damned, coddled and indulged by their respective undead "parents" until they die and lose their souls. If not for their extreme loyalty to their camarilla bordering on the psychotic, living vampires would be a disruptive influence in today's modern society.

■ Living vampires have an emotional need for taking blood, and high-blood living vampires are often indulged beyond what is prudent as they practice the skills of luring prey with both other living vampires and humans. Witches and Weres are not immune to a living vampire's attentions but are more often the targets of more sophisticated living vampires slated for a higher position in the vampire hierarchy.

■ Living vampires are able to bind others to them much as an undead can, using a diluted form of the same neurotransmitters and toxins that change pain into pleasure, instilling a euphoric sensation when taking blood. If taken to extremes, such "blood shadows" will become addicted to the unhealthy state where they will seek attention from any vampire, not just their chosen lover.

■ Living vampires are employed in every aspect of society at or above the mean average income. Most of the day-to-day work in the I.S. is carried out by living vampires.

LIVING VAMPIRE

- Living vampires are the preferred blood donors of the undead, a burden they are happy to bear even as it warps their minds and destroys their bodies.
- A scion is a living vampire chosen by a dead vampire to do its daylight work, generally receiving special favors and having extra responsibilities.

Political Strengths

- Living vampires are extremely political among themselves but generally not outside their camarillas, bowing to their masters in this area.
- Though appearing to be content and stable, living vampires are often walking a thin line between lucidity and a debilitating depression, addicted to the passions that their undead masters can instill with the taking of blood. Much like abused children, the older, more experienced living vampires will often shield the younger, often sacrificing themselves to protect those they love. The wise master will recognize this and maintain a greater distance from his children's children, allowing them the illusion of security as he nurtures and promotes the most stable, ensuring the next generation of undead will be healthy and long-lived.
- Living vampires will often police themselves at both the street and family level, curbing or eliminating a disruptive influence before it comes to the attention of their undead masters. Most of the I.S. street force is made up of living vampires, and without them, much of the uglier side of Inderland would be exposed to humanity.

Species Assets

- Almost superhuman with their strength, hearing, and sense of smell.
- Are born with small, sharp canines that allow them to better practice the skills they will need when undead.
- Although living vampires cannot see auras, they can "read" an area for recent emotional output, allowing them to almost see where a crime has taken place. (See Moulage.)
- Loyalty to their masters is strong.

LIVING VAMPIRE

Species Vulnerabilities

■ Can be easily manipulated by those who know how, be they vampire or otherwise.

■ Infant mortality is higher than human norm, but this normalizes after the first year.

■ Are often mentally unstable due to the severe manipulation from their bored, undead masters.

■ Will "pull an aura" when angry or afraid. Eyes dilate and control over their bloodlust slips.

■ Instincts can be triggered by pheromones and emotions to their detriment.

Overall Assessment

■ Living vampires are a large group, covering a wide range of socioeconomic levels. The Turn allowed an unprecedented amount of freedom, and a corresponding rise in the number of living vampires has resulted. Society has adapted well, and living vampires are the middle ground, helping to keep the rest of Inderland stable. Without them, humanity would be preyed upon mercilessly, and they would undoubtedly rise up and destroy entire Inderland societies.

Notes: _____

_____

_____

Reviewed by _____

Print	Date	No FFHC

_____

Signature	PIC	Green Level

UNDEAD VAMPIRE

CREATED: August 25, 1967
LATEST REVISION: February 14, 2001

200473-0226-37

DOCUMENT SHEPHERD: Shanny M. Michaels
Officer of Internal Documents
555-6979 (ext 772)

ORIGINAL PRESENTER: Jennifer Cormel

UNDEAD VAMPIRE

OVERVIEW: Body type is modified human. Difficult maintaining human façade before Turn due to blood needs and sunlight restrictions.

INTEGRATION: Moderate to high

DISRUPTION POTENTIAL: High if unbalanced

POPULATION: Undocumented

OLFACTORY: Second only to pixies

AUDITORY: Significantly greater than human baseline

ENDURANCE: Can be extremely high

LIFE SPAN: Indefinitely, but generally 200 years after passing the first 40 years

DIET: Sanguinivore, modified auravore

CULTURE: Solitary

T4 SENSITIVITY: Negative

Sleep Patterns

- Nocturnal. Doesn't actually sleep, but will occasionally rest during daylight hours.

Reproduction

- Living vampires cross into their undead existence naturally at the end of their first life.
- Secondary reproduction: Infecting a human with enough vampire virus to create a ghoul will prime a body for life after death, but additional, undead assistance is needed to survive death and become an undead.

Species Origin

- Unknown, but believed to originate in several demon curses sometime around the advent of agriculture.

Interaction with Other Species

- As one of Inderland's apex predators, undead vampires interact carefully with other species, almost ignoring humans in their efforts to maintain a harmless image. The reality is understandably different, but human predation is limited since the careless undead is fatally reprimanded by his or her older brethren.
- The undead prefer to remain out of the working sector, but inflation often forces them to resume a 9–5 job or freelance work within the I.S. Most other work environments are unable to meet the undead's physical and emotional needs, but the occasional entrepreneur can be quite successful in the private sector.
- Clashes between rival camarillas are few. The undead are patient, especially the old.
- The undead prefer to feed upon living vampires, but will occasionally seek new experiences with witches or Weres. Humans are generally too fragile for all but the oldest and wisest undead to keep alive long enough to be of any pleasure.

Political Strengths

- Highly political both in and out of their own species, undead vampires control a large fraction of companies not owned by elves.
- The undead retain their intelligence and memory from their previous existence and will continue to work within established agreements and judiciously create new ones as needed, making them highly effective in the political arena. They are utterly without conscience, remembering love but not understanding it.
- Undead vampires instinctively condition entire living vampire family lines to obedience and will breed generations of living vampires for their blood needs. Loyalty goes beyond death and is absolute, hence vampires are forbidden from running for office unless they first sever all ties with their camarilla.
- Undead vampires police themselves to help hide the danger that they represent to humanity. Stepping outside accepted boundaries brings swift and unforgiving correction. The only time vampires will work unquestioningly together is to eliminate threats. It's no accident that undead vampires comprise 90 percent of the decision-making offices in the I.S.

UNDEAD VAMPIRE

Species Assets

- One of the physically strongest Inderland species, they can only be destroyed by beheading, light poisoning, or blood poisoning from a blood exchange with another undead vampire.
- Temperature tolerance is untested, but extreme.
- Do not need to breathe or carry on any metabolic function beyond the soft digestion of blood to maintain and repair the soul-less body.
- Excellent senses enable them to survive in a world that is mostly toxic to them.
- Able to "bespell" potential blood donors with a complex neurotoxin cocktail of pheromones.
- Possess neurotoxins that, when injected with saliva, change the body's processing of pain into pleasure, furthering the undead's ability to find and keep blood sources by combining bloodletting with sex, and able to mentally bind both human and Inderlander to them with repeated exposure.

Species Vulnerabilities

- Unable to tolerate even the smallest amount of reflected sunlight. Must remain six feet under to prevent light sickness leading to death.
- Abhorrence to holy or blessed objects. Because this has its origin in witch magic, not religious beliefs, this can be easily surmounted by the prepared.
- "Infant mortality" among the newly undead is high, with an average of 95 percent of the undead dying their second death before their fortieth undead birthday. This is due to the difficulty in establishing permanent emotional bonds with a new generation. It's only in the strongest of bonds that the auratic intake is sufficient for the undead, but the undead who are able to learn the task of how to create new emotional bonds have an almost unlimited undead "life span."
- The undead need an almost daily intake of blood. Blood from a bag lacks the aura that comes with living blood, and so will not sustain the undead. Without an aura, the body will realize the soul is absent, and the undead will walk into the sun to bring mind, body, and soul back into balance.

■ Favorite individuals, called scions, are the undead's voice aboveground and do the undead's daylight work. The bond can be as limited as a handshake but more often involves blood and a deep symbolic relationship. When taken to unhealthy extremes, the undead can literally see through his or her scion's eyes and control the scion's body. Such an extreme connection is risky for both the scion and the undead and is very rare. While serving as an undead's scion, a living vampire enjoys a greater strength and ability to bespell the living.

■ Need to employ witch magic to maintain their youthful appearance.

Overall Assessment

■ As individuals, the undead are powerful both physically and psychologically. Their needs place them as predators, but their intelligence and traditions help disguise the danger they represent. As the governing body of what is usually a large collection of individuals, the undead is very much alone, able to remember love, but not why they loved.

■ Highly intelligent and often with a lifetime of resources and experiences to draw upon, the undead have an undeniable place in society, offering stability in an often unstable world.

Notes

■ A living vampire, Rynn Cormel, became the world's first publicly undead vampire when he was assassinated the first month of the Turn. He then continued to publicly run the US government through the first four years of the Turn, being highly instrumental in giving Inderlanders back the rights that they enjoyed as "humans." He was never sworn in as president, however, for at that time, legislation did not grant the undead any rights.

■ The mechanism of how a virus keeps an undead alive has been studied in great detail and is still being deciphered. Current accepted theory is that the vampire virus lodges itself in the bone marrow and pineal gland, stimulating a need for blood intake. Blood intake is actually a mechanism to draw in an aura from the blood donor. The siphoned aura bathes the brain in a false sensation of life,

tricking the mind into believing that a soul is still present. If an aura is allowed to completely dissipate from the undead, the brain realizes the soul is gone and the vampire is in danger of committing sunicide as the mind tries to bring body, soul, and mind back in balance.

Reviewed by _____

No

| Print | Date | FFHC |

Green

| Signature | PIC | Level |

WERE

CREATED: May 29, 1967
LATEST REVISION: February 9, 2001

487660-2702-44

DOCUMENT SHEPHERD: Shanny M. Michaels
Officer of Internal Documents
555-6979 (ext 772)
ORIGINAL PRESENTER: Mark Smith

WERE

OVERVIEW: Primary body type is human. Blends easily with humanity.
INTEGRATION: High
DISRUPTION POTENTIAL: Low to moderate
POPULATION: Undocumented
OLFACTORY: Slightly higher than human

AUDITORY: Significantly higher than human
ENDURANCE: Higher than human
LIFE SPAN: Commensurate with human
DIET: Omnivore
CULTURE: Gregarious
T4 SENSITIVITY: Negative

Description

■ When in primary body form, Weres have slightly larger teeth, but still well within human norms.

■ Secondary body type is a wolf, unremarkable apart from the large body mass carried over from primary body. Intelligence is constant across body types.

■ Nocturnal/Diurnal: Ten-hour sleep schedule is optimum. Prefer a nocturnal existence, but will adapt to a human clock without problem.

Reproduction

■ Normal reproduction allows a slow and steady increase in population. Weres cannot be created with an exchange of body fluids, despite long-standing folklore. (Currently under investigation, see DOX: 3.18.) Fertile within normal human standards. Ovulation triggered by phase of moon. Slight but telling genetic differences prevent hybrids with any other species, including humans.

Species Origin

- An almost identical genome to humans has made dating the beginning of a stable Weres population difficult. Estimations range from three thousand to six thousand years ago. Because of the close similarity to humans, it's thought that Weres originated from a demon curse.
- Subspecies: Were Fox. Endangered species in the US. More prevalent in European countries. Were foxes are able to lose or gain mass from the ever-after when shifting and therefore are thought to have their beginnings in witches or elves instead of humans. They're not able to perform any other form of magic.

Interaction with Other Species

- Weres have probably been with humans as long as, if not longer than, witches. Their retiring nature has put them on the outskirts of society for much of their existence, but with the advent of the Turn, Weres have begun to freely mix within Inderland and human society.
- Weres rely on their tattoos to help ease tensions between packs in close quarters, and the best tattoo artists are invariably Weres.
- Despite long-standing myths, Weres do not lose their intelligence when in their wolf form and are no more likely to attack under a full moon than at any other time.
- They do not prey upon other species and coexist with little friction among themselves.
- Weres are not generally hunted by either living vampires or the undead. The undead, especially, run the risk of bringing down the wrath of an entire pack by bespelling a Were, turning a usually placid, easygoing family group into a savage, ruthless pack bent on revenge or retrieval.
- Weres cannot be turned into vampires and are rarely bound to the undead.

Political Strengths

■ Despite their strong family bonds, Weres don't possess much political strength as any attempt to make a political statement is hampered by their inherent pack rivalry.

■ Weres handle internal problems at the pack level, decisions being made and enforced by either the alpha male or female depending upon the need. Pack justice is swift and absolute, and there is seldom a situation where a more formal intervention from the I.S. is necessary. Alpha females generally hold more sway than alpha males within the pack.

Species Assets

■ Weres shift into form without the intervention of witch magic.

■ It is possible for Weres to bind into a "round" where all the members of a pack will take on the pain of one individual, allowing him or her to shift quickly or ignore pain entirely. Once one of the Weres' best-kept secrets, the practice is policed in sporting events.

Species Vulnerabilities

■ Shifting body types is painful, eased by the ingestion of wolfsbane.

■ Have a deeply engrained wariness of holy places, but it has been proven this is entirely superstitious and not based on any physical discomfort.

■ Suicides are always on the full moon.

■ Do not return to a human shape if they die as a wolf, requiring witch magic to turn them back.

Overall Assessment

■ Unlike most Inderland species, Weres cover a wide span of tax brackets, their incomes ranging from destitute to very wealthy depending upon their pack standing. Personal pack standing can limit or accelerate a Were's standing

outside the pack as well, and a significant number of Fortune 400 businesses are owned or managed by alpha males or alpha females.

■ The higher a Were is in the pack, the more "respectable" he or she appears.

■ Weres excel in physical tasks and have a determination that borders on the certifiable. Not known for their business smarts, they nevertheless have the ability to accomplish surprising things through loyalty and sheer determination.

■ Weres constitute a significant tax base in the areas of insurance and sports and are the largest consumer of wolfsbane.

Notes:_____

_____

_____

Reviewed by _____

           Print   Date   FFHC

No

Green

_____

    Signature   PIC   Level

WITCH AND WARLOCK

CREATED: June 14, 1967

LATEST REVISION: February 2, 2001

652117-8452-00

DOCUMENT SHEPHERD: Shanny M. Michaels
Officer of Internal Documents
555-6979 (ext 772)

ORIGINAL PRESENTER: John Templeton

WITCH AND WARLOCK

OVERVIEW: Body type mimics human. Blends easily with humans. Warlock designation is an indication of a lack of formal magical training, not ability.

INTEGRATION: High

DISRUPTION POTENTIAL: Moderate

POPULATION: One-third of Inderland society

OLFACTORY: Slightly higher than human

AUDITORY: Slightly higher than human

ENDURANCE: Within normal human parameters

LIFE SPAN: 160 years

DIET: Omnivore

CULTURE: Gregarious

T4 SENSITIVITY: Negative

Sleep Patterns

■ Modified diurnal: Eight-hour sleep schedule, able to mimic humans, but prefer an 11:00 A.M. wakeup and 3:00 A.M. end of the day.

Reproduction

■ Normal reproduction allows a slow and steady increase in population. Generally fertile from twenty to one hundred years of age. Ovulation is not moon based and occurs only after intercourse with a witch or warlock. Severe genetic differences prevent hybrids with other species, and many pre-Turn sterility issues were from witch/human pairings. Sterility can be circumvented with

magic, but this is not a common practice as witch morals freely accept the practice of "borrowing" a witch for a night to serve as a birth-father stud.

Species Origin

- Pre-Turn genetic studies indicate witches evolved in the ever-after, migrating to reality as early as 5,000 B.C. But a recent, unsubstantiated statement indicates that witches are actually a bastard species springing directly from the demon genome and are a product of an ancient demon/elf war. (See DOX: 979.3.)

Interaction with Other Species

- Because of their close mimicry of humans, witches have long enjoyed a close relationship with the pre-Turn, dominant human species. The few exceptions stem from the witch's ability to tap into the ever-after and execute magic. Witches do not prey upon humans, and they coexist with little friction apart from their varied sleep schedules.
- Witches are hunted by living vampires to a small degree, a practice closely monitored to prevent any magical backlash or withholding of magical charms that dead vampires enjoy. Witches cannot evolve into vampires, and will suffer a decrease in magical abilities if they become bound to an undead.
- On the whole, witches get along with most Inderland species.

Political Strengths

- Witches are generally solitary or family oriented, with little inclination to increase their political power as a species.
- The political body responsible for making species decisions is the coven of moral and ethical standards, an elected body of six witches balanced in ages and magic specialties. Highest form of species punishment is a collective shunning.

WITCH AND WARLOCK

Species Assets

- Witches are able to tap directly into the ever-after using ley line magic and perform dramatic changes in reality including but not limited to physical changes, mental adjustments, and distant-effect magics. The blood enzyme that kindles earth magic was identified as early as the 1960s and is likely the source of the claim that witches evolved from demons.
- Witches are the single largest source of Inderland magic, quietly bringing in a tremendous income at both the state and federal level through the cottage industry of spell crafting and selling, as well as state license fees for creating and selling magic products.
- Reference DOX: W.54.12 for more information on magic systems available to witches.

Species Vulnerabilities

- Infant mortality is slightly higher in the witch population than humans, mostly due to a genome sensitive to change.
- Witches tend to be more susceptible to lower temperatures than the human baseline.

Overall Assessment

- Witches are usually a low-maintenance species both at the street and governmental level.
- Pre-Turn traditions instilled an almost fanatical desire to maintain a low profile, a practice still prevalent today. Witches self-police themselves to a high degree, and only the most high-profile cases of black magic or magic misfire are released to the general public.
- Witches are stable in both their political standing and their physical numbers.

WITCH AND
WARLOCK

Notes

- The creator of a spell or charm can be determined using standard detection methods, helping to curtail black magic practitioners.
- The more a witch partakes in crafting magic, the stronger he or she smells of redwood.

Reviewed by _____

Print	Date	No
		FFHC
Signature	PIC	Green
		Level

The Hollows Gazette

Wednesday, April 5, 2006

LOCAL / STATE

C

PUBLIC FORUM FOR PROPOSED MUSEUM EXHIBIT

By Winifred Gradenko
winniegrad@hollowsgazette.com

Cincinnati has long been known for bringing new ideas and old history to her people. But have we gone too far?

That's the question city officials will try to answer this Friday at a hearing concerning documents found during renovations at the university.

The pre-Turn documents, dubbed the Periwick Papers, highlight the genetic research later outlawed. Outraged citizens are calling for their disposal. Proponents of Safe Genetic Research (SGR) want to determine if it's possible to reclaim knowledge that could end leukemia and diabetes again. "Not all genetic research was bad," SGR president Cavas said as onlookers booed. "We've a right to see."

Historians also decry the possible destruction, claiming the documents should be displayed. "Cincinnati is the right place for this," Sarah McCavin said. "We have one of the most stable, productive human and Inderland populations in the US. Our children deserve the truth." But is it truth, or a sugar-coated pill to disaster?

As any elementary student knows, the Turn began 40 years ago when a military virus unexpectedly attached itself to the genetically altered, widely distributed, Angel T4 tomato.

Within 3 years, humanity teetered on extinction in the US and Europe, the situation worse in the third worlds.

But in saving humanity, it became clear Inderlanders weren't human, and on October 31st, 1966, future president and living vampire Rynn Cormel addressed a frightened population, saying "You are not alone. We have always been here. Today we saved our society, tomorrow, we will build it anew. Witch, vampire, Were, and human."

Bold words that rang through history, unmuffled even after the successful as-

Protesters at City Hall show their teeth as proponents clash.

sassination upon Cormel. His death only galvanized the man into a stronger position of equality, truth, and honesty that marked his presidency.

Genetic research has been outlawed, and now it's the scientist who hides, not the witch or Were. Will a physical reminder of that dark time serve as a warning, or a beacon to brighter days?

WANT TO GO?
A public meeting will be held at the City Offices, Friday, April 7th, to discuss the Periwick Papers.

New Tax Laws Scrutinized

By Cindy Strom
cstrom@hollowsgazette.com

Proposed tax laws impacting thousands of Cincy residents are again under scrutiny as lawmakers near the June deadline to ratify or strike down changes.

Councilman Trent Kalamack said he

See Taxes **C 6**

The Way I See It

Devin Crossman

BAD LUCK, or BAD RUNNER

I didn't shave today. I'd like to say I decided to grow a beard, but I was the victim of a disturbing and often unreported crime of spell misfire, struck by a badly trained Inderland Security runner in her attempt to bring injustice to heel.

Misfire I can tolerate, but when my calls to the I.S. seeking information were ignored, I couldn't help but wonder if it was a misfired charm, or incompetence. You can be sure I'll be investigating. These are our streets, and we've a right to feel safe around those who protect us.

Devin Crossman is a guest columnist, bringing his uniquely human point of view to the Hollows. Comments concerning any Devin Crossman article will reach Mr. Crossman at: dcrossman @hollowsgazette.com

---

@ A Glance April 5, 2006
Average High/Low: 63° / 40°

	Today	Tomorrow
Sunrise	6:16 AM	6:15 AM
Sunset	7:06 PM	7:07 PM
Moonrise	11:24 AM	12:27 PM
Moonset	2:26 AM	3:08 AM
Phase 50% first quarter		

SEE ALMANAC C 6

Kalamack Industries, Inc

Trenton A. Kalamack
CEO Kalamack Industries
Kalamack Industries, Inc
Building A
15 Rolling Acres
Cincinnati, OH 45239

I N T E R O F F I C E   M E M O

TO: Jonathan Davaros
FROM: Trenton Kalamack
CC:
DATE: 4/6/06
RE: Contact Flag on Rachel Morgan

Jon, I acknowledge your reluctance to allocate any resources to Mr. Crossman, but after reading yesterday's *Hollows Gazette,* I'd like you to compile a dossier on him, going back to his grandparents and inclusive of his medical history. His entire work history, please. Perhaps a day of surveillance by Quen if he feels it might yield something of interest.

I'd like this by Monday.

Also, please include a copy of the *Hollows Gazette* into my morning reading from here out.

TK

Chapter 2

Kalamack Industries, Inc

Jonathan Davaros
Chief Personnel Officer
Kalamack Industries, Inc
Building A
15 Rolling Acres
Cincinnati, OH 45239

I N T E R O F F I C E   M E M O

TO: Trenton Kalamack
FROM: Jonathan Davaros
CC: Quen Hansen
DATE: 10/2/06
RE: Devin Crossman

Sa'han,

I'm clearing this Friday's morning schedule for you and Quen to discuss Mr. Crossman in further detail. Quen has increased surveillance on him since Crossman acquired public files upon you, Piscary, and Leon Bairn, in his continuing investigation of Morgan. The best we can figure, he's trying to tie her to you. Crossman has also gotten onto the grounds of Morgan's church, though not inside, and that's the main aspect that Quen would like to discuss. If Crossman does gain access, however brief, it might require decisive action. I advise creating ties to close this possible gap in security and would like to meet with you and Quen next week to go over some possibilities.

I also have samples ready for your approval for the entertainment scheduled for your October orphans' benefit at the end of the month.

Yours,

Jonathan

Devin's
Journal
Entry

October 3, 2006

I found a few things out this last week. Watching the church is almost useless with those pixies Morgan has living at her church. I can't bribe them no matter how much honey I bring. About all I managed was to make a sketch of the church by looking in the windows. I'll do more if I find out what moves the pixies. They seem to be an entire family unit, and a big one. Interestingly, I saw a dead vamp go in the back, so only the front is holy. (Note—numbers are on the wrong side of the street. Weird.)

The city records say deed is in Piscary's name. An undead vampire owns property he can't go into? Huh.

The belfry would be a great place to watch for people coming and going. Looks like the bell is still up there.

INSIDE

Tumbling mats in the sanctuary, no pews. Nice hardwood. Stained glass still there. Big, knee-to-ceiling windows. Probably worth a fortune. There's a shadow of a cross on the old altar, but otherwise, no religious anything.

Two institutional bathrooms converted into a standard bathroom and combo bath and laundry. Clergy offices turned into bedrooms with original oak floors. The vampire's room has a huge closet. Probably for storing the bodies. Ha, ha.

Kitchen and living room look added on, which would explain why they aren't holy. The kitchen has been remodeled. Two stoves, lots of stainless steel. Big vat of what's probably salt water on counter by the window. The witch scraped a gouge in her linoleum in the kitchen for a circle. It looks like she does her spelling in there.

The vampire has her office in the kitchen as well. It takes up the entire table. Huge fridge. There's a rack of cooking stuff over the center counter, and tons of books under it. Spell books, I think. There's enough copper bowls in there to wire an entire subdivision.

The back living room has a huge fireplace. Works by the look of it, and I've seen pixies going in and out through the flue. There is a back door to the garden off of it, but watch the steps, they creak.

OUTSIDE

There is a small garden and graveyard patrolled by pixies. City records say that no one has been buried there since the Turn. Both car gates are rusted shut. The property stretches the entire block, bordered by road on two sides.

The graveyard takes up most of the property. It's fenced with a high stone wall you can climb if you're careful. There's a smaller, knee-high wall that divides the graveyard from the witches' garden out back. It looks like Morgan grows her spell ingredients there—sweet setup for a witch.

The oaks lining the street are huge. There's a sad excuse of a carport out front with the vampire's cycle in it. Parking is allowed on the street, but no one does much.

Back Door

Living Room

Fridge

Table

Ivy's Room

Rachel's Room

W   D

Shower

Sanctuary

Front Door

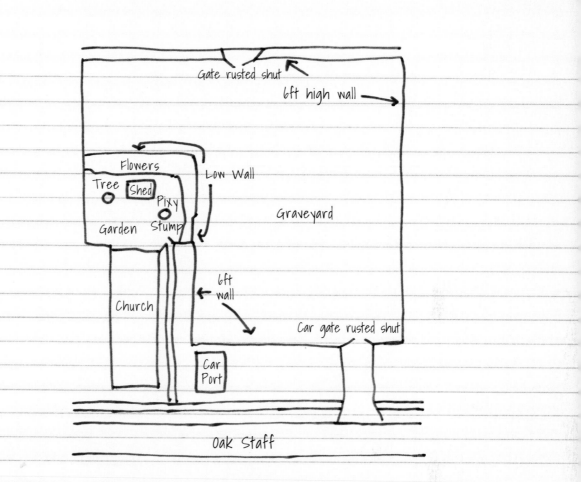

This doesn't look like an independent runner firm to me. A front, maybe? The vampire's master vamp is Piscary, so it's possible.

I found Piscary's fact sheet at work while looking up exactly what the I.S. and FIB are supposed to be doing in keeping us safe. Piscary is one scary individual. He nearly runs the city in that he's responsible for keeping the vampires in line. It might be my healthy human skepticism, but I'm not buying the friendly restaurant owner face he shows the world, even if he does have a Mixed Public License so he can safely serve humans and Inderlanders in the same establishment.

I pulled up Kalamack's file, too, since Morgan went to "visit" him last June in a sweet little red convertible. I'm not sure what's going on there. Rumor has it Morgan quit the I.S. And then she goes to talk to Kalamack?

I had better luck in the city files, digging up Morgan's last evaluation—which sucked. And that's what I have a problem with. Leon Bairn was an experienced runner who tried to quit the I.S. and he was pasted. Yet Morgan survived? It's been months since she quit, and she's still alive.

I find it very interesting that Bairn was investigating Kalamack Sr.'s death before he quit and was killed. I pulled Bairn's death certificate, and though it looks legit, I think his death was faked, and I think I know who helped him. Kalamack.

I'm guessing that Bairn exchanged his silence on whatever he found on Kalamack Inc. for Kalamack faking his death so he could get out of the I.S. Morgan might have been looking for the same deal, but I doubt that's what she got since she tried to pin a biogenetic crime on Kalamack shortly after talking to him. (It didn't stick.)

The <u>Gazette</u>'s fact sheets say that the I.S. is a generous employer. They would have to be with that 30-year contract.

I'm also willing to bet that Captain Edden of the FIB bought out Morgan's contract in exchange for her help with that Brimstone bust at the bus depot she was involved in since Kalamack clearly didn't. Normally I'd say that a witch is the last person the FIB would go out of their way to help, but after seeing Edden's fact sheet from the paper, him helping her is a definite possibility.

Edden has some radical ideas about working with Inderlanders. I might try to get an interview with him. See what I can dig up. Morgan actually wrote up some species guidelines for his department. I've got a copy of them here since they have more useful information than the species descriptions I got out of the I.S.'s dumpster.

Wish I'd known earlier that pixy dust can make you itch.

RETIRED I.S. RUNNER PRONOUNCED DEAD

by Yevon Darling
ydarling@hollowsgazette.com

I.S. officers were shocked today to find that the ooze that I.S. forensic teams scraped off former I.S. runner Leon Bairn's front porch was indeed the remains of the longtime I.S. officer.

"It's a shame," an investigating officer who preferred to remain anonymous was quoted as saying. "I knew Bairn, and he was more careful than to be blown away by a misaligned spell. We're going to miss him. And right after he retired, too."

Claims by the FIB of foul play have been filed but the human-run institution has no jurisdiction to pursue a court case unless a human link can be made, unlikely since the spell that killed Bairn was witch in origin.

"It's probably a disgruntled Inderlander out for revenge," Ms. Petter, public relations at the I.S., told us. "That's why we frown on early retirement. You have to give the felons you put behind bars a chance to cool off." Bairn's memorial is being arranged by Divine Departure, Cincinnati. The family asks for donations to Displaced Witches in lieu of flowers. Bairn is survived by a daughter and granddaughter.

See I.S. RUNNER **C8**

63

Of Vampires, Living—and Not So Living

By Rachel Morgan

*Published in conjunction with Cincinnati's FIB Inderland Department;
FIB Inderlander Handbook, issue 7.23*

Even before the Turn, vampires have held a place in literature as figures of power and terror, lusting after both our blood and will. They're capable of horrific actions with no sense of remorse, instilling humans and Inderlanders alike with a healthy respect born in fear. But even more dangerous than a hungry vampire is trying to confront one in ignorance. It is with this in mind that I agreed to put on paper the distinctions that separate the big-bad-ugly wannabes from the really big-bad-uglies. Both can kill you, but if you know their limits and liabilities, this very powerful, manipulative branch of the Inderland family can be understood and handled in a successful manner.

Living vampires are either high-blood, vampires conceived within a living vampire and therefore having an inactive vampire virus fixed into their fetal genome to modify their development, or low-blood, humans bitten by an undead and existing in a tenuous, halfway-turned status. Only an undead vampire has the active form of the virus that can infect a human. The virus happily settles itself within cells of the blood-producing bone marrow of its new host and immediately goes dormant. Very little of the vampire's abilities or liabilities are imparted to the hapless human apart from their liking for human blood, and that might be conditioning rather than any physical need.

Bitten humans half-turned are at the bottom of the vampiric rung, constantly currying the favor of their undead sires for a chance to ingest more of his or her blood in the hopes of achieving a higher level of vampire characteristics. With their human teeth, human frailties, and lacking any blood lust but in their imaginations, these ghouls are little more than a willing source of blood to the undead and an object of hidden ridicule to the rest of Inderland.

Ghouls rightly live in fear that the undead who feed on them will become careless and accidentally kill them, conveniently forgetting to finish the job and bring them back as an undead. And whereas a high-blood vampire is born with status that he or she carries into vampiric death, low-blood vampires must fight for theirs. They can be very dangerous if they start to overcompensate, becoming ruthless in their attempts to measure up to their sire's expectations.

The other extreme of the vampiric existence are the true undead. These are the soulless, alluring vampires who exist only to satisfy their carnal urges, and it's their incredible strength coupled with their utter disregard for life that makes them such a threat. They experience no compassion or empathy, yet retain all their memories; they remember ties of love, but they don't remember why they love. It's a dead emotion, and in my limited experience, it brings untold grief to the living they interact with and once cared for.

The liabilities of the undead are few, and while they have lost their souls, many don't consider that a drawback but a blessing. If sanctified, crosses can inflict real damage on undead tissue, but it's a charm that causes the hurt, not a religious belief. Bringing out a cross will most likely only irritate a vampire, not get him or her to back down, so have something more potent to follow it up with.

In theory, the charm to burn undead flesh can be put into any bit of redwood or silver, but the magic is older than agriculture, and those that craft the spell—be they human or witch—insist the charm won't stick to anything but a cross. Personally, I wouldn't trust anything but a sanctified cross to distract a vampire in a tight situation.

I've found that unblessed artifacts of any religion are little more than a bother, ticking off the undead with the reminder that because their soul has already moved on, there will be nothing to carry their awareness to a higher plane when their body fails. Undead vampires are intimately aware that if their body dies, not only will their spark of life cease, but it will be as if it had never existed, a thought intolerable to the immortality-seeking vampires.

It's with the undead that light becomes a liability. The virus that allows vampires to continue their existence after the loss of their soul is rendered inactive by light, and they will undergo a remarkably undramatic death.

Only the undead are capable of bespelling an unwilling person, luring them into a state of bliss by way of sophisticated pheromones. This is perhaps the most dangerous aspect of the undead and should be treated with the utmost caution. Don't bother averting your eyes; it won't help and only pushes a hungry vampire's buttons. Fear is a blood aphrodisiac; try not to make things worse.

Fortunately, unless you have pissed the undead off or are quivering in terror, they will likely ignore you. The undead are fastidious in choosing their blood partners and will generally target living vampires to avoid legal battles with humans. A word of caution: luring and betraying humans to their ruin with false promises gives the undead a feeling of lustful domination that stirs them almost as much as the blood. Try not to get involved.

The newly undead can be very cruel to those they don't fear or have never loved, but with time they regain a veneer of morality, most attaining elegant social skills to beguile and charm. It's all the better to eat you with, my dear, so be careful. A good rule of thumb is the nicer a vampire is, the more depraved he or she can be.

As their sophistication grows, undead vampires' lust for domination mixes equally with their desire for blood, making the blood of someone they betrayed far sweeter than the blood of the merely stupid. The older the vampire, the longer and more emotionally devastating the hunt can be on the hunted. The "long hunt" is a skill that even living vampires practice unconsciously.

* * * *

Caught between the living and the undead are the high-blood living vampires, existing in a state of grace most other vampires envy. They embody the best of both worlds and are the cherished living children of the undead, both protected and plagued, loved and abused, warped, manipulated, and coddled by the undead who hunt and feed upon them.

High-blood living vampires are not bitten but born with the vampire virus already having molded them into a state of in-between. As a result, high-blood living vampires possess an increased strength and reflexes, better hearing, and an incredible sense of smell, all of which fall between normal human and an undead vampire. Even more telling is that they can bespell the willing, becoming deadly if their lust for blood overrides their other emotions.

The bloodlust in living high-blood vampires doesn't kick in until puberty, and even though they don't need blood to remain sane as the undead do, the dormant virus does impart a craving for it. You can spot living vampires by their magnetic personality and their sharp canines, but don't rely on the teeth to give them away as they can be capped.

Because the virus is fixed into their DNA, living high-blood vampires are guaranteed to become undeads even if they die with every last drop of blood in them. If you accidentally kill a living vampire, be responsible and call an ambulance before the sun comes up. They have the right to settle their affairs even if they might want to take you out later. Chances are good that if you apologize, they may thank you for ending their first life.

Living vampires possess rank based on bloodlines both living and dead, sometimes stretching back generations. This gives many of the more affluent living vampires a "prince in waiting" status honored by all wise vampires and should be honored by you. A blood sire often charts the path of his living children with the careful study of breeding thoroughbreds, so if you insult a living vampire, you may hear about it from his or her master. Whether you agree with their lifestyle or not, you should respect someone who was around at the signing of the Declaration of Independence.

Through the generations, living and undead vampires have evolved many ways to capture and keep a ready supply of companionship and blood, most of which hinge on pheromones both consciously and unconsciously emitted. Supporting the pheromones is a veritable cocktail of neurotransmitters and endorphin-inducing compounds in the saliva of a vampire. With any bite, the compounds settle into the tissue surrounding the wound, and when stimulated, even years later, may cause pain to be recognized as pleasure. Don't be fooled. It's a trap.

With experience, a living vampire can sensitize the bite so that he or she is the only vampire able to stimulate the scar, effectively preventing easy poaching from another vampire's stable. The person is mentally bound to the vampire and is called a shadow. A shadow belonging to a living vampire is generally cared for, though there's a significant loss of will.

If bitten and left unbound, there's no dependency upon any particular vampire and life can soon return to normal. However, if enough vampire saliva has been introduced into the wound, the victim is left in a dangerous state where he or she is highly susceptible to vampire pheromones without the usual loss of will. These unbound shadows are almost irresistible to a vampire's blood lust, and if not under a strong vampire's protection, they're taken as fair game for any vampire. Unclaimed shadows have a very short life expectancy, passed from vampire to vampire until they lose first their individuality and then their vitality, dying alone and unmourned.

For better or worse, vampires are here, living among us but forever apart. When on the streets, knowledge is the ultimate weapon, and it's up to you to protect yourself from the dangers engendered by contact with vampires. They will always be ready to play upon our desire for perfect love, and the dangers of seeking out that perfect love in ignorance can lead to your death or worse. I hope that I have frightened you enough to be careful and given you enough knowledge to realize that vampires are the ultimate predators of mind and body. The danger lies in that they're more human than human, and for that they deserve our respect and understanding. ■

Pixies and Fairies. Yes, There Is a Difference
By Rachel Morgan

Published in conjunction with Cincinnati's FIB Inderland Department;
FIB Inderlander Handbook, issue 7.23

Pixies and fairies have lived among humans for longer than any other Inderland group, but less is known about them than any of their larger kin. For ages, artists and poets have tried to capture the distinctions between them gained in glimpses, ultimately falling short as both pixies and fairies worked to preserve the truth of their existences. Now that they live among us openly, it's time to recognize the differences in these two highly inventive groups of citizens so that we may treat them with the respect they deserve.

To the uninformed, pixies and fairies might be considered the same species with minor changes in size and wings. Nothing could be further from the truth, and the easiest way to incur the anger of either of these resilient peoples is to say so. Pixies especially have an incredible culture, and understanding this will lead to a greater appreciation of what motivates them.

Pixies have dragonfly-like wings and are slightly smaller than their fairy kin, coming in at about four inches. Their faster metabolism and hard wings make them wickedly fast fliers, necessitating a diet of mainly nectar and pollen, supplementing it with the odd bit of meat before hibernation. A sustained temperature below forty-five degrees Fahrenheit will drop them into a torpid state that is unwise to break until spring.

They invariably marry for love and are said to die of heartache when their spouse passes on. Their life span is fifteen to twenty years, largely hinging upon their living conditions. Children are born in batches from two to a dozen, gestation being about six months depending on the season and the availability of food.

Big families are indicative of a good provider and a nurturing mother, giving the entire pixy clan status since it takes a large plot of land to support many children. It's not uncommon for the first year or two of children to be lost because of bad conditions and the inability to defend against encroaching fairies. Death during hibernation is another constant threat to the very young and very old, but pixies can expect a long life once they make it past the first few years.

Tradition dictates that children are named after their father, the eldest having short names, the youngest given longer, more elaborate titles. Children leave to tend their own gardens when about nine, shortly after puberty.

When lured into paying jobs, pixies use their natural talents to excel in surveillance, camera maintenance, and general sneaking around. They will not work as gardeners for anyone but themselves. Though loyal and honest to a fault with those they respect, they will lie like the devil to those they don't, and friendships mean more to them than life itself.

Most metals burn pixy skin, acting like a poison should it get into their blood system, whereupon the survival rate drops to almost nothing. Pixy dust is still much of an enigma, but shedding dust is a sign of high emotions and can act as an irritant on human and Inderland skin, much like poison ivy. A lesser-known aspect of pixy dust is its ability to clot blood, an adaptation necessary for sword-toting gardeners who can afford little blood loss before becoming comatose.

Most pixies live in the country since gardens sophisticated enough to support a growing clan are understandably scarce within city limits, but once established, an elaborate city garden is safer than one in the country and vigorously defended. It's the rare pixy who is attracted to the danger and excitement of living among people a hundred times larger than pixies are, but the safety found within the city is often lure enough to risk starvation.

Even city-living pixies generally avoid people, existing on the fringes as citizens without rights or responsibilities to the point where they're actually considered an expense, not an employee, when working for the I.S. They cannot hold property and have no legal rights. It's a situation that pixies promote, preferring to swallow the indignities heaped upon them by their fellow Inderlanders and humans so they can remain free to settle their much more pressing differences with fairies using a sword rather than in the human/Inderland-run courts.

Pixies are in constant conflict for territory with the larger, more aggressive fairies. If you see a pixy wearing red, he is out of his territory and not looking for trouble. It's a sign of truce. Don't ask him to violate it; you'll likely get pixed and spend the rest of the day with a bad case of hives.

Despite their small size and fun-loving, peaceful appearance, pixies will not hesitate to kill fairies in defense of people they care for or to defend their territory—and they're good at it. Their natural skills of subterfuge, quickness, and their mind-set of putting their own beliefs above the law could lend itself to a life of crime, but a pixy is at his or her best in the garden. They could rule the world through fear if they wished, but all a pixy desires is a small plot of land and the right to defend it. I've never heard of a pixy harming a person other than making the individual's life miserable in retaliation for a slight or insult. In pixies' minds, we're simply below notice, not worth the risk of attracting a human or Inderland court and changing the status quo.

* * * *

Fairies also keep to themselves, but they're far more likely to hire out for questionable jobs for large pay. Their small size and inward-directed morals make them very effective assassins, so don't mistake small with harmless. They have butterfly-like wings and a slower metabolism, but their ability to float high unseen for long periods seems to be a good trade-off for the faster but more calorically expensive flying that pixies are capable of.

Fairies are far more prevalent in the cities, and adolescents of both sexes will brave the streets to set up packs in parks or green spaces, looking for adventure and a chance to prove themselves and earn the right to start a family. Might makes right is their mentality, compared to the individual morals guiding pixy decisions.

Being insectivores, fairies often vie for the same space as pixies, and this often brings the two species into conflict. They could exist peacefully on the same territory but for a fairy's tendency to ruin an area in search of food. The balance of power is fairly equal, with fairies being larger—coming in at about six inches—but slower. Fairies share the same allergic reaction to silver as pixies, and they migrate to Mexico with monarch butterflies for the winter instead of hibernating. Not much is known about their home life.

* * * *

Despite their small size, pixies and fairies are potentially dangerous and can cause untold grief when insulted or slighted. Treat them with respect, and these deservedly proud, intelligent members of Inderland will respond with professionalism and grace. ∎

I checked out Cincy's DMV files and found out that the sweet little red car Morgan's tooling around in used to belong to the same I.S. agent who died in the car bomb last June. He's dead, and she's got his car. There's more here, I know it.

I'm going to bust this wide open. I just need a little more time.

With that in mind, I started creating a description of everyone who comes to the church more than once. There aren't too many. I think the vampire, Ivy Tamwood, scares them away. It's a good thing my scope has a camera on it, or I'd never get close enough to take a shot. Those pixies are murder!

Oh, and I've got a date with that woman at the paper who started the same day as me. Winnie and I are sharing space at the paper, apparently, since she got herself a real column, too.

Subject: RACHEL MORGAN

Species/Sex: Witch/Female
Location: Hollows
Employer: Self-Vampiric Charms
Gets Around: Bus or red convertible

Home: 1597 Oak Staff, Hollows, KY
Work: Same

Height: 5'8"
Weight: ~130#
Build: Athletic
Age: 24, Birthday is July 27, 1981

DAYS/TIMES OBSERVED

9/8 6:00 am-6:45 am   9/13 3:40 pm-2:00 am
9/9 6:00-2:00 pm   9/29 all day
9/12 noon-4:00 pm

OBSERVED

DESCRIPTION: Wears a size 8 dress and 8 shoe. Carries her spells
in a large shoulder bag. The only sensible thing about her wardrobe
are her shoes or boots. She has red, frizzy, shoulder-length hair
and green eyes. Flat chest, narrow hips, minimal makeup. Somehow
she pulls it off. I've seen guys turn around. Must be a witch thing.
She dresses trashy most of the time and likes charms and big hoop
earrings.

HAUNTS: Mostly the Hollows, but her work takes her into Cincinnati. I'm sure she's the witch who naired me—the bus won't pick her up. Ha, ha!

HABITS: She likes her coffee black. She runs almost every evening, ending up at a spell or coffee shop more often than not. Keeps a fish in the kitchen on the windowsill.

ACQUAINTANCES / FAMILY
- Ivy Tamwood: The vampire she quit the I.S. with.
- Jenks: Pixy. Entire family lives in the stump in garden.
- Mother: Alice. Lives in Cincy. Crazy mom.
- Robbie: Older brother, not speaking; Portland.
- Kisten Felps: Boyfriend, or Piscary's watchdog?

RESEARCHED
Not much on this woman—It might be I.S. policy to clear the records of their employees, but even so, I couldn't even find out her middle name. I was lucky to find her birth date.

EDUCATION: Two-year degree at a small local college, majoring in earth magic and criminal justice. Not a spectacular standout, but she graduated HS almost a year early, probably due to homeschooling for several years.

EMPLOYMENT: First real job was I.S. runner, straight out of college. She quit the I.S. and either bought her way out of her contract or slept with someone, because the woman isn't smart enough to survive

73

an I.S. death threat. She currently works for herself with Ivy Tamwood as an independent runner. They both seem to be using pixies as backup.

HISTORY: Father died when she was 13. He used to be an I.S. operative in the Arcane Division, which explains the I.S. job. Her medical history is of some note. She was diagnosed as having Rosewood syndrome, but she's alive, meaning they misdiagnosed it. She's sensitive to sulfur, though, and reads the back of almost everything she puts in her shopping cart. It looks like she's got a recent vampire bite on the left side of her neck. Probably from that Felps vampire.

I've watched this woman for three weeks. She's a nutcase, living with a vampire in a church!! Bi? Or just clueless?

APPLICATION FOR TITLE AND REGISTRATION KENTUCKY

Rachel Morgan	Phone Mobile:	(513) 555-4893
Name of Buyer(s)	Phone Home:	(513) 555-7762

Primary Address:	1597 Oak Staff	Hollows	KY	41011
	Street	City	State	Zip Code

KY845220894	07/27/81	NA		
Buyer's Driver's License No.	Date of Birth /Death		Co-Buyer's Driver's License No.	Date of Birth/Death

YES	NO	NO		
New Title and Tag	Tag Transfer	New Title, no Tags	Motorcycle Engine Number	Truck/Tractor/Trailer Weight

If Transferring Tags from a vehicle that you sold to this vehicle, give the following	Class of Vehicle	Tag Number	Validate

Subject to a Lien?			Kind of Lien
NO	Amount	Date	

Name of Secured Party	Address of Secured Party
	Were Insurance 710 Vine, Cincinnati OH, 45702

Certificate of Insurance		Name / Address of Insurance Co	Tammy LeForne
	20060877825		Name of Agent
	Policy or Binder Number		

I certify that the odometer reading made by the seller is correct to the best of my knowledge.

I/we certify under penalty of perjury that to the best of my/our knowledge that the vehicle's VIN number and the one on this document agree with the plate on the vehicle.

Signature of Buyer(s)	*Rachel Morgan*	*Rachel Morgan* Date 10/02/06
Printed name of Buyer(s)	Rachel Morgan	

EMPLOYEE PERFORMANCE REVIEW

Employee Name: **Rachel Morgan**   Period of Evaluation: **May 2006**

Employee Number: **200106WR48**   Department: **Street Force**

Job Title: **Street Runner**   Supervisor: **Denon Gradey**

PERFORMANCE

	Unacceptable					Superior
Abilities, Knowledge, Skills: Does employee show the required knowledge and skills to perform his job?	❏	❏	☒	❏	❏	❏
Quality of Work: Does the employee complete projects within the required quality standards?	❏	❏	☒	❏	❏	❏
Work Habits: Does the employee show a positive and cooperative attitude to his or her assignments?	❏	☒	❏	❏	❏	❏
Communication: How well does the employee communicate with others both verbally and in writing?	❏	☒	❏	❏	❏	❏

BEHAVIOR

	Unacceptable					Superior
Cooperation: Does employee work with others?	❏	❏	☒	❏	❏	❏
Initiative: Does the employee seek ways to improve job functions or take on more responsibility?	❏	☒	❏	❏	❏	❏
Adaptability: Does employee show a willingness to take on unexpected tasks or constructive criticism?	❏	❏	☒	❏	❏	❏
Judgment: Does employee analyze issues and find ways to solve problems?	❏	☒	❏	❏	❏	❏

Attendance/Punctuality: Absences, excused and non.   ❏ Unacceptable   Superior ☒

Overall Performance	❏	❏	❏	☒	❏	❏

EMPLOYEE: I have seen my review and discussed it with my supervisor. My signature doesn't imply agreement.

Employee: _**Rachel Morgan**_   Supervisor: _**Denon Gradey**_

Subject: IVY TAMWOOD

Species/Sex: Vampire/Female
Location: Hollows
Employer: Self-Vampiric Charms
Gets Around: Nightwing 2000. Borrows mom's car a lot.

Home: 1597 Oak Staff, Hollows, KY
Work: Same

Height: 5'10"
Weight: ~140#
Build: Athletic or model
Age: 27. Birthday in January 1979

DAYS/TIMES OBSERVED
9/8 6:00 am-6:45 am   9/13 3:40 pm-2:00 am
9/9 6:00-2:00 pm   9/29 all day
9/12 noon-4:00 pm

OBSERVED

DESCRIPTION: This woman is stunning. More sexy than most undead vampires I've seen. She has an Asian cast, with an oval face, pale skin, and long, straight, black hair. Small nose. Very white teeth. Her canines are not as long as an undead's, but longer than a human's. No jewelry but for a large crucifix. I think she wears it to keep her undead mother at arm's length, even if she's always borrowing her car. No nail polish, little makeup. She's a dresser, too, with lots of leather because of the bike, I guess, and silk.

HAUNTS: I've seen her everywhere, from the ugly parts of the Hollows to Cincy, and even up in Carew Tower's restaurant.

HABITS: Likes her coffee black and drinks a lot of orange juice. She's got a big-ass katana and practices martial arts when Rachel is out. She's got two owls she keeps up in the belfry. I think she's a little obsessive about organization. Something isn't right with her. I think she was abused as a kid. I think she's bi. Seems to have a thing for Rachel. Rachel seems oblivious.

ACQUAINTANCES / FAMILY

- Rachel Morgan
- Jenks: Pixy. Does her backup work.
- Mother: Don't know her name, but she's dead. Lives in Cincy.
- Dad: Living vamp. Takes care of mom. He looks ill. Goes by the last name Randal.
- Erica: Sister. Last name Randal.
- Kisten Felps: Living vamp. Ex-boyfriend?
- Piscary: Master vampire. Hollows.

RESEARCHED

EDUCATION: Four-year degree in criminology at University of Cincinnati. Graduated with top honors.

EMPLOYMENT: Hired into the I.S. out of college. Skipped entry-level position of runner and went into homicide where she worked with an undead vampire until he was convicted of underage predation. She bought her I.S. contract out and is now one-third owner of Vampiric Charms. She's the money behind the firm. The woman is loaded. Rachel owns another third. I don't know who has the last.

HISTORY: She's one of Piscary's favorite vampires. She was his scion at one point, but was stripped of the position when she went on a blood fast. They are currently on the outs, which is probably why she's living in a church, but a vampire, even a living one, can't leave the maker of their family line. Her mother and grandmother were Piscary's as well. Ivy is the last living heir to the Tamwood line. Her younger sister, Erica, took their father's name of Randal so as to keep his family line from dying out.

Subject: JENKS

Species/Sex: Pixy/Male
Location: Hollows
Employer: Vampiric Charms

Home: 1597 Oak Staff, Hollows, KY
Work: Same

Height: ~4"
Weight: Few ounces?
Build: Athletic
Age: Looks about 18 (and has a mouth to match)

DAYS/TIMES OBSERVED

9/8 6:00 am-6:45 am   9/13 3:40 pm-2:00 am
9/9 6:00-2:00 am   9/29 all day
9/12 noon-4:00 pm

DESCRIPTION: I never thought I'd make a report on a pixy, but this one is around too much to dismiss. I'm thinking he's the final third in the partnership of Vampiric Charms, but since pixies aren't real citizens, I don't know how that's going to work. At any rate, the church grounds are infested with them. Honey won't bribe them like every other pixy I've run into, and I'm tired of being pixed. I've started parking half a block away and watching through a high-powered scope.

Jenks is blond, like all pixies. He wears black silk when on a run. He usually has a red bandana on when he leaves the church grounds. I think it protects him from other pixies.

He is heavily scarred. He carries a sword the size of an olive pick, and I've watched him use it to kill a blue jay bothering his kids. His wings and dust change color according to moods. He's got strong shoulders, a thin waist, angular face. He looks about 18, but I've counted almost four-dozen kids. They must have them in batches.

HAUNTS: He stays at church unless on a run. Goes out for coffee a lot with Rachel.

HABITS: Flies around and curses a lot. Has a thing for Tink. I noted his best curses.

For the love of Tink.
Sweet mother of Tink.
What in Tink's knickers.
Tink's diaphragm.
Tink's titties.
Tink's contractual Hell.
Damn it all to Disneyland.
Tink knocks your knickers.
Tink's a Disney whore.
Son of a Disney whore.
What in Tink's garden of sin.
Tink's daisies-crapping on or pissing in.
Tink's little red shoes or thong.
Dumber than Tink's dildo.
Tink's tampons.
Tink loves a duck.
So sweet I could fart fairy balls.
Tighter than a straight man's butt cheeks in prison.
Before the sun goes nova.
Poop ice cream cones, do you?
Pissing on my daisies.
Worthless as a pixy condom.
Slicker than snot on a doorknob.

ACQUAINTANCES AND FAMILY

- Ivy Tamwood: they get along very well.
- Rachel Morgan: good partnership, if weird.
- Matalina: I think this is his wife. Sweet voice.
- Kids: He's got about 50 of them. I listed them below.

Jenks's kids and how often he yells at them.

Jax ///	Jalaheel //	Jocelynn
Jerrimatt /	Jezabel //	Jacklyn
Jolivia ////	Joshua	Jamilla
Jack ////	Jorel //	Jessie //
Jessica //	Jaiden /	Jalan /
Jrixibell //	Janie /	Jixy ///
Jariath //////	Jih	Jamantha
Jristofer ///	Jillian /	Jumoke /
Jenry /	Jannie /	Junis
Jistina ///	Jake ////	Jacey
Jarlies //	Jhem //	Jhan //
Josie //	Juniper /	Jicholas
Jiselle //	Jacen	Jarie
Jinn /	Joce ///	Jindrew /
Josbelle //	Janthony	Jichael
Jeorge /	Janice /	Jeremy /
Jagan /	James /	Josephine
Jaul /	Jinni /	

Subject: KEASLEY

Species/Sex: Witch?/Male
Employer: Retired
Gets Around: Walking

Home: Across the street from the church
Hollows, KY

Height: ~5'8"
Weight: About 160
Build: Arthritic
Age: Old. Really old.

DAYS/TIMES OBSERVED
9/8 came over ~2:00 pm
9/13 came over for dinner.

OBSERVED

DESCRIPTION: Brown eyes, dark skin. Keeps his hair tight to his skull, but it's graying. Looks worn out and tired. Wears thin clothes. Clearly on a fixed income. Has bad arthritis, even with the charms he wears to fight it. Voice is raspy. Looks like a vagrant. Teeth are stained from coffee. Doesn't leave the house much.

HABITS: Likes to garden, and I've seen him trying to fix up his house, but he hurts too much to do anything. Looks like he's broke, but I've seen him give money to kids to get ice cream.

Subject: KISTEN FELPS (KIST)

Species/Sex: Living Vamp/Male
Location: Hollows
Employer: Pizza Piscary's
Gets Around: Black Corvette

Home: Pizza Piscary's
213 River St
Hollows, KY 41011
Work: Same

Height: 5'10"
Weight: ~160#
Build: Athletic, slim
Age: 26. Birthday is January 29, 1980

DAYS/TIMES OBSERVED

9/9   Came over to church ~2:00 pm
9/10   Spot check at dinner hour at Piscary's

OBSERVED

DESCRIPTION: Small nose, small chin, lightly stubbled. Blue eyes, blond hair, but I found hair dye in his trash. He's really brown-haired, I think. Lean, but strong. I saw him cart a huge man out of Piscary's like a baby. Talks with a British accent, again fake. Wears a chain of black gold—not fake. Twin stud earrings in one ear, the other lobe is torn. (ouch) No visible scars apart from one right over his eye. Sharp, small fangs make him a living vampire.

Wears leather on occasion. More silk and cotton. Dresses well, sophisticated. Keeps a slight stubble for the ladies, but otherwise tidy. This guy is a player. Moves with a predator's grace and has a voice women would probably call sexy. I've had to stay too far back to hear much of it.

HAUNTS: Hangs out at the church or Pizza Piscary's. He's Piscary's scion. He's got a huge boat at the quay called SOLAR, and he stays on that when Piscary's pissed at him.

HABITS: Likes to play the submissive, but this guy has a temper. Likes his women. Works as a manager/bouncer at Pizza Piscary's.

ACQUAINTANCES / FAMILY

- Rachel Morgan
- Ivy Tamwood: I think they dated, seem like friends now.
- Piscary: His master vampire. Hollows.
- Lots of bar friends, but none seem serious.

RESEARCHED

EDUCATION : Bachelor's in marketing and business at U of C. Graduated from local HS. Nothing of note.

EMPLOYMENT: Has always worked for Piscary, first as a cook at the restaurant, then a bouncer, now manager. The Gazette's fact sheet says he's Piscary's scion, but he's in too good a mood most of the time. Maybe it's because Tamwood is picking up the nasty stuff.

Hollows Gazette
Fact Sheets

INTERNAL FACT SHEET

Document Shepherd: Anne Cardan (513) 555-7735 ext 15
Updated 1/05

Kalamack in a word: Powerful. Charismatic. Enigmatic.

TRENTON ALOYSIUS KALAMACK
Fortune 20 member "since birth"

IN BRIEF

Species	Undisclosed
Born	Oct. 21, 1979
Height	5'10"
Weight	155 pounds
Eyes	Green
Build	Slight, Athletic
Hair	Blond
Marital Status	Single
Children	None

Trent Kalamack is one of the most enigmatic and popular figures in today's polite society. It's still open to speculation if he is Inderland or human, but his wispy hair, trim physique, and small teeth eliminate most Inderland species.

Trent graduated from CA State in 1999 with a business degree, which he put to good use developing his father's considerable estate.

Trent maintains many of the city orphanages and donates generously every year to the zoo's herbology department.

Mr. Kalamack is best known for his city council seat and his annual October 31st party benefiting the Greater Cincinnati area's underprivileged. He resides at the Kalamack estate outside of Cincinnati's city lines, where he employs hundreds of humans and Inderlanders alike in industrial research and development.

Trent is also known for his prizewinning gardens and his world-renowned stables that have produced not one but six Kentucky Derby winners if his father's efforts can be included. He also breeds and shows hounds.

He's been voted Cincy's Most Eligible Bachelor three years running. He favors Earl Grey tea and golfs regularly with the mayor's son.

The taint of biodrugs shadowed his father's death, a shame that still follows Trent even today and may be why he remains single and very private despite his numerous public appearances.

TRENTON ALOYSIUS KALAMACK

HIGHLIGHTS

QUEN HANSEN Trent's bodyguard and chief security officer. He has worked for the family for years, beginning with Kalamack Sr.

JONATHAN DAVAROS Once a personal friend of Kalamack Sr., he now works for Trent as his chief personnel officer.

SARA JANE GRADENKO Trent's personal secretary. New hire, June 2006. She's a warlock, as all of Trent's secretaries are.

PARENTS Both deceased under questionable circumstances. Trent's mother, Felecia, was very active in Cincy's social circles and is still missed today. Kalamack Sr. created the industrial empire Trent now gainfully wields. He was said to be a harsh man.

Contact: Mr. Jonathan Davaros
Chief Personnel Officer
Kalamack Industries, Inc.
15 Rolling Acres
Cincinnati, OH 45239
513-555-4242

Interviews are granted for: city issues, industrial concerns (local and abroad), and public relations, including but not limited to his stables, gardens, inner-city revitalization, and his underprivileged outreaches. The occasional human-interest story is entertained in an election year. Film and photos are not allowed.

Expect a thorough search upon entering the grounds. Confiscated equipment will be returned.

TO INTERVIEW

Interviews are a strict 40 minutes unless otherwise arranged. It is advisable to arrive 40 minutes ahead of time to allow processing. Mr. Kalamack is an easy interview, but do not push an issue that he clearly skirts. Topics to avoid are underemployment of Inderlanders (unless it's currently a hot topic in an election year), biodrugs, Brimstone, questions as to his species, his marital/relationship status, and anything concerning his deceased parents.

Though Mr. Kalamack is a tactile person and initiates an introductory handshake, professional hugs are not acceptable.

No perfume or strong cologne.

Business attire is required regardless of the time of day, even when at the stables or gardens.

TO CONTACT

Interviews with Mr. Kalamack are most readily available before noon and after 7:00 P.M. at Kalamack Industries. Expect 2 days to 2 weeks before confirmation.

Document Shepherd: Anne Cardan (513) 555-7735 ext 15
Updated 1/05

Captain Edden in a Word: Determined. Honest. Misguided?

CAPTAIN S. EDDEN

Captain of street detail of FIB

IN BRIEF

Species: . . . . Human
Born: 1958
Height: . . . . 5'9"
Weight: . . . . 180#
Eyes: . . . . Brown
Build: . . . . Stocky/Ex-Military
Hair: . . . . Black, cut short
Marital Status: . . . . Widower
Children: . . . . Adopted son, Mathew Glenn

Captain Edden has worked for the FIB his entire adult life, beginning his career on the streets of New Orleans. He is currently captain of the Cincinnati FIB's street force division, a post he doesn't seem to be eager to leave, keeping enough clout to advance his questionable attempts to work more closely with Inderlanders, and maintaining enough anonymity to do the same.

His desire to form an Inderlander branch within the current FIB system is meeting internal resistance, but if successful, it will be the first time since the Turn that Inderlanders and humans have worked together on a state level since the evolution of the FIB and the I.S.

His adopted son, Mathew Glenn, has taken over much of the responsibilities of developing this human/Inderlander task force and has enjoyed some minor success in solving several crimes that the I.S. and the FIB have been unable to resolve on their separate devices. It's believed that Edden's ideas concerning Inderlanders have kept him from further advancement.

Well liked by his men despite his efforts to work with Inderlanders, he's known for his straightforward responses; not necessarily PC, but effective.

Edden maintains his relationships with

INTERNAL FACT SHEET

CAPTAIN S. EDDEN

HIGHLIGHTS

FIB Worked for the FIB following four-year enlistment, hiring in at New Orleans. Moved to Cincinnati to take advantage of promotion to captain.

LENORA EDDEN (GLENN) Wife, deceased after a violent mugging.

CPL. ROSE SMITHE Office manager and Edden's acting secretary. She's been with Edden since he moved to Cincinnati.

FIB OFFICER MATHEW GLENN Adopted son from his wife's previous marriage. Mathew hired into the FIB after a brief stint in the military. Transferred to his father's division to head up the new Inderland Division. Uses his mother's maiden name to avoid claims of nepotism.

high-ranking members in the I.S. while brushing up his bowling and golf scores.

TO CONTACT

Interviews with Captain Edden are available during human business hours at the FIB's downtown office.

Contact: Cpl. Rose Smithe
FIB 5th floor
513 Bur Oak St
Cincinnati OH, 45202
513-555-6900 (ext 6)

Interviews are granted for city concerns, trends in crime, and public relations and will generally need 48 hours advanced notice unless it's a timely story needing immediate damage control.

Film and photos are allowed with advanced notice.

Five-minute "Can I quote you" sessions by phone are preferred.

TO INTERVIEW

In-depth interviews are 30 minutes unless otherwise arranged. If you're on time, he will be too.

Topics to avoid: his personal opinion on noncity issues, his personal relationships, and his time spent in New Orleans.

Document Shepherd: Anne Cardan (513) 555-7735 ext 15
Updated 3/05

The Hollows Gazette

Piscary in a word: Dangerous. Necessary. Scary-as-All-Hell.

PISCARY

AKA Ptah Ammon Fineas Horton Madison; Parker Piscary

IN BRIEF

Species. . . . . Undead vampire
Born. . . . . Presumed 1700s
Height . . . . 5'8"
Weight . . . . 150#
Eyes . . . . Brown
Build . . . . Slight
Hair . . . . None
Marital Status . . . . Widower
Children . . . . No biological children

Piscary's name has been a part of Cincinnati's history for almost as long as the city has had a name. He currently operates most of Greater Cincinnati and the Hollows-area gambling cartel, a task he began under the name Parker while running bootleg whiskey out of KY during Prohibition.

Piscary is best known now for Pizza Piscary's, a relatively safe eatery for Inderlanders and curious humans alike. His MPL is ironclad and has a long-standing tradition of safety.

One of Cincinnati's more benevolent master vampires, Piscary is owed a debt of gratitude by the city for keeping the living and undead vampires under his umbrella healthy, happy, and mostly away from the human population.

Piscary has been a Cincinnati and Hollows fixture long before the Turn, coming to this area first to help escaped slaves across the Ohio River for a small payment of blood.

There have been many ugly crimes linked to Piscary through the years, dismissed due to lack of evidence and his excellent work in keeping Cincinnati's vampires in line. His possible history with the I.S. supports this, and indeed most law-abiding citizens are willing to overlook a few foolish humans for the illusion of safety.

He speaks with a hint of an Egyptian accent, is aggressive to large dogs, and unsettlingly kind to children. Though appearing harmless, especially when

INTERNAL FACT SHEET

PISCARY

playing the part of the kind restaurateur, Piscary should be interviewed with the utmost respect.

HIGHLIGHTS

PIZZA PISCARY'S
Piscary's restaurant located in the Hollows, serving stout bar food downstairs and elegant gourmet dining upstairs. MPL is current.
> 213 River St
> Hollows, KY 41011
> 513-555-9777

KISTEN FELPS Piscary's current scion. Pretty, but less effective in the ugly but necessary parts of the job.

IVY TAMWOOD Scion-in-waiting, currently on the outs with Piscary. Doing the ugly work in exchange for him ignoring her. Piscary began her living-vampire line in the early 1700s.

INDERLAND SECURITY
It's rumored that Piscary is one of the original I.S. backers and is consulted upon occasion. Also rumored that he's on the I.S. shit list after a falling out with a top I.S. executive.

TO CONTACT

Interviews with Mr. Piscary are most readily available between midnight and two hours before sunrise at his restaurant. Occasional daylight interviews are accepted at his home.

Contact: Mr. Kisten Felps
> Manager of Pizza Piscary's
> 213 River St
> Hollows, KY 41011
> 513-555-9777

Interviews are granted for: city issues concerning vampires, gambling regulation, and Inderland public relations. Occasional interviews with a historical aim are accepted.

A limited amount of film and photo is allowed with advanced notice.

Expect a thorough search for unauthorized filming equipment, holy artifacts, and weapons. Confiscated items will not be returned.

TO INTERVIEW

Interviews are 40 to 60 minutes, and a magic-using chaperone posing as a photographer is advised.

Treat with utmost respect. Follow the do's and don'ts.

Do:
- Wear a citrus-based perfume/cologne.
- Limit physical contact to a brief handshake.
- Wear professional attire.

INTERNAL FACT SHEET

PISCARY

- Leave immediately if Piscary's pupils dilate for longer than thirty seconds.
- Feel free to laugh to alleviate stress.

Do not:

- Interview Mr. Piscary if you possess a vampire scar. The *Gazette* will not be responsible for your safety.
- Eat crunchy food even if invited. (Liquid refreshment is okay.)

- Try on an article of clothing if offered.
- Feed his instinct by showing fear.
- Topics to avoid are vampire cronyism, past alliances, and deceased friends. It's advisable to drop a subject if Mr. Piscary shows a reluctance to divulge information.

MPL
MIXED POPULATION LICENSE

Pizza Piscary's

Has complied with current standards of safe operation and filed emergency plans with the city of Cincinnati and is hereby awarded level "A" and licensed to serve Inderland and human species.

December 12, 2005

_____
Office of Health and Safety

_____
City Inspector

INTERNAL FACT SHEET

Document Shepherd: Cathy Reddon (513) 555-7735 ext 21
Updated 1/05

INDERLAND SECURITY

Inderland Security evolved shortly after the Turn when frightened humans rebuilding the domestic security system forcibly excluded Inderlanders from the employment rolls believing that having Inderlanders on the force would result in cronyism and corruption. State jurisdiction was abandoned for a nationwide system in an effort to quicken response time and eliminate loopholes in the law.

Inderland-based crime understandably skyrocketed, and unregulated for-hire Inderland services sprung up as frustrated Inderland officers, who had been working in the former system of FBI, CIA, and local police forces, struck out on their own to right the same magical-wrongs they'd been secretly righting before the Turn, using a network that is the basis for the I.S. today.

Many of the for-hire services at that time were little more than organized crime centers, and seeing all their forward progress in achieving equality in danger of being destroyed, several of the stronger U.S. vampire camarillas took it upon themselves to expand their long tradition of self-policing their younger, more enthusiastic vampire brethren to include the significant demographic of witches and Weres.

Titling themselves Inderland Security, these very old, very experienced vampires were later highly instrumental in working with the FIB to help define Inderland crimes, ascertain proper procedures for incarnation, due process, evidence gathering, as well as helping set up a system of self-policing and information sharing to ensure that internal abuses were kept to a minimum and confidence with their FIB counterparts was held to a high standard.

Today, the I.S. is a nationwide police force that works at both the street level and in the courts to deftly handle a wide range of domestic and espionage crimes.

Though encompassing more manpower and demanding more resources than the outdated local police force they replaced, a city-based I.S. tower is well structured to handle a variety of tasks with a minimum of expenditure.

Street detail consisting of traffic control, light security, handling domestic complaints, and maintaining Inderland incarceration facilities is handled by highly trained individuals called Runners. Runners consist of 70 percent of the I.S. task force. Runners are continually licensed and regulated, ensuring the highest standard of behavior and magic abilities in their duties.

Crime investigation is the realm of the Arcane Division, and it's here that the I.S. pulls away from its FIB counterparts, relying heavily upon the undead and high magic users to gather information to bring to the courts. The Arcane Division

INTERNAL FACT SHEET

INDERLAND SECURITY

is heavily populated with vampires, both living and dead, with the occasional highly trained witch or Were.

Information gathered by the I.S. is presented in a traditional court system, unchanged since before the Turn. Both I.S.- and FIB-gathered data is permissible in court. The current court system is balanced in terms of human and Inderland magistrates and works surprisingly well.

It's the I.S.'s responsibility to safely incarcerate Inderlanders found guilty of serious crimes. Most large cities have at least one high-security facility within the city limits to hold undead vampires, the location allowing for their blood needs. It's up to the I.S. to keep these most dangerous individuals both happy and behind bars.

City-based Runner and Arcane Divisions are managed by a handful of I.S. operatives in what can only be compared to a backroom brother- and sisterhood of the same vampires who started the I.S. forty years ago. The I.S. has often come under fire for allowing secret meetings and unseen individuals to manage an entire nation's police force, but these observations are few and far between as the current system works well.

The I.S. is known to be a generous employer, with a very low turnover among its operatives. Most new hires fulfill their 30-year contracts and retire without incident.

AT A GLANCE

WHAT IT IS: An Inderland-based, state-line-crossing police force run by Inderlanders, for Inderlanders, designed to apprehend and incarcerate individuals with unique needs and abilities.

WHO CAN CALL THEM: Crimes that are Inderlander in origin revert to the offices of the I.S. Humans can request an I.S. investigation even if evidence doesn't support Inderland involvement, but this situation is less than ideal.

PROS: Many human institutions don't trust the I.S., feeling as if it's rife with cronyism and cover-ups that hide illegal Inderlander activity instead of bringing them to justice.

CONS: The I.S. is a necessary force to safely apprehend and contain the worst that Inderland has to offer.

DIVISIONS: Runners: street force. Arcane Division: investigate and gather evidence for trials.

For more information, contact:

Audrey Robin
I.S. Publicity Officer
816 Vine St.
Cincinnati, OH 45202
513-555-1005 (ext 120)

INTERNAL FACT SHEET

Document Shepherd: Cathy Reddon (513) 555-7735 ext 21
Updated 3/05

FEDERAL INDERLAND BUREAU

The Federal Inderland Bureau, or FIB, was begun during the Turn when the existing city, state, and nation security force broke down. It was intended to be a "humans only" club as a way to police the "new" demographic of Inderlanders without fear of corruption. It was a poorly thought out idea born in fear, and even more poorly implemented as it excluded the very Inderlanders who had been secretly policing Inderland from the start.

The FIB has since publicly apologized, but the two branches of security remain separate to this day. Unfortunately, the mistrust that prompted the separation still exists, and neither branch has seen fit to even try to strike down the archaic law that makes it illegal for the FIB to employ an Inderlander.

It's understandable why the FIB is often thought of as the I.S.'s poor cousin. Lacking in extended senses and magical abilities that their I.S. counterparts have, the FIB often falls behind in the task of apprehending both human and Inderland suspects.

However, it's important to note that in the areas of investigation, evidence gathering, maintaining databases, and compiling those databases into functional, easily accessible formats, it's the FIB who excels, leaving the I.S. in the dark age of pre-Turn techniques.

It's only in the human-on-human crimes that the FIB maintains its individual status, but the information they gather has served to put away more Inderlander criminals than the I.S. could ever hope to, and they remain to this day an effective force in keeping both humanity and Inderland safe.

For more information, contact:

> Bob McTarvis
> Public Relations Department
> Federal Inderland Bureau
> 513 Bur Oak St.
> Cincinnati, OH 45202
> 513-555-6980 (ext 10)

AT A GLANCE

WHAT IT IS: A human-based, state-line-crossing police force manned by humans that often serves as a source of information in the processing of Inderland and human crimes.

WHO CAN USE IT: Crimes without an Inderland association can be handled by the FIB.

PROS: Often looked down on by their I.S. counterparts, the FIB excels in nonmagic crime-scene data gathering, often supplying the hard data to bring an offending Inderlander to justice.

CONS: Officers are at a severe disadvantage when fronted with an Inderland crime.

DIVISIONS: Current divisions mimic pre-Turn designations of captain, detective, officer.

The Hollows Gazette

Tomatoes, myths/dangers **C 2**
City street party planned **C 3**
Spells: Is it legal? **C 4**
Almanac **C 4**

Wednesday, October 4, 2006

LOCAL / STATE

C

WHO YOU GOING TO CALL?

By Winifred Gradenko
winniegrad@hollowsgazette.com

As we begin October, Inderlanders and humans alike are looking to their closets and spell cupboards for costumes to celebrate the day, be it the traditional pre-Turn begging extravaganza, the holy Samhain, or what has become the unofficial marking of the Turn.

The FIB and the I.S. are preparing with candy inspection stations, free safety spell-checks, and preholiday clinics on removing tomatoes from your car or home. Neither the I.S. nor the FIB are capable of handling every emergency, and knowing who to call when trouble arises this holiday season can save you time.

Federal and local police forces that dissolved during the Turn were replaced by a single entity with the power to cross state lines. A frightened human population denied Inderlander hire-ins, frustrating the out-of-work paranormal officers who'd been keeping the pre-Turn streets safe.

Not surprisingly, crime skyrocketed and the I.S. was formed to police, apprehend, and hold its more violent members, a task that it still performs today.

That doesn't mean that the cop giving you a speeding ticket is human. Most new hires in the I.S., called runners, are given low-entry jobs while developing the diverse and detailed knowledge to apprehend the worst Inderland has to offer.

A friendly rivalry has developed between the I.S. and the FIB, keeping them both sharp as they police Cincinnati together.

The FIB is required to turn jurisdiction of a crime to the I.S. when an Inderlander is involved, but FIB-gathered data is often used in I.S. courts, generally being more detailed and far reaching.

So who do you call when your neighbors start to howl on the 31st? If you're not joining in, start with the I.S., who will likely do little more than make a report. The FIB won't be able to do anything either, but they might have the chutzpah to ask them to quiet down.

And if you are smeared with a tomato this Halloween, don't bother the I.S. or the FIB. Just wash it off. The species that caused the Turn has long been eradicated.

City Prepares For Halloween

By Cindy Strom
cstrom@hollowsgazette.com

The ideas are flowing at City Hall over Cincinnati's annual October street party. "It'll be the best one yet!" Mayor Martson was heard to say. "We've a howlathon for the homeless, a petting zoo, and a mini-car race downtown."

Festival opponents claim the yearly event breeds trouble, but the FIB and I.S. have long supported it, saying it helps reduce Halloween hijinks.

The three-day celebration starts Monday. Volunteers are needed.

WANT TO HELP?

Contact Phoebe Kelts at
555-7730 (ext 14),
pkelts@hollowsgazette.com

Partygoer at the 2005 festival, showing off his new face paint.

The Way I See It
Devin Crossman

RETIREMENT?

In my three months investigating the I.S., I've been stalled, ignored, and threatened as I sought a name, nothing more. In my search, an uglier snake than the one named incompetence reared its ugly head. Corruption.

Is it possible that the I.S. has become so corrupt that employees can't quit alive? The last person to try to break his I.S. contract, one Leon Bairn, was found dead shortly after serving notice, reduced to a thin smear on his porch ceiling. My investigations show he's not alone.

Is it conceivable that I.S. eliminates those who wish to leave before their contract ends? I'll let you know.

Devin Crossman is a guest columnist, bringing his human point of view to the Hollows. Comments will reach him at: dcrossman@hollowsgazette.com

---

@ A Glance Oct 4, 2006
Average High/Low: 69˚ / 48˚

	Today	Tomorrow
Sunrise	6:37 AM	6:38 AM
Sunset	6:16 PM	6:14 PM
Moonrise	5:04 PM	5:31 PM
Moonset	3:21 AM	4:38 AM
Phase: 3 days to full		

SEE ALMANAC C 4

Kalamack Industries, Inc

November 6, 2006

Ms. Maria Gonzalez
Senior Editor
Hollows Gazette
Hollows, KY 41011

Dear Maria,

I wanted to personally thank you for the favorable print that I've been seeing coming from your small but insightful press, specifically the wonderful front-page spread that you ran showcasing my yearly bid for Cincinnati's monies to help bolster the coffers at the city-run outreach programs. It's wonderful when all can work together for a positive end.

I also have a favor to ask. I couldn't help but notice that you're experimenting with new ways to increase both your circulation and promote better human/Inderland relations by hiring an already popular blogger, Devin Crossman, for a daily column. I can think of no better way to foster understanding than communication. Could I impose upon you to find out how effective this out-reach has been? Perhaps over lunch at your convenience?

All the best,

Trent Kalamack

Trent Kalamack

Trenton A. Kalamack ~ CEO Kalamack Industries
Kalamack Industries, Inc, Building A • 15 Rolling Acres, Cincinnati, OH 45239

9 8

Kalamack Industries, Inc

Jonathan Davaros
Chief Personnel Officer
Kalamack Industries, Inc
Building A
15 Rolling Acres
Cincinnati, OH 45239

INTEROFFICE MEMO

To: Trenton Kalamack
From: Jonathan Davaros
CC:
Date: 12/8/06
Re: Crossman Meeting

Sa'han,

Quen has arranged to meet with you Monday concerning his findings about
Crossman. Quen is currently planning on taking advantage of the upcoming
business holiday to conduct a more thorough investigation of Crossman and
possible steps to curtail him. In my mind, this has the potential to draw the very
scrutiny you're trying to avoid. As to date, nothing that Crossman has learned is
outside normal parameters of a human investigating a new audience, despite his
I.S. dumpster diving and increasing curiosity concerning magic.

It's my opinion that Quen is giving this entire situation more merit than it
deserves, and I recommend pulling Quen from heavy surveillance or hiring
someone else to conduct his regular duties before anyone else becomes curious
as to why we are watching him so closely.

Yours,

Jonathan

Chapter 3

DEVIN'S
JOURNAL
ENTRY

DECEMBER 27, 2006

I'm keeping my notes on Morgan at home now. Someone very professional went through my desk at work. Even worse, my editor, Maria, warned me off Kalamack when I was researching the archives on him. I'm clearly on to something, and Morgan, Kalamack, the I.S., and the FIB are all mixed up in it.

It's unreal, the lengths people will go to avoid the truth. There's a video circulating on the Internet of Morgan being pulled down the street by a demon, and they still look the other way! "You can't prove it was Morgan," Maria tells me. Like what other redhead would be dragged down Oak Staff road?

And what is it with Morgan being Kalamack's escort on that boat that blew up? And then surviving? I don't think Morgan was his security. I think Morgan was the one who blew it up.

This stinks like a dead vamp, and I'm going to find out what's going on.

I found Vampiric Charm's Yellow Pages ad. Nice, huh?

It looks like a hooker site the way it's worded, but it does prove that the pixy is at least a member, not just backup. Weird. If it wasn't for the snow, I wouldn't be able to watch the church anymore. The pixies are on to me even when I'm a block away. I've tried to get a camera up on a light post, but they keep finding them and shorting them out. I keep waiting for them to go into hibernation, but they aren't. I think they are going to winter in the church. Sounds like fun.

The pixies outside of the I.S.'s dumpsters are a lot more friendly, and right before it got cold, I traded a jar of peanut butter for a hard drive from a computer they were throwing out. I don't think they would have gone for it, but they needed the protein for hibernation, apparently. I feel bad for the little guys.

Most of what I found on the drive was garbage, but I did find something from Morgan's Juvie record. Seems she started this pattern of making trouble and getting away with it when she was young with a "public disturbance" at Fountain Square on file when she was 18. She was caught with a naked witch when they were closing the circle at the winter solstice. Streaker or spell? I'll probably never find out. I printed out a hardcopy of it since I've been having trouble with all my computers, both at home and office.

If Morgan was human, she would have been processed as an adult, but her report says Juvie, which threw me until I did some checking. Witches aren't considered adults until they are 20. 20?! I was on my own with an apartment at 20. But it might explain her stellar life choices so far.

So Morgan walks after the stunt because her dad used to work for the I.S. before he died. More corruption, more cronyism. It as much as admits it on the report.

I also got Morgan's health and school records, which shouldn't have been as hard as it was. My God, the woman I got them from is going to be a pain in the ass. She thinks I want to get into her pants, not her computer files. She's called me twice already. I'd much rather go out with Winnie. I almost got a kiss under the mistletoe at the paper's solstice party. She's got this weird mix of innocence and

LEVEL 1 INFRACTION REPORT
JUVENILE

INDERLAND SECURITY
KEEPING YOU SAFE WHEN OTHERS FAIL

Cincinnati / Hollows Division
Cincinnati, OH 45202
Phone: 555-6979 • Fax: 555-6800

DATE:	12-22-1999		NAME:	Rachel Morgan
OFFICER:	Miltast		SPECIES:	witch
CASE:	122200JV622		AGE:	18
OFFENSE:	fleeing officer		Use adult form for pixies, fairies, & imps over 5.	

PERSONAL INFORMATION

NAME:	Rachel Morgan				ALIAS:		
DOB:	7/27/81	DOD:	N/A	SEX:	F	SPECIES:	Witch
ADDRESS:	3370 Kroger Ave, Cincy 45226				SS #:		
PREVIOUS ADDRESS:	N/A				PHONE:		
OTHER INFORMATION:	Rachel is the daughter of deceased Monty Morgan from Arcane. (1995) Was told to "cut her some slack" by basement floor as a personal favor.						
PERSON RESPONSIBLE:	Mrs. Alice Morgan			PHONE:		513-555-7762	
ADDRESS (if different):							

INFRACTION

OFFENSE:	Fleeing officer. Mr. Robert Morgan (brother), Ms. Rachel Morgan, and an unidentified male fled on foot after suspected unauthorized witchcraft and consequent indecent exposure of unidentified man at public celebration.		
OBSERVERS:	Ms. May Blufford	CONTACT:	513-555-0848
LOCATION OF INCIDENT:	Fountain Square, Cincinnati		
ACTION TAKEN:	None. Busy night and couldn't spare the manpower to get Morgan's mother down to office to question Rachel. Told to write it off as solstice prank. Mr. R. Morgan was excused after Rachel and unidentified man fled the building during an exchange of destructive magic.		
ASSIGN COURT DATE:	no		

KENT HIGH SCHOOL

471 Kent St., Cincinnati, OH 45208

STUDENT MEDICAL INFORMATION

NAME OF STUDENT: __Rachel Morgan__

PARENT/GUARDIAN __Alice Morgan__

DOB __7/27/81__ DOD _____

HOME PHONE __555-7762__

WORK PHONE __Same__

FAMILY DR. __Dr. A. Tessler__

PHONE _____

IN CASE OF EMERGENCY CONTACT PARENTS

OR _____ PHONE _____

STUDENT OR MEDICAL INFORMATION

ABOUT STUDENT MAY BE RELEASED __Robert Morgan__

MEDICAL INSURANCE:

__I.S. Health__

Please explain any health and/or behavioral issues that may impact your child or other children around your child while on school grounds or participating in school activities.

__Rachel is easily fatigued due to recovering from Rosewood syndrome. Please excuse her from strenuous activity.__

Are student's immunization shots current? ☒ YES ☐ NO

If human, has he or she been exposed to T4 Angel? ☐ YES ☐ NO

STUDENT IS SUBJECT TO:

☐ asthma
☒ general fatigue
☐ mistrust of other species
☐ allergies (explain)

For Weres only

☐ wereing inconsistencies
☐ pack tendency
☐ spontaneous howling

For vamps only

☐ light restrictions
☐ history of "binding"
☐ diet restrictions

****

In case of emergency, I hereby give permission to the physician selected by the school to provide necessary treatment for my child.

Parent/Guardian signature: __Alice Morgan__   Date: __7/27/81__ world-wise that has me curious. She must have had a hard childhood. I hear the big farms are hard to escape.

Anyway, Morgan has a longer medical history than a hypochondriac. If she didn't have Rosewood syndrome, then she had something just as bad—in and out of the hospital until she was about 12—until she got better after three summers at one of Kalamack's Make-A-Wish camps.

Everything ties in with Trent Kalamack, I just have to figure out how. They were seen together looking very fine on one of Cincy's gambling boats. <u>Right before it blew up.</u>

The paper is treating it as an accident, but I don't believe that BS about a boiler blowing up. Not if Morgan and Kalamack had time enough to survive it. That boat going up was a hit. The only question in my mind is was it aimed at Saladan, muscling in on Piscary's gambling, or Saladan trying to take out his "dear old friend Trent." The best of friends can often become the best of enemies, and both of these yahoos are too rich to care if they hurt innocents in their power games.

Saladan still hasn't surfaced. I'm guessing if he's still alive, the West Coast rich kid is either thawing out somewhere or nursing his burns in a private hospital. I can't get within a quarter mile of his place.

If it was a hit, it's Saladan's own fault. Trying to shake Piscary out of the protection business was stupid. What, like we're going to trust a witch to keep the vamps in line? I may be only a human, but I know it takes power to keep us safe.

I tried to talk to Kalamack this week, but his publicity adviser Jonathan is a freak of good manners crossed with Lurch from that

Charles Addams documentary. No interview, he tells me. I didn't want an interview, I just wanted to shake Kalamack's hand. I bet I could figure out what he is just by looking at him. He isn't human. Not after surviving that boat explosion. I can't get any dirt on him, either. No history at all except birth dates and anniversaries. Nothing. The Midwest's most powerful bachelor doesn't exist but for newspaper articles and Internet pictures? That's going to change whether Maria backs me or not.

I went back to investigating Morgan, who at least exists in the system. I'm pretty sure she's an earth witch after looking over the fact sheets for the Gazette. God, these things are about worthless, but it did give me a lead to Dr. Anders since she was the "for more information contact" person in regards to ley line magic.

I tried to arrange an interview with Anders only to find out she is dead, her car having gone over a bridge this last September.

The most recent thing I could find on Dr. Anders was an article in JOLLS. I'd never heard of it, but it's THE journal for ley line witches. It doesn't make much sense to me, but I kept a copy of it. About all I got out of her article was that Morgan doesn't practice ley line magic.

My computer got a bug and I lost everything but what I wrote down and included here. Some of it I don't know if I can find again. I gotta stay off those Brimstone sites trolling for leads. Stupid-ass cyber termites.

I bought a new camera and microphone this month, but Sandra in reimbursement is giving me crap about it being a legit claim. "Toys," she called them. It was worth a shot.

Hallows Gazette
EXPENSE REPORT

Employee:	Devin Crossman		
Employee ID:	84-1698		
Phone:			
Fax:			
E-Mail:	dcrossman@hollowsgazette.com		

Invoice No.:	0416201983
Month/Year:	Dec 29, 2006

Description	Date	Amount	Approved	
Dinner out with information source	12/1	89.57	Partial	40.00
Jar of peanut butter (pixy bribe)	10/31	2.95	Yes	2.95
Anti-itch cream	11/15	15.95	No	
High-powered microphone	12/18	512.95	No	
Zoom camera	12/28	295.99	No	
Total:		917.41	Total:	42.95

Review:

Reviewed by:	Print	Sign
Approved:	Sandra Stamford	Sandra Stamford
Comments:	I can't authorize over 100, Devin. No toys. Take the microphone and camera up with Maria if you want, but I can tell you now she's not going to go for it. I can't authorize your half of dinner. Sorry.	

Failure to attach original receipts will result in decline of reimbursement. Do not fill in shaded areas.

Hollows Gazette
Fact Sheets

Document Shepherd: Ralph Carlton (513) 555-7735 ext 3
Updated 8/05

Earth Magic Is Quietly Running Most of Inderland Society

At first glance, earth magic seems to be a poor cousin to ley line magic. It's not flashy and is painstakingly slow to prepare. Often it won't work, for no apparent reason. But this very complex magic has the ability to physically change a person, such as vampires turning into bats. It can put you into a sleep you never wake from. It can relieve pain, find a missing loved one, and even bring back a loved one from purgatory, though not true death.

Earth magic gets its strength from ley lines, filtered—some say strengthened—through plants and animals. Using "recipes," witch spell-crafters will "stir" a spell, invoke it with the enzymes in their blood, and then either use it directly, such as in a potion, or store it in a redwood charm, or amulet.

The physical changes are real, and sometimes painful, until complete. This makes earth magic generally more expensive, but far more reliable.

Earth magic is one of the oldest magics in existence, showing itself in the classic, pre-Turn idea of a hearth witch. It's a highly specialized magic and is unforgiving to mistakes or experimentation.

Charm crafting is an important cottage industry, helped made safe in that all charms can be traced back to their maker by way of aura residue. Spell manufacturing is a source of pride, and it's seldom that there's an issue. Quality is maintained through steep licensing fees.

Though often looked down upon by their ley line witch counterparts, earth witches are responsible for more magic being produced than any other spell-crafting branch of magic.

Earth magic practitioners seldom dabble in black magic due to the ingredients (such as body parts) needed for black-magic charms. Even so, the dangers inherent in black earth magic is greater here than in black ley line charms because of earth

INTERNAL FACT SHEET

EARTH MAGIC

magic's ability to physically change someone, not just glamour, meaning it's harder to detect an unwelcome or illegal change and rectify it.

Earth witches that practice black magic are more difficult to catch than their ley line counterparts because they generally don't flaunt their power, fully acknowledging the "wrongness" of their black magic, unlike ley line witches who stray into a gray area and call it acceptable.

Demon magic is a mix of earth and ley line magic that has yet to be reproduced.

AT A GLANCE

WHAT IT IS: Ley line energy stored in plants, animals, or even people.

WHO CAN USE IT: Witches are the only species able to invoke earth magic due to an enzyme in witch blood needed in most earth magic recipes. Once invoked, anyone can use it.

PROS: Do not need a familiar to safely practice earth magic. Magic can often be targeted to individuals using a focusing object incorporated into the potion.

CONS: Easily broken with salt water. Can be circumvented with anticharm gear. Does not work well within 50 miles of a salt coast.

LONGEVITY: Potions degrade after a week unless stored in an amulet. Shelf life is a year thereafter.

For more information, contact:

Dr. Martin Marrion
Professor of Spells
University of Cincinnati
Cincinnati, OH 45221
513-555-2240 (ext 99)

The Hollows Gazette

Document Shepherd: Ralph Carlton (513) 555-7735 ext 3
Updated 8/05

Ley Line Magic—Potentially Disruptive, Highly Dangerous

Ley line magic draws power from ley lines using ceremony (gestures) and symbolism (tools) to control it, causing change on a visual level as well as within one's mind.

Charms are typically stored in metal rings and invoked with a pull pin. This magic can work by glamour—you look taller, but you aren't—or can cause real change such as in sleep charms or slowing or speeding up your heart. They can even cause temporary mental shifts, such as alleviating depression or love charms; admittedly though, charms that work by imagination are easily overcome.

Ley lines can be worked sympathetically, as in finding charms, or create physical barriers to protect the magic user or help better harness a complex charm or spell—such as the well-known circle charms able to bind demons or stop bullets.

Unlike earth-based magic, ley line amulets don't need to touch your skin to work, making them far more discreet. They need only be within your aura, such as in a pocket. And though ley line charms often need witch blood in their construction, they do not need the biological trigger of witch blood enzymes to invoke. Once crafted, even nonmagic people can invoke them, making ley lines the most accessible magic practiced.

Ley lines can be seen as a shimmering band of red haze at shoulder height when using second sight. When holding on to a ley line, power continues to build in the user until the witch lets go, and refusing to release their hold is said to cause insanity.

Ley lines are energy gateways to the ever-after, used by demons to travel between our reality and theirs. This might be the origin of the claim that witches align themselves with demons and is thought to be the cause for the pre-Turn witch trials.

There are far more black ley line witches than black earth magic witches. Repeated use of black ley line magic will stain a person's soul with "smut," which can only be gotten rid of by transferring to another person.

INTERNAL FACT SHEET

LEY LINE MAGIC

Ley lines are the basis for much of the Grimm Brothers' historical record. The "dead lines" in the Arizona desert are believed to have been drained when the demons created the ever-after.

It takes a curse to travel the ley lines.

AT A GLANCE

WHAT IT IS: Energy lines running parallel to the earth's surface.

WHO CAN USE IT: Witches, leprechauns, and demons can use ley lines. Were foxes use them unconsciously, as do wishing fishes. Elf magic was based on ley lines, and humans who can use ley lines are said to have elf blood.

PROS: Can use at a distance by employing focusing objects. A very fast magic useful in defense.

CONS: Need a familiar to pull on a line across water belowground or in flight. Can be circumvented with anticharm gear. Ley lines are inaccessible belowground or on water.

LONGEVITY: Uninvoked charms last indefinitely. Invoked charms fade within a year depending upon quality. Can be broken with countercharm.

For more information, contact:

Dr. Anders
Professor of Ley Line Studies
University of Cincinnati
Cincinnati, OH 45221
513-555-2440 (ext 71)

JOLLS

The Journal of Ley Line Studies

PO Box H36653
45702

Bringing ley line practitioners together to uplift, enlighten, and educate

The relation between familiar choice and ability for the serious ley line practitioner.

SUPPORTED BY DR. ANDERS
PROFESSOR OF LEY LINE STUDIES
UNIVERSITY OF CINCINNATI
CINCINNATI, OH 45221

It's long been theorized that the intelligence of a familiar is proportional to the ability of a practitioner to manipulate ley lines, or in lay terms, the better you are at magic, the smarter your familiar needs to be. I've observed this to be true with nearly 4,000 individuals over a span of 40 years, ranging from novice to highly experienced as I taught high-level ley line manipulations at the University of Cincinnati, and basic ley line courses at local colleges.[1]

Familiars serve two main functions besides companionship, the first being a bridge to a ley line when we are cut off by way of water; the second, protection.

Many a ley line witch has survived a badly spun charm because the familiar took the brunt of the backlash with no apparent detriment. Demons, too, will often snag a familiar in error when we come too close to the black arts.

But by far a familiar's most common function is to filter the ley lines, protecting their masters from surges and drops that exist naturally in a line's force, much as a capacitor. And as anyone knows, you need a higher capacitor the more amps you can channel.

. . . Proving that familiar intelligence impacts practitioner strength is the first step, and at the very least, will offer us a new set of tools with which to help teach the next generation . . .

Most witches in the U.S. who take advantage of the benefits of a familiar have adopted domestic cats, a choice that has been with us through the ages not only because of availability, but because 95 percent of witches fall into the strength category that cats resonate with. Also used as familiars are parrots, dogs, mice, and in extreme cases of ineptitude, fish. But even the lowly fish can serve as an effective

bridge to a ley line. How this is so when a fish lives in water isn't known, and I won't delve into theories in this study.

It is in the other extreme, the high practitioners, that the phenomenon of intelligence matching to ability is easiest studied, and indeed, the most necessary. Table 1 below is an example of just one group of students, but the effect can be seen repeatedly.

The trend is obvious, the question is—how do you measure ley line ability? The unhappy truth is that ley line ability still cannot be quantified as easily as

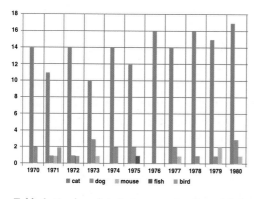

Table 1: Number of students over a decade and their familiar choices [2]

intelligence. I've seen the most foolish of students possess the strongest abilities, and tragically the most intelligent, capable students fall short when it comes to fieldwork through no fault of their own apart from a lack of talent.

Through countless familiar evaluations, I have observed that a practitioner's circle strength is an excellent indicator of present and indeed future ley line ability, and whereas we still do not have anything more than arbitrary numbers, knowing that ranges parallel familiar types does give a measure of confidence.

I'd like to outline the most rudimentary of tests so that you can begin to see for yourself the clear linkage between ley line ability and familiar intelligence.

Creating a circle is one of the most fundamental abilities available to a witch, easily grasped and taught to laypeople to facilitate a wider sampling of the populace at large. Ideally such a large study could be performed with middle-school-aged children where witches typically begin to experiment on their own with their ley

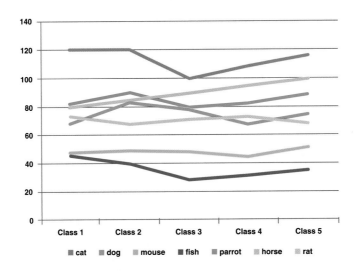

Table 2: Familiar strength reflected in auratics[3]

line abilities, but this remains for future witches to discern.

Once mastered, the subject would be asked to set a circle of a standard size using magnetic chalk. I would suggest using the same circle for all subjects to eliminate variances of circle strength due to imperfection in the circle itself. The administrator can then measure the thickness of the barrier either visually with an aurautic scope (giving a reading in nanometers) or mechanically with a simple volt meter adjusted to measure such small variances. Within a span of a dozen tests, the correlation between circle strength and familiar will become obvious.

As can be seen by Table 2, there is a clear tendency for a familiar's endurance to mimic the narrow parameters of our own limits, stretching or shrinking only when the familiar itself is outside the norm (Table 3). Whether the heightened or lessened abilities of the practitioner is due to his or her stamina or the familiar itself, we do not yet know.

But what is clear is that the parrot and horse are able to facilitate the thickest circles, the fish and mouse the least. Also note the clustering of familiars in the 70 to 90 auratic range where most practitioners are.

So what does all this mean to the average person? To be honest, it doesn't mean much right now. Perhaps the question we should be asking, and possibly the ultimate

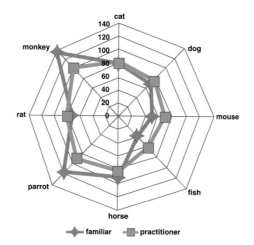

Table 3: The expected correlation between familiar and practitioner strength

goal, is to ascertain if it is the familiar that chooses the practitioner, or the practitioner who chooses the familiar, allowing us to potentially increase our own strength by forcing a union with a stronger familiar. For if the relationship between familiar intelligence and practitioner strength can be proven, it might be prudent to attempt to find the way to circumvent the natural selection of a familiar for something that can serve us even better.

But that is for the next generation.

Proving that familiar intelligence impacts practitioner strength is the first step,

and at the very least, will offer us a new set of tools with which to help teach the next generation, and possibly a warning for the serious practitioner to look outside the normal venues of cat and dog to the more intelligent of species around us for protection.

Dr. Anders has taught at the University of Cincinnati since before the Turn, having developed and promoted such ideas as white smut, spindled energy, and the relationship between the ever-after and time.

---

[1] Please see addendum for complete list of subjects and recorded familiars.

[2] This data was not used in calculating overall adherence to the proposed theory due to the student with the fish dropping the class before circle strength could be evaluated.

[3] Classes are a compilation of data gathered from random university classes.

The Hollows Gazette

Tuesday, December 19, 2006

LOCAL / STATE

C

OHIO RIVER BOAT CASINO EXPLODES

By Gary Brown
gmbrown@hollowsgazette.com

Wreckage from Saladan's floating casino.

Residents on both sides of the Ohio River were rocked late Sunday when a faulty boiler in one of Cincy's casino riverboats is thought to have exploded, killing all but two of the boat's dozen guests.

The I.S. is continuing to investigate, pulling bodies and wreckage from the icy river in the hopes of positively identifying the cause of the mishap.

I.S. experts are concerned this might be the start of a citywide power struggle between gambling boat operator Piscary and Cincy newcomer Stanley Saladan, owner of the destroyed floating casino.

Surviving the encounter was Councilman Trent Kalamack, who was back at work yesterday appearing somber but unhurt. Kalamack claims he was at the boat to persuade his longtime friend Saladan to desist in his attempt to cut into Piscary's gambling empire. According to Kalamack, Saladan wasn't there at the time of the explosion. Saladan has been unable to be contacted for comment.

Kalamack's security that night also survived despite early claims of her demise. Piscary, well-known master vampire, couldn't be reached for comment, but Kisten Felps, manager of Pizza Piscary's, was able to tell us that Piscary is concerned and is doing all that's possible to ensure the city's safety.

Piscary has kept the Cincinnati area nearly incident free for over 40 years, maintaining a benevolent but iron fist on its many Inderland denizens. His gambling boats have been a mainstay for the

See Boat **A 2**

@ A Glance Dec 19, 2006
Average High/Low: 28° / 45°

	Today	Tomorrow
Sunrise	7:53 AM	7:53 AM
Sunset	5:18 PM	5:18 PM
Moonrise	7:17 AM	8:19 AM
Moonset	4:13 PM	5:10 PM
	Phase: New	

SEE ALMANAC C 4

The Way I See It
Devin Crossman

SURVIVAL, AT WHAT COST?

The obituary was premature, and Rachel Morgan, listed as dead after a boat explosion rocked the Hollows waterfront Sunday, is alive and well. Magic, yes, but what kind? A clip of a witch being demon-dragged down Oak Staff St., Hollows, KY, has me worried.

Is this is the same witch who recently separated from the I.S. and survived their mythical "death squads"? The same who flouts tradition and works for the FIB upon occasion for "favors"?

And if so, what is going to be the eventual cost?

Calls to Vampiric Charms, Morgan's independent runner firm located on Oak Staff, have gone unreturned. Kalamack is silent as well, ruing, perhaps, having trusted his life to Morgan and Co. It's a mistake I hope the city doesn't make as well by continuing to allow a demon-summoning witch her freedom.

Devin Crossman brings his uniquely human point of view to the Hollows. Comments will reach Mr. Crossman at:
dcrossman@hollowsgazette.com

Takata Concert Canceled?

By Winifred Gradenko
winniegrad@hollowsgazette.com

Security concerns have city officials and Takata himself considering canceling his yearly solstice concert.

"I can't afford to pay two organizations for security," Takata said when asked. "Cincy had better figure out who is providing protection, and fast."

Hometown Cincy boy Takata has given the proceeds from his solstice concerts to Cincy charities for years, joining Councilman Trent Kalamack in helping to improve the lives of underprivileged children in the Cincinnati area.

This year's concert sold out in record time, and local radio stations are staging outrageous contests to give away their promotional tickets.

All could come to a fast halt if Takata can't produce a security contract for the show, demonstrating his ability to enforce the much-needed MPL.

See Concert **A 6**

Kalamack Industries, Inc

December 28, 2006

Ms. Maria Gonzalez
Senior Editor
Hollows Gazette
Hollows, KY 41011

Dear Maria,

I understand that the *Hollows Gazette* has enjoyed a substantial gain in readership these past few months, no small amount of credit due to Devin Crossman's insightful, sometimes quirky columns. I will be honest. I would dearly love to woo him from your paper to a full-time position within my public relations department, but upon investigation, discovered that you managed to get him to sign a no-compete clause, one that puts my legal department to shame and would prevent him from working for me in any capacity whatsoever.

First, brava, Maria, for a hand well played. Second, is there any way we can come to some arrangement that would free Mr. Crossman from his obligations and allow him to come to work for me?

I hope the solstice has bestowed the best of the season upon you and yours,

Trent Kalamack

Trenton A. Kalamack ~ CEO Kalamack Industries
Kalamack Industries, Inc, Building A • 15 Rolling Acres, Cincinnati, OH 45239

The
Hollows Gazette

SERVING THE GREATER CINCINNATI AREA SINCE THE TURN

12/29/2006

Trenton A. Kalamack
CEO Kalamack Industries
Kalamack Industries, Inc
15 Rolling Acres
Cincinnati, OH 45239

Trent, you fox. That soaking in the Ohio River must have addled your perception. Don't think I can't see through you, but it's flattering nevertheless. You want to buy Crossman to shut him up! He's a good man, and a good reporter, and I'm curious myself as to what he can dig up on you. The bottom line is the man is selling papers. You can't have him. However, I understand your concerns, and in light of the situation, you have my assurances that I'll try to bring him back into a more sensitive frame of mind in regards to reporting the facts.

Are you free next week for lunch, perhaps? I'd love the chance to chat with you concerning your reluctance in granting an interview on your family history. I'd even let you preview the article for errors, and you know what a concession that is from me. If you're going to try to take my star attraction, give me something to replace him with!

All my very best regards,

Maria

Ms. Maria Gonzalez • Senior Editor • Hollows Gazette • Hollows, KY 41011

Kalamack Industries, Inc

Jonathan Davaros
Chief Personnel Officer
Kalamack Industries, Inc
Building A
15 Rolling Acres
Cincinnati, OH 45239

I N T E R O F F I C E   M E M O

To: Trenton Kalamack
From: Jonathan Davaros
cc:
Date: 5/29/07
Re: Interview Policies

Sa'han,

The *Hollows Gazette* informs me that you've agreed to an extended, ninety-minute, human-interest interview and wishes to schedule it immediately. Such changes to policy are easier for my staff to handle if you'd inform me before you make them.

I have a block of time open June 4th, which is a Monday, unless you would like to reschedule your tux fitting from June 19th to the 26th. Please advise.

Yours,

Jonathan

Kalamack Industries, Inc

Trenton A. Kalamack
CEO Kalamack Industries
Kalamack Industries, Inc
Building A
15 Rolling Acres
Cincinnati, OH 45239

I N T E R O F F I C E   M E M O

To: Quen Hansen
From: Trenton Kalamack
CC:
Date: 5/29/07
Re: Devin Crossman's Hard Drives

Quen, I want Crossman's hard drives wiped if he gains access to Morgan's church again. Maria is a sharp businesswoman, but she's in the business of selling papers. No telling what the two of them will come up with using assumptions backed by a few facts. Also, will you make sure Maria knows that she's not getting anything but a history lesson of the Turn from me until she actually begins to curtail this man's statements? I'd ask Jon, but he's not taking this seriously.

I'm becoming increasingly uncomfortable with how good Crossman is getting at figuring things out. If the paper won't sell him to us, increase your surveillance and give me three reasonable-assumption end-case solutions by the weekend.

Thank you, Quen. I know you're busy, but I appreciate you taking the time to do this yourself.

Trent

June 2, 2007

I don't believe this. I've been censored! I didn't think they could do it, but there apparently is some tiny clause I signed when I agreed to give them a daily column. I would've bagged it all and walked right out the door if Winnie hadn't calmed me down.

That memo I got from Maria is total crap. Total CYA. She comes into my office yesterday at lunch, shuts the door, and hands it to me like it's an invitation, then stands there telling me to stay away from the church and Morgan. That I've been seen watching her, and there have been complaints of harassment. That my interests in the witch or the vamp might be "misconstrued" and "unhealthy." That I might end up as someone's blood toy. Not that vampire, though. She's got the hots for the witch.

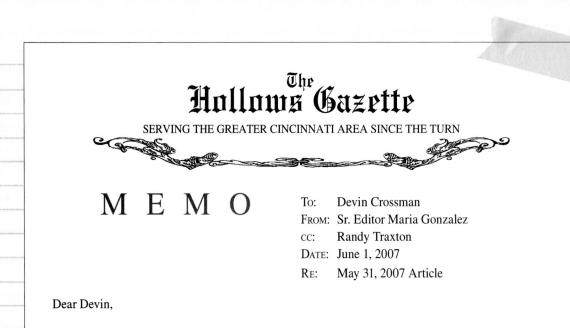

The Hollows Gazette

SERVING THE GREATER CINCINNATI AREA SINCE THE TURN

MEMO

To: Devin Crossman
From: Sr. Editor Maria Gonzalez
cc: Randy Traxton
Date: June 1, 2007
Re: May 31, 2007 Article

Dear Devin,

The accusatory and inflammatory nature of your recent article entitled DON'T FORGET YOUR TASER in last Thursday's issue has become a problem to both me and the paper. Hate mail I expect, and interspecies tensions are always a hot button, but you've crossed the line by naming Rachel Morgan as the cause for the recent trouble among the Weres. I'm now looking at a potential liability problem. Any further unsubstantiated attack upon Rachel Morgan, Ivy Tamwood, or even that pixy, will result in a withdrawal of protection by the paper and suspension.

You have put me in an unwelcome position, and I reluctantly take the following steps:

- You hereby will submit all articles to Randy Traxton for review a full twenty-four hours before paper deadline or forfeit your space.

- Failure to edit an article to Randy's satisfaction will result in suspension of your article until such time as you submit an acceptable article.

- Sensationalizing your restrictions will result in immediate termination and a withdrawal of the paper's protection.

If at such time that I feel these restrictions can be removed, they will be. I'm all for freedom of the press, Devin, but you're pushing your opinions as facts. So far, the Tamwood family is taking this in stride, but I'm not going to embroil the paper in a freedom of speech circus because you're finding terrorists in your teacup.

Maria Gonzalez

Sr. Editor, *Hollows Gazette*

Maria crabbed at me for a good fifteen minutes before telling me to back off or get fired. I wouldn't care, but I can't even go back to blogging for an entire year, and I am not going to flip burgers for twelve months. Clearly I'm close to something, and I think it has to do with Morgan. I'm sure she's summoning demons again. I just need to find the proof.

I doubt very much that it's coincidence that the trouble in Cincy with the wolf packs started the same week Morgan left. I know it ties in with the focus, seeing as she's not only in a pack, but a female alpha according to Winnie. I've got a request in for a Were Registry, so we'll see. Sounds off to me. Why would a witch join a Were pack?

I can play this game. I'll submit my column for review from here on out, but Maria can eat fairy dust if she thinks I'm dropping my investigation of Kalamack and Morgan. I'll clear out my desk and keep everything at home before I give this up. Clearing out my desk might not be a bad idea, anyway. Someone's been through it, <u>again</u>.

Good news is I got into the church for a few minutes when Morgan and the pixy hightailed it out of state to rescue her boyfriend, and then Tamwood followed her a few days later. I didn't get to look at much except the kitchen before the pixy kids chased me out. God! I itch everywhere!

Even as brief as my snoop was, I hit pay dirt. Morgan has what I think are demon texts hidden between her cookbooks. They don't have any titles, the paper is yellowing, the bindings are cracked, and they smell bad. Really bad. Like burnt rubber.

I took pictures so I could get a witch to look at them and tell me if they're demon magic, but I can't find the pictures on my hard drive.

The shots I took of the cookbooks I can find, but not them. (By the way, Morgan seems to be allergic to eggs, and her roommate puts Brimstone into cookies.) If I can't get back into the church, I might have to send my hard drive off to recover them. The pictures are the proof.

I've been meaning to write up some descriptions of a few people who I've seen at the church lately. That old witch across the street from the church has someone living with him now. I would say she's his live-in caretaker, except I know Keasley doesn't have enough money for a nurse. I've heard the pixies call her Ceri, and the old man uses her full name when he's mad at her. Ceridwen Dulciate.

Tamwood has a new/old girlfriend, I think. As soon as Rachel lit out after Sparagmos, some blonde moved in. Tamwood calls her Skimmer, but I followed her to work and found out her real name is Dorothy Claymor.

I did a profile on Rachel's old boyfriend, Nick Sparagmos, too. I was waiting until I got a picture, but he hasn't been around much lately. I think they had a falling-out, seeing as he is in trouble in Mackinaw. I'm going to try to find this guy if he shows back up in Cincy again, if only to get a picture. So far, no luck. I don't have a picture of the woman across the street, either. My new camera hasn't been working right.

Subject: CERIDWEN MERRIAM DULCIATE (CERI)

Species/Sex: Human?/Female
Location: Hollows
Employer: None
Gets Around: Walks or goes with Rachel
Home: Across from the church, Hollows, KY
Height: 5'4"
Weight: ~120#
Build: Slim
Age: Mid-30s??

DESCRIPTION: Green eyes, from what I can tell, thin, slight build. Not athletic, but frail. Pale complexion, heart-shaped face, angular features, and cheekbones are prominent. Goes barefoot a lot, even when it's cold. She has very fair, thin hair that goes to her midback. It's usually free, but I've seen the pixies braid it. Pale eyebrows.

Her voice is high and musical, and she sings in Latin. She swears in Latin, too, and she's not afraid to raise her voice at Keasley when he teases her, or to the neighborhood kids when they throw stones at stray dogs.

She is usually wearing something casual but sophisticated, and it's usually purple, green, or gold. She has a crucifix that I think used to belong to Tamwood.

RESEARCHED

I can't find anything on this woman, either at the FIB or I.S. It's like she doesn't exist, which is about what I would expect for some reason. She seems to be chummy with Rachel, so maybe the old witch took her in as a favor. The pixies love her. Maybe if I learned to sing in Latin, they'd quit pixing me.

She carries herself as if she's freaking royalty, having both a wicked temper when she feels slighted, and a huge capacity to forgive when she makes a mistake.

I can't figure her out. I've seen her do magic, but I'd swear she's not a witch or human. Or if she is, she's been stuck under a rock since before the Turn. She is obviously smart if she knows Latin, but I watched her struggle to figure out Keasley's new camera as if she'd never seen one before.

Subject: DOROTHY CLAYMOR (AKA SKIMMER)

Species/Sex: Living Vampire/Female
Employer: Piscary
Gets Around: White BMW convertible
Home: Piscary's Pizza, Hollows
Height: 5'4"
Weight: ~120#
Build: Sleek, sexy
Age: Mid-20s?

DESCRIPTION: Slim, dancer's body. Blond hair to her shoulders, straight. Keeps it in a ponytail sometimes when she rides with the car open. Blue eyes. Delicate facial structure with a small nose and long, dark eyelashes. Fair skin. No scars that I can see easily. European descent. Maybe Scandinavian?

Dresses in pastels, with a lot of style and money. Silk, linen. She reeks of confidence. The woman is as smart as a cracked whip.

I'm guessing Claymor is one of Ivy's old lovers. Morgan knocked her flat on her ass on the street during a loud conversation about Ivy.

RESEARCHED

EDUCATION: Claymor and Ivy went to the same high school out on the West Coast. Roomed together their last two years at an all Inderland college. Claymor graduated at the top of her class, went on to pass the bar in a frighteningly short amount of time. She makes all the right moves.

EMPLOYMENT: Works for Piscary as his lawyer. Previously she handled a myriad of cases for her camarilla on the West Coast. She's done a share of trials, but specializes in settling things before they go to court. Slick, the woman is slick. Don't let her baby-doll, angelic voice and face fool you. I've seen her fangs.

HISTORY: Belongs to a West Coast camarilla and is on leave from her master vampire as a favor to get Piscary out of jail.

Subject: NICK SPARAGMOS

Species/Sex: Human/Male

Location: Hollows/Cincy

Employer: Used to work for City Art Museum

Gets Around: '92 Blue Ford Truck, if I remember right

Home: Shady Creek Apts, 728 W. Blvd, Hollows

Height: 5'10"

Weight: ~160#

Build: Bookworm, but tough

Age: Mid-20s??

DESCRIPTION: Brown eyes, pale skin. Dark, straight hair. Spare, narrow build. He's got a lot of scars, thick and badly healed. Something happened to this guy, so he's tougher than he looks. His ears are notched, like someone bit them. He's clean shaven most of the time. Looks smart, which makes me wonder what he was doing with Morgan. Maybe what they say about female witches is right. Doesn't like dogs, even little ones.

RESEARCHED

EDUCATION: High school degree at local Hollows HS. Mediocre grades. Tough school for a human, but that would explain why he's comfortable hanging out with Inderlanders.

EMPLOYMENT: City records say this guy has had more jobs than a bus of teenagers, and none of them paid much. Still, I've noticed if he wants something, he gets it. His truck, for example, is a rat trap, but it's tricked out with NOS. His work patterns indicate he's good with electronics and artifacts.

HISTORY: Not much on this guy, but his mother was a single parent who still lives in the Hollows in a low-income area. He was an only child. Raised in a poor Hollows district. That's probably where he got the scars. No medical history on this guy.

"Refreshingly Honest." —*Inderlander Cuisine*

BETTY BOB'S
EVERYDAY RECIPES
FOR THE STOVETOP IDIOT

THE ULTIMATE RECIPE BOOK FOR THE KITCHEN NOVICE, WRITTEN BY THE TURN'S MOST CELEBRATED INDERLAND CHEF,
BETTY BOBSON

"Both entertaining and functional, Betty gives it to you straight. A must-have for the new adult on his or her own, dead or alive."
—*Rynn Cormel*

MAPLE CANDY

BETTY BOB SAYS . . .

There's nothing like the smell of maple candy simmering on the stove, especially on a cool spring day. Candy can be tricky, but if you pay attention to detail, and the barometer is low, chances are good that even the most inept dunce can create something tasty, if not always exactly what he or she wanted.

4 cups maple syrup
1 cup whipping cream
$1/4$ cup butter
$1/2$ teaspoon rum extract

1. Heat the maple syrup, cream, and butter in a thick-walled, medium-size pan on medium heat, stirring constantly with a wooden spoon until it starts to boil. (Don't use a metal spoon, it just doesn't work!)

2. When it starts to boil, remove the spoon and let the water boil out until the temp reaches 245°F exactly. It will boil up high when you start before it settles, so feel free to panic if you picked a pot too small and it boils over. Lowering the temp on the burner helps.

3. While it's boiling off the water, prepare the pan by smearing the bottom and sides with a thin layer of butter. We're talking really thin, almost not there, or your candy will be greasy. If you're

using candy forms, melt 1 tablespoon butter and "paint" the inside of the forms with the melted butter. If you don't have a candy pan, you can make one out of buttered tinfoil. (This is Betty's preferred method.)

4. After reaching 245°F, remove from heat and add rum extract. Start to stir.

5. You'll stir for about 10 to 15 minutes, nice and slow to keep from adding air to the candy. It will be syrupy at first, but will thicken fast at the end and lose its gloss. You will hear sugar crystals scraping.

6. When it hints at thickening, pour it into the pan. Betty Bob usually has help at this point, because it smells so-o-o-o good and draws people to the kitchen like vamps to burning Brimstone. One person holds the still-warm pot, and the other scrapes it out. Yes, Betty Bob knows you're not supposed to scrape candy pots, but if you work fast, you can get it all out before the sides cool and the candy crystallizes.

7. Once the candy is firm but still moist (approximately 10 to 30 minutes), pull the sides of the tinfoil pan down, and, with a butcher knife, cut it into squares.

Betty Bob Says. . .

Make a pan by greasing a sheet of tinfoil and folding up the sides. Betty does this so she doesn't scrape her 9"x9" pan, and it's "a hell of a lot easier to cut."

No candy thermometer? Dribble some candy into a glass of cold water. If you can take that blop of candy and make a ball out of it and that ball holds its shape, there's a 50-50 chance it's done. Get a thermometer.

If it never sets up, pour candy back into the pot and heat it up until you can stir it, and try again. It took Betty eight years to learn when to pour it out. But even the failures were yummy.

WAFFLES

BETTY BOB SAYS . . .

Waffles you make out of a box are okay if you're 12 (or 40, for Weres). But for us adults, take the time to whip up a batch of this batter for your honey on the weekend and you'll find out why it's called a quick(ie) bread. Mmmmm.

4 ~~egg yolks~~ *egg beaters*

1³/₄ cups milk

¹/₂ cup cooking oil

1 tablespoon mayonnaise

¹/₈ teaspoon vanilla

¹/₂ teaspoon salt

1³/₄ cups all-purpose flour

1 tablespoon baking powder

¹/₈ teaspoon allspice

4 tablespoons sugar

4 egg whites

1. Beat egg yolks with fork, then beat in milk, cooking oil, mayonnaise, and vanilla.

2. Mix the dry ingredients in a second bowl.

3. Add the egg mixture to the dry ingredients and stir until blended, but still lumpy. Set aside.

4. In a small bowl, beat egg whites until stiff peaks form. Fold this into the egg and flour mixture. Don't overmix; leave some egg white intact.

5. Pour batter onto a preheated, lightly greased waffle maker.

6. Garnish with fresh fruit and maple syrup.

BRIMSTONE COOKIES

THINGS YOU'LL NEED

Rolling pin

Pastry cloth

Baking tins

Wax paper

Cookie cutters

Good attorney if
you're caught

³/₄ cup butter

1¹/₂ cups sugar

2 ~~eggs~~ *change out to egg beaters for Rachel*

¹/₄ cup milk

³/₄ teaspoon vanilla

³/₄ teaspoon salt

3 teaspoons baking
powder

3 tablespoons Brimstone

3¹/₂ cups all-purpose
flour

Betty Bob Says . . .

How did this
get in here?

1. Soften the butter in the microwave on low or let it
   sit out for a couple of hours. Don't melt it. Cream
   the butter with the sugar.

2. Add the eggs, milk, vanilla, salt, baking powder
   and Brimstone. Mix until blended.

3. Slowly add the flour while mixing. When
   uniform consistency, divide the dough, wrapping
   in wax paper.

4. Chill dough for at least an hour.

5. Roll dough ¹/₄" to ¹/₈" thick on the pastry cloth.

6. Cut with a cookie cutter. Betty Bob likes fat lips
   and scary cats so she can frost them and really
   give herself a sugar high.

7. Using a spatula, shift the cut cookies to an ungreased baking tin. Leave enough room between cookies for them to rise a bit.

8. Bake in a preheated oven at 375°F for 7 to 10 minutes—thin, 10 to 12 minutes—thick.

9. Let cookies cool for no more than a minute before removing to wire rack to finish cooling.

10. Eat naked, or frost. (Betty Bob made us put that part in. She means eat the cookies with no frosting [naked] or frost them with butter frosting. Anything else is up to you.)

Betty Bob Says. . .

Don't skip the fridge. If you do, your cookies will be too gummy to roll out. Wrap the dough in wax paper or plastic wrap to keep it moist.

Don't have a pastry cloth? Roll cookies out on a counter heavily dusted with equal parts of flour and powdered sugar.

Dough sticking to cutter? Dip the cutter into equal parts flour and powdered sugar.

If your kitchen smells like Brimstone, your roommate bought cheap Brimstone. Light a candle. Pray no one calls the I.S. Next time, buy better stuff or have a lawyer on speed-dial.

The Hollows Gazette

Thursday, May 31, 2007

LOCAL / STATE

C

The Way I See It
Devin Crossman

DON'T FORGET YOUR TASER

Going to the mall? The store? Pack your Taser.

Some may call my response harsh, but after the recent attacks taking place throughout Cincinnati and the Hollows, I'm going to be packing some personal protection for a while. The moon is a day from full, and the city is already feeling the pinch.

Sure, you can't become a Were by way of a bite, but if this focus is to be believed, all bets are off. Packs are packing up due to the lure of the focus, brought to Cincy by our favorite witch, Rachel Morgan.

Is it coincidence that she's the first witch to not only join a Were pack but also to become its alpha female? I think not. And it's going to get worse before it gets better as this demon-summoning witch keeps flaunting her

See Unsafe **C 6**

Mall where brawl occurred last night, now peaceful

MALL BRAWL ENDS IN FIVE ARRESTS

By Winifred Gradenko
winniegrad@hollowsgazette.com

Residents are still reeling from a brawl that took place at their local mall last week, resulting in several hospital admissions and a full call-out of both the I.S. and the FIB to stop the free-for-all that began with an exchange of insults between the large Cincinnati Barrows pack and the small, but history-drenched Hollows pack, Chewed Leaf.

Investigations from both the I.S. and FIB have turned up little, hampered by a lack of cooperation, but bystanders say a thrown slushy began the confrontation that ended with five hospitalized and released for minor injuries.

Three from the Barrows pack were taken into custody and released on bond. Two Chewed Leaf members are still being detained, alpha male Dan Banden and current beta female Sara Smith.

"The last thing a Were wants to do is make their territorial squabbles public," public relations Wayne Wheredon told us. "Most times, tattoos tell everyone who's on top. It's a long-standing tradition that has its beginnings pre-Turn and enables multiple packs to share the same space. It's highly unusual for two packs to go from taunts to tearing. It isn't like Weres to do this."

But "do this" is what happened, and the I.S. is on high alert, coming down hard as similar squabbles between ordinarily peaceful packs are appearing all over the city.

"Something has them stirred up," Captain Edden of the FIB said when questioned. "I think it's that focus thing that none of you believe in."

The courts are moving forward now that banshee involvement is eliminated.

See Mall **C 6**

Were Artifact A Hoax?
By Cindy Strom
cstrom@hollowsgazette.com

The focus. The very name invokes a shiver to those who can run on paws, and fabled or not, focus fever has taken Cincinnati by the throat and is being blamed for the recent squabbles between peaceful packs and leaving humans and Inderlanders alike asking, "Why the fuss?"

The answer is power. Though pack-oriented, Weres seldom look beyond their alphas as a political force. That's where the focus comes in play, imbuing the holder with the ability to bind alphas to him, and with the alphas go their packs, giving one Were more political sway than the average master vampire.

A nice biscuit treat indeed, and it's obvious why even the hint of the focus has Cincy and Hollows packs on the sniff looking for it as the vampires watch and worry.

See Packs **C 6**

@ A Glance May 31, 2007
Average High/Low: 76˚ / 56˚

	Today	Tomorrow
Sunrise	5:14 AM	5:14 AM
Sunset	7:57 PM	7:58 PM
Moonrise	8:11 PM	9:11 PM
Moonset	4:29 AM	5:11 AM
Phase: 1 day to full		

SEE ALMANAC C 6

Kalamack Industries, Inc

Jonathan Davaros
Chief Personnel Officer
Kalamack Industries, Inc
Building A
15 Rolling Acres
Cincinnati, OH 45239

I N T E R O F F I C E   M E M O

To: Trenton Kalamack
From: Jonathan Davaros
cc:
Date: 6/08/07
Re: *Hollows Gazette* Interview

Sa'han,

I have reviewed the enclosed *Hollows Gazette* article and found it to be secure if you are comfortable with what you divulged concerning your family's origins. I will, of course, check it against the copy that makes it to print and inform you of any changes. If you would like any modifications to the article as it stands, please let me know immediately. The proposed run date is Sunday.

Yours,

Jonathan

Enclosure: *Gazette* submission sheet

SUBMISSION SHEET

For salaried employees only. Freelance, please use submission form FL16008B.	SUBMITTED BY:	Cindy Strom—human interest
	TITLE OF ARTICLE:	Trent Kalamack. Turning Ashes into Gold
	RUN DATE:	June 10, 2007
	CHARACTER COUNT:	7412 w/ spaces

In a rare opportunity, Cincinnati's own Trent Kalamack, the multibillionaire bachelor, opened up to the *Hollows Gazette* concerning his family's struggle during the Turn and their ultimate rise to success. Unable to reconstruct the conversation into article form without destroying the subtle feelings evoked by chatting with such a beguiling man, the interview has been printed as it was taken to preserve the intimacy of the moment. Here now is my conversation, set among the lush interior gardens and accompanied by a birdsong and pot of tea. Earl Grey, served hot.

Hollows Gazette: Thank you, Mr. Kalamack, for this opportunity.

Trent Kalamack: Please, call me Trent.

HG: Trent. I appreciate you taking the time to talk to me concerning your family's rise from obscurity to one of the most well-known names in the U.S., if not the civilized world. I'd like to begin with your father at the onset of the Turn.

TK: It's my pleasure, Cindy. Ask away.

HG: Most people now relate the Kalamack name to the large farms east of the Mississippi and the extensive railroad system that your father gathered under one protective umbrella during the Turn. Most don't know that your family actually started on the West Coast, in what most would call a modest situation.

TK: [Crosses leg upon knee] You've done your homework, Cindy.

HG: I have. Some might say that without the Turn, your father might never have had the opportunity to turn the few thousand dollars in his pocket into an industry that spans the globe and has a gross income greater than most small countries.

TK: [Smiles charmingly] And others might counter that society would have collapsed utterly if able

Checked By: _____ Date _____

Comments _____

The Hollows Gazette

individuals hadn't gathered what resources they could to preserve them from loss for the greater good.

HG: Of course. It was an employee of your father's, wasn't it, who is credited with the discovery of the link between the T4 Angel virus and the plague?

TK: [Sips his tea] No, it was actually the Saladan family who made the connection. My father only made it public, despite the governmental cover-ups.

HG: Please, can you elaborate?

TK: As you learned correctly, my father was manager of a large number of tomato fields in California at the time, owned by the Saladan family. My father's practice of setting aside a field for the workers to take fruit home turned out to have disastrous results. It was meant to keep profits up and employees happy, but when he opened the field for harvest and 90 percent of his workers and their families died by the end of the week, Mr. Saladan made the correct correlation.

HG: So you are lucky to be here then.

TK: My father loathed tomatoes. I can't say that I disagree with him. [Smiles]

HG: Still, you might say that the downfall of civilization was the beginning of the rise of your family as your father went from a field manager to—

TK: To owning more land and infrastructure than a small country? [Laughs] You could, but that makes it sound as if he took advantage of another's losses when he was simply trying to save what he could by consolidating it into a more manageable package. The whole is always more powerful than the parts, and my father knew this very well. He never made a dime by capitalizing upon any individual's loss. He saw a need, and he filled it. I try to do the same myself. It's how I honor his memory.

HG: Of course. I meant no disrespect.

TK: None taken. It's the orphanages and outreach programs he started that are the core of my father's successes, not the railroads he bought in order to keep them moving or the hospitals he worked to keep stocked with acceptable medicines of the day.

He nearly lost his life when he

Checked By: _____ Date _____

Comments _____

The Hollows Gazette

broke from the Saladan farms to get the word out concerning the source of the virus, fleeing through a plague-torn continent with my mother, informing those he encountered of the source of the plague until he made it to my mother's family in Cincinnati and found a radio station at the bottom of the tunnels, functioning independently of the government. He was very young. I don't know if I could have done so well if given a similar task.

HG: Then you believe the rumor of the governmental cover-up?

TK: I do. Or perhaps I should say that my father did. We may never know, since society murdered most if not all the bioengineers of the time who might have had a hand in the virus's development.

Like many, my father subscribed to the belief that the virus probably began in a remote U.S. military lab, thought to be made safe for military use because it was effective only if ingested, and therefore easily contained. But it escaped, traveling in what most experts agree was probably a now extinct species of ladybug. The insect harbored the virus until it was introduced into Mediterranean fields of tomatoes by farmers trying to combat an influx of scale without the use of pesticides.

It might have ended if the now-famed T4 Angel tomato in production there didn't possess a loose genetic structure, engineered to facilitate quick changes in growth and habit at will.

HG: A practice which is now thankfully curtailed.

TK: Curtailed? I suppose the bioengineer trials and executions that were little more than legalized murder could be considered curtailing. [Pours a cup of tea] The T4 Angel tomato had been a mainstay of drought-stricken areas for the last three years. My father told me they called it the miracle fruit. It was being grown worldwide, all the seeds in distribution coming from one field since it was a copyrighted genome, a practice which has now been outlawed, regardless of patents and trademarks. The virus slipped into a gap in the plant's DNA, the fruits harvested for seed production, and then sent out for next year's crop.

HG: And the Turn began.

Checked By: _____ Date _____ _____

Comments _____

The Hollows Gazette

TK: [Inclines his head] Because the T4 Angel had been accepted as safe for three years previous, it took longer than it should to have made the connection between it and the exponentially rising numbers of deaths. And as you said, government cover-ups were thought to have added months to the realization that ingesting the tomato was to blame until it was too late to do anything but minimize the damage.

HG: So you believe that the hidden Inderland population in the government at the time was to blame?

TK: No. [Smiles] I do not subscribe to the belief that the plague was Inderland's attempt to rid the world of humanity, merely frightened people trying to cover their tracks. That a vampire was in the White House at the time probably saved humanity, not damned it. Personally, I've found too many friendships among Inderlanders to believe it was a conspiracy. They have nothing to gain by our loss, and everything to lose if we die out.

Our past is joined by bonds of common suffering through world wars and depressions since before the pyramids, and our future will be all the more glorious by the open sharing of our varied skills and wisdoms. That is my father's true legacy. [Finishes tea and smiles pleasantly]

HG: Thank you, Trent, for your candor. I know the *Gazette*'s readers would love to hear more of your family history. Your father's race across the desert in a plague-torn America with your mother has bestseller written all over it.

TK [Laughs as he tidies the tea tray and stands] Perhaps someday, Cindy. Allow me to escort you out through the gardens. Your photographer simply must get a photo of the orchid pond. It's stunning this year.

Checked By: _____ Date _____

Comments _____

Kalamack Industries, Inc

Trenton A. Kalamack
CEO Kalamack Industries
Kalamack Industries, Inc
Building A
15 Rolling Acres
Cincinnati, OH 45239

I N T E R O F F I C E   M E M O

To: Jonathan Davaros
From: Trenton Kalamack
cc:
Date: 7/30/07
Re: Property Acquisition

Jon,

Please make arrangements to purchase Morgan's church from Piscary's estate.

TK

Devin's
Journal
Entry

July 30, 2007

Morgan is a demon practitioner. Not only that, but I think she's working with Kalamack. I've seen too much over the last year to doubt it. From the freaky neighbor across the street who sings in Latin, to that demon Morgan summoned into the courtroom to put Piscary away, she's bad news.

Morgan was <u>in</u> that room at the FIB when Piscary died, and you can't tell me that she didn't have something to do with it. Skimmer, that blond vampire friend of Tamwood, might have done the deed, but I bet Morgan witched her into it.

Morgan wanted Piscary dead, not Skimmer. Piscary blood-raped Tamwood, Morgan's roommate, then he tried to kill Morgan herself, and when that failed, he gave Morgan's boyfriend, Kisten, to another vampire as a blood gift, which is nothing less than giving him away to be legally bled to death for someone else's enjoyment. Sort of like giving a bottle of wine to a business associate. Vamps are not human. I got a copy of Felps's second-death certificate. He is dead and gone, and he's not coming back. Not from blood poisoning. I cut his obituary out of the paper. It almost makes him sound respectable.

A CITY GRIEVES FOR ONE OF ITS OWN
Piscary's Scion Inspired Unification and Tolerance

Hollows leaders applauded the efforts of respected Greater Cincinnati businessman Kisten Felps for bringing a new level of tolerance and respect among humans and vampires.

The proposed changes in human and vampire interactions drafted by Mr. Felps could have brought the relations of human and vampire cultures to a new level of co-operation.

Mr. Felps died on his boat in what authorities believe to be an assassination. Services will be held this Saturday at 10:00 pm in the Hollows Cathedral.

A native of Cincinnati, Mr. Felps was a graduate of the University of Cincinnati where he studied international and inter-species businesses. He was a member of Piscary's camarilla from birth and became principal scion three years ago after former scion Ivy Tamwood renounced her position.

Following Piscary's arrest and incarceration, Mr. Felps became principal camarilla leader for the greater Cincinnati area. He closed Piscary's restaurant and reopened the site as a vampire-only nightclub after the restaurant lost its mixed public license. Mr. Felps did not contest the loss of the MPL, which many believe was the biggest step in reducing the anxiety between humans and vampires. Mr. Felps was quoted as saying, "This establishment is not a hunting ground for our species, and humans should not be treated as a source of amusement."

Mr. Felps is survived by a sister and nephew, both of whom reside in the Cincinnati area, and an aunt and uncle who reside on the East Coast.

I ran into Maria again over content with Monday's piece. I had to soften it up, take out the hard statements. They even slashed my word count. If I didn't have a contract, they might have cut it altogether. This isn't like Maria at all, and I wonder if it has something to do with that article Cindy did on Kalamack a few months ago. It felt like a bribe piece when I first read it. I have a copy of my original article in case I get a chance to reprint it once I blow this thing open. At this point, I don't care if they sue me for breach of contract. Something is seriously wrong, and no one is listening to me.

I don't even want to guess what's going to happen now that Piscary is dead. The bastard might have given one of his own people to another vampire to be bled to death, but Piscary kept us humans safe. The next couple of months are going to be hell until a new vampire comes out on top.

The Hollows Gazette

SUBMISSION SHEET

For salaried employees only.
Freelance, please use submission
form FL16008B.

SUBMITTED BY: Devin Crossman
TITLE OF ARTICLE: Morgan Is a Menace
RUN DATE: Monday, July 30, 2007
CHARACTER COUNT: 1250 w/spaces

Though curiously free from suspicion of the murder of Piscary, Rachel Morgan of Vampiric Charms had plenty of motive to kill. It was her vampire lover who was found murdered twice, just hours after Piscary's death. The FIB and the I.S. might be ignoring that Kisten Felps was a blood gift to an as-yet-unidentified vampire, but I think that's motive enough for the dangerous, hot-tempered witch known for dabbling in demonology.

The FIB is in Morgan's pocket, having gone so far as to issue the black witch the warrant allowing Morgan to arrest Trent Kalamack at his wedding under the charge of murder to prevent her secret lover from marrying another woman. I can only hope that the I.S. is ignoring her motive in the Piscary slaying because Morgan is a suspect in her former lover's death herself, and they're hoping she'll make a mistake that links her to both deaths.

It would be a pleasant surprise if indeed the I.S. and FIB are giving the woman the rope with which to hang herself since the FIB is bewitched and Morgan continues to wreak havoc on the city—a city now bereft of one of its most powerful protectors, thanks to her. Who will keep us safe as minor camarillas prepare to make a bloodbath of our streets and take Piscary's place? Morgan herself? I think not.

Checked By: Randy Traxton   Date   7/30/07

Comments   Devin, I can't clear this. Take out the libelous statements, especially the demon remark and black witch comment. It's too long, as well. Keep it under 660 characters. -RT

And then there's the Kalamack angle. Trent was in the FIB building when Dorothy Claymor decapitated Piscary. I've got a copy of the warrant and arrest papers that Morgan used to get Trent there in case they get "modified" in the interim.

I hate to say it, but I'm impressed. Kalamack is slicker than a wet frog. He's got lots of people skills, but he's only showing what he wants us to see.

So I did a little more digging at the FIB and found out that Kalamack's father and Morgan's father (who used to work for the I.S. in the Arcane Division) not only knew each other, but worked together on the sly on something that caused their deaths only a few weeks apart. Something that had to do with the ever-after, if the rumors are true. I can't get any paperwork on it though. Nothing.

All of which begs the question of how did Morgan miraculously survive a 100% lethal childhood disease? Occam's razor says the Kalamacks are dabbling in a little illegal biodrug production, developing and marketing illegal medicines to those who can afford it.

Why not? Kalamack's father had to have a hobby other than dogs, race horses, and making money. Rachel got a freebie at that camp because her dad and Trent's dad were close, and now Rachel and Trent are continuing the relationship. At least, I think they are. She really seemed intent on bringing him in. Unless she did it just to break up the marriage to that cold bitch of a West Coast woman, Ellasbeth Withon.

I did a little research on Withon, and none of it came up good. The woman is like ice. Morgan did him a favor by stopping the wedding if you ask me. The paper got an invite to the wedding, and

WARRANT FOR ARREST

Cincinnati / Hollows Division
Cincinnati, OH 45202
Phone: 555-6980 • Fax: 555-8001

EASTERN ALLIANCE FOR EXPEDIENT JUSTICE VS.

NAME:	Trenton A. Kalamack				ALIAS:	
DOB: 10/21/79	AGE:	27	Sex:	Male	SPECIES:	Undeclared
ADDRESS: 15 Rolling Acres, Cincy 45239				SS#:		xxx-xx-xxx
DRIVER'S LICENSE: OH008341874				PHONE:		513-555-4242
PREVIOUS ADDRESS: N/A						
DEFENDANT'S EMPLOYER:	Self-employed			ADDRESS:		
CASE NUMBER:	OH-H-072720077119					
OFFENSE CODE(s): HPR			OFFENSE IN VIOLATION OF O.G.S: no			
DATE(s) OF OFFENSE: 7/28/07			DATE OF ARREST: 7/29/07			
COMPLAINT: (NAME, ADDRESS, DEP)	Det. M. Glenn Cincy FIB		NAME/ADDRESSES OF WITNESSES:			
DATE ISSUED: 7/29/07	Magistrate	Assistant CS		Deputy CSC:		Clerk of Sup. Court XXXXX

STATE OF OHIO and/or KENTUCKY, in the court of justice district court division:

To any officer with authority to execute a warrant for arrest for the offense(s) charged below:

I, the undersigned, find that there is probable cause to believe that on or about the date of offense shown and in the state(s) named above, the defendant named herewith unlawfully, willfully, and feloniously did

> Kidnap and hold Brett Markson, directing and allowing his torture
>
> for information until said victim died by either wounds inflicted
>
> by said torture, or his own suicide.

This act was unlawful, and this warrant has been issued by statements made under oath. You are directed to arrest the defendant without delay to answer the charge(s) above.

SIGNATURE:	*Dr. Ambrooen*	COURT DATE:	
LOCATION OF COURT:	Detroit, MI	COURT TIME:	

CO-CR-2007, Rev 1/2005 (Structured, Expedient Sentencing)

ARREST REPORT

Cincinnati / Hollows Division
Cincinnati, OH 45202
Phone: 555-6980 • Fax: 555-8001

DATE:	07-27-2007		NAME:	Trenton A. Kalamack
ARRESTING OFFICER:	Runner: Rachel Morgan		SPECIES:	Undeclared
			AGE:	25
CASE OFFICER:	Captain Edden			
CASE OFFICER:	072720077119			

PERSONAL INFORMATION

NAME:	Trenton A. Kalamack	ALIAS:	N/A
DOB:	10/21/79	SPECIES:	Undeclared
ADDRESS:	15 Rolling Acres, Cincinnati, OH 45239	SS#:	xxx-xx-xxx
DRIVER'S LICENSE:	OH008341874	PHONE:	513-555-4242
PREVIOUS ADDRESS:	N/A		
PREVIOUS OFFENSE:	No convictions		

INFRACTION

OFFENSE:	Wanted for questioning concerning a series of		
	Were deaths that the I.S. is ignoring.		
OBSERVERS:		CONTACT:	
ADDRESS OF INCIDENT:	Cincinnati, OH; Hollows, KY		

even the announcement is cold. Now I wish I'd gone. Who knew Morgan would be there to arrest Kalamack?

Either way the I.S. and the FIB had better get their heads out of each other's asses and do something about Morgan. A demon practitioner witch

Mr. and Mrs. Walter A. Withon

Request the honor of a member
of the Hollows Gazette's staff
present at the
marriage of their daughter

Ellasbeth Olivia
with
Mr. Trenton A. Kalamack

Sunday, the 29th of July
Two thousand and seven
At nine o'clock in the evening
Hollows Basilica

and a rich human dabbling in illegal genetics is a problem. And I know the woman is doing black magic. I paid a witch to look at her aura, and she told me it had a black rim around it. That means black magic.

Frankly, I'm surprised that I got the cost for the aura reading past Sandra in accounting. The woman thinks she's a damn comedian, writing snarky comments on my expense reports. At least she cleared the itch cream this time. I'm keeping a copy of my expense report with her signature until the check clears. I've grown very suspicious lately, what with Maria watching everything I write and someone going through my desk on a regular basis.

Hallows Gazette
EXPENSE REPORT

Employee:	Devin Crossman		Invoice No.:	0416202157
Employee ID:	84-1698		Month/Year:	July 2007
Phone:				
Fax:				
E-Mail:	dcrossman@hollowsgazette.com			

Description	Date	Amount	Approved	
Aura reading for interview	7/14	75.00	Yes	75.00
anti-itch cream	7/8	15.95	Yes	15.95
Total:		90.95	Total:	90.95

Review:		
Reviewed by:	Print	Sign
Approved:	Sandra Stamford	Sandra Stamford
Comments:	You got a bad rash or something, Devin? This the third month you've submitted itch cream. Stay away from the pixies, you idiot!	

Failure to attach original receipts will result in decline of reimbursement. Do not fill in shaded areas.

The Were registry I bought finally came in. Apparently a new edition was being printed, and it slowed everything down. Morgan is indeed a female alpha, and even fought off a couple of challenges. Which is weird, because I didn't think witch magic could change a witch to a wolf. I wouldn't have believed it if I hadn't seen the paperwork.

Joining a pack could be a scam to get her insurance cheap, seeing as her alpha male is an insurance adjuster for Were Insurance named David Hue. He's really stiff-necked, but I wouldn't have pegged him as a Were by his looks. Most are covered with tattoos, and he has very few. Morgan and Hue are clearly not having sex, so what's the deal? What is Hue getting out of this? Is it the focus? I've been over the Gazette's fact sheet, and it looks like something that would be worth joining a pack for.

Document Shepherd: Cindy Strom (513) 555-7735 ext 7
Updated 6/07

The Hollows Gazette

The Focus: Fact or Fiction

Once thought to be a fable, it's now believed the focus, a long-lost Were artifact of magical significance, is not only fact, but has resurfaced.

The focus is said to be demon crafted, made of ancient bone of unknown origin and possessing a consciousness of sorts, with the drive and desire to survive and dominate. It's said to change its appearance according to the phases of the moon, being a human female on the new moon, and the bust of a howling wolf on the full.

Rumor says the focus was unearthed by a human in 2007, found in a basement in Detroit, MI, where it had lain with the bones of a long-dead master vampire who had gone missing in the early 1800s.

Shortly after being discovered, the focus went off the Mackinac Bridge during an attempt by the Celtic Knot pack to acquire it. Neither the body of the man fleeing with it, nor the focus was recovered. Even more telling is that there was no search performed by any Were-based operations at the site. Most experts agree that the focus is likely again in hiding, probably in Cincinnati or the Hollows.

The greatest evidence that Cincinnati is now home to the focus is the suicidal deaths of three human women found as wolves. It is believed that two other human women have been successfully turned and are now members of the Black Dandelion pack. If so, this would be the first recorded instance of such happening since the Anderson texts.

The ability to turn a human into a Were is said to be one of the properties of the focus, accomplished by way of bite, scratch, or sex.

Though seemingly insignificant, this has the potential to cause a spike in the Were population. Combine this with the focus's foretold ability to garner the loyalties of other alphas,

INTERNAL FACT SHEET

THE FOCUS: FACT OR FICTION

this Were artifact is a serious threat to the vampire superiority in numbers and political strength.

Worst-case scenario: the focus is indeed in play, and a worldwide power struggle is about to ensue. Best-case scenario: it's a fable whose power is limited to what we give it.

WHAT IT MEANS TO YOU

WERES: Highly coveted, seen as the "holy grail" of were-wolves, and the potential beginning of a new age of respect and power.

VAMPIRES: Thought to have put the focus into hiding several centuries ago to slow the political power that the Weres are capable of.

WITCHES: Currently watching the situation, trying to remain neutral. Interesting to note that it's likely only witch or demon magic can destroy the focus.

HUMANS: Should be paying more attention since the focus, if it exists, has the ability to turn a human into a Were, possibly without consent.

For more information, contact:
Dr. Pandorn
Professor of Human Studies
University of Cincinnati
Cincinnati, OH 45221
513-555-2440 (ext 77)

UNITED WERE REGISTRY

2007 ISSUE 3

CINCINNATI: RANGE 293
UNITED STATES, CANADA

WERE REGISTRATIONS

ADDITIONS OR CORRECTIONS: PO BOX WR66, 45702

Pack:
BLACK DANDELION

Number...O-C[H] 93
Established .... December 20, 2006
Tattoo Registered......... Currently unratified
Established 2006.........................5 members
Influence ....in flux

Tattoo is not ratified due to
insufficient number of members

ALPHA MALE:
DAVID HUE

Number...........................O-C[H] 93AM
Claimed Status.................At Inception
Inclusion.....................Charter Member
Address ....611 Ash St Apt D1
                          Cincinnati, OH 45202

ALPHA FEMALE:
RACHEL MORGAN

Number................O-C[H] 93AF
Inclusion........ Charter Member
Witnessed ....Kisten Felps
                     Ivy Tamwood
                     Jenks Pixy
Claimed Status......At Induction

BETA FEMALE:
SERENA McTAVEN

Number................ O-C[H] 93BF
Inclusion....... Inducted 7/16/07
Witnessed ....Rachel Morgan
                   Tod McTaven
                   May McTaven
Current
Rank Won ....At Induction

Compiled by Anne Garfield

PACK MATTERS

ALPHA MALE:
DAVID HUE

Number	O-C[H] 93AM
Inclusion	Charter Member
Marital Status	Single
Active	Yes
Prior Pack Affiliations	Oak Tree (family)
	Warriors (teen)
	Were Insurance
Address	611 Ash St.
	Cincinnati, OH 45202

DESCRIPTION: Hue is 5'8", has thick, shoulder-length black hair, dark eyes, brown eyes, short fingers. Dislikes stubble and dresses like a loner. Not a big man but has a large presence that has seemed to have strengthened since taking on the responsibilities of a pack. Athletic. Habitually runs on two or four legs. As wolf: Hue is gray with black paws.

IDENTIFYING MARK(s): Dandelion pack tattoo on left neck. Family's Oak Tree tattoo on back. Were Insurance logo on inside right wrist.

HISTORY: Hue recently started a pack with a witch in an attempt to maintain his job and avoid pack responsibilities. He currently has a small pack of four, but it is probably one of the more influential packs in Cincinnati because of his choice of alpha and her rumored acquisition of the fabled "focus."

Hue was questioned by the I.S. concerning a spate of Were deaths, including Elaine Yevon and Felicia Borden, but was released due to lack of evidence.

CHALLENGES: None. Registered loner until late 2006. Hue has no males in his pack, a situation that has several top alphas concerned, but his pack is young and most of his peers are willing to "wait and see."

LEADERSHIP: Hue's leadership style is still evolving as his pack of nonconforming Weres grows. He seems to be unusually protective and tolerant of his members while ruthless with those who threaten them. Hue spends a lot of time with everyone in his pack, excluding his alpha, and isn't pair-bonded to either of his subordinate bitches.

CONNECTIONS: Hue works for Were Insurance as an adjuster. Supervisor is Mr. Finley. Hue is currently one of the company's highest-paid insurance

ALPHA MALE: DAVID HUE (cont.)

investigators. He's familiar with working with other species, which might account for his choice in alpha. Hue's partner at Were Insurance was a witch named Howard Keden until Keden recently retired. Hue is also a notary.

OF NOTE: Hue collects Civil War sabers. Until recently, he lived alone in a town house in an upscale, mixed neighborhood. Keeps a cat. Hue was markedly sexually active until taking on pack responsibilities. Hue listens to country music and knows how to shoot a shotgun. He drives a gray sports car. Hue now lives in an informal live-in relationship with two of his subordinate, single bitches.

OTHER: It's interesting to note that the female members of his pack have no history of prior pack affiliation and are not even in the Were database. This is the strongest evidence to date that Hue does indeed possess the focus and is able to turn humans into Weres with a bite or sex.

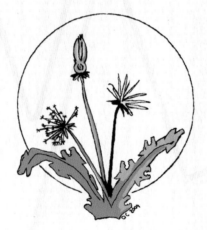

Compiled by Anne Garfield

ADDITIONS OR CORRECTIONS: PO BOX WR66, 45702

PACK MATTERS

ALPHA FEMALE:
RACHEL MORGAN

Number...................................... O-C[H] 93AF
Inclusion .... Charter Member
Witnessed............................... Kisten Felps
Ivy Tamwood
Jenks Pixy
Marital Status .... Single
Claimed Status .... At Induction
Address............................ 1597 Oak Staff
Hollows, KY 41011
Phone 513-555-4893
Alt Phone............................ 513-555-7762

DESCRIPTION: Morgan is 5'8", red hair, green eyes, fair skin, slim build. As wolf: Morgan uses witch magic to Were into a into a true, red-coated wolf.

IDENTIFYING MARK(s): Demon mark on right wrist. No marks as wolf. No pack tattoo as it fails to survive her witch-wearing process.

HISTORY: Rachel Morgan has no previous history of pack affiliation as she is a witch and was chosen by her alpha David Hue as a way to maintain his employment status in Were Insurance and avoid true pack responsibilities. It's of note that shortly after becoming an alpha in name that David Hue added to his pack and has become an alpha in the truest sense of the word.

CHALLENGES: Morgan has accomplished two challenges to her alpha status, the first by Karen Clauss (O-C 81F) where Morgan did not Were, but bested her using witch magic. This could be a contested loss, but the matter was never pursued, evidence that there were issues present in the challenge itself. The second challenge was registered by Pam Vincent (MI-D(CS) 153AF) who was taken to ground and killed during the challenge by the feral wolves she was studying. There have been no further alpha challenges to Morgan, probably due to Pam's death and the belief that the wolves wanted Morgan to maintain her alpha status. Morgan was not held responsible.

LEADERSHIP: Morgan is a paws-off alpha, letting pack matters be handled by her betas unless trouble arises. If she weren't a witch, she'd be a model alpha.

CONNECTIONS: Morgan is a freelance runner and met her alpha while he was investigating her for possible insurance fraud.

OTHER: There's an ongoing controversy whether Morgan should be allowed to maintain her pack status. Most claims come from rival packs after rumors surfaced that the fabled focus was in her possession in the hopes that if she were discounted, the focus would be more accessible.

Compiled by Anne Garfield

Pack:
SILVER KOI

Number...O-C O7
Established ....November 3, 1966
Tattoo Registered ....November 6, 1966
Charter Pack........................500+ members
Influence ....High

ALPHA MALE:
SIMON RAY

Number...............................O-C O7AM
Inclusion....................Charter Member
Claimed Status.............................1982
Address .... 17 Spring St
Cincinnati, OH 45202

ALPHA FEMALE:
CARRIE RAY
(FOLLY)

Number......................O-C O7AF
Inclusion........ Charter Member
Claimed Status................. 1982

BETA FEMALE:
SAVANNA HURON
(FOLLY)

Number......................O-C O7BF
Inclusion....... Inducted 7/21/67
Witnessed ....Ken Turson
Anne Gabs
Simon Ray
Current Rank Won........... 1985

BETA MALE:
GARY HURON

Number....................O-C O7BM
Inclusion........ Inducted 4/1/84
Witnessed ....Ken Turson
Sharon Vandell
Angie Diver
Current Rank Won........... 1999

Compiled by Anne Garfield

PACK MATTERS

ALPHA MALE:
SIMON RAY

Number.......................................O-C 07AM
Inclusion ....Charter Member
Marital Status... Married: Carrie Ray (Folly)
Claimed Status 1982
Offspring:..................Christine Ray (1984)
Jessica Ray (1985)
Brittany Ray (1986)
Lauren Ray (1988)
Address................................. 17 Spring St.
Cincinnati, OH 45202

DESCRIPTION: Ray is short and round due to a sedentary lifestyle, but he's well liked by his peers and subordinates. As wolf, Ray is heavy and has an abundance of gray around the muzzle.

IDENTIFYING MARKS: Missing his right big toe in both forms. His tail is broken, and he suffers from arthritis when in wolf form, but not human. His Silver Koi tattoo takes up his entire back and right buttock. Ray took his wife's family tattoo, which is a swallow in flight, to honor her.

HISTORY: Ray is a charter member of the Silver Koi pack, which he helped organize during the Turn with his new wife, Carrie (Folly), and later her sister, Savanna Huron (Folly). Both Carrie and Simon began at the bottom of this large, Turn-originating pack, gaining status as Ray spent sixteen years becoming a valued member in his workplace and pack until he accepted the alpha male position from retiring CEO Charlie Bruster.

CHALLENGES: Though gained without the traditional fight, his position and standing in his pack are well assured.

Shortly after gaining alpha male status, his wife successfully challenged the previous alpha female, and, in a battle that nearly killed both women, Carrie achieved her alpha female status. It was only then that Simon and Carrie had their children, and the entire pack is watching the four girls grow up.

LEADERSHIP: Simon is an excellent leader in the corporate world, and his choice of beta male reflects this. It has unfortunately left the pack unbalanced should a military situation arise. Simon has a great respect for his pack members and demands utter obedience.

CONNECTIONS: Simon is CEO of a major manufacturing company in Cincinnati. He employs hundreds, many of whom are pack members.

OF NOTE: Simon breeds and shows koi. He was recently accused of stealing some of his livestock, a claim that would be laughable except he did not file a claim when said fish was stolen.

Simon Ray drives a black Hummer and likes to show off his alpha status. Simon Ray has a bitter rivalry with the Broken Fence pack, which he acerbates whenever he can.

Compiled by Anne Garfield

Pack:
BROKEN FENCE

Number...O-C 03
Established ....November 1, 1966
Tattoo Registered .... November 7, 1966
Charter Pack........................500+ members
Influence .... High

ALPHA MALE:
YALE VERNON

Inclusion.......................Inducted 2000
Claimed Status.............................2001
Address .... 600 Sirius
Cincinnati, OH 45202

ALPHA FEMALE:
ELLEN SARONG

Number.................... O-C 03AF
Inclusion........ Charter Member
Claimed Status................ 1979

BETA FEMALE:
PATRICIA SARONG

Number....................O-C 03BF
Inclusion................ Birth 1976
Witnessed .... Ellen Sarong
Troy Sarong
Heather Adams
Current Rank Won...........2006

BETA MALE:
ALLEN NEWELL

Number....................O-C 03BM
Inclusion...........Inducted 1979
Witnessed .... Ellen Sarong
Patricia Sarong
Troy Sarong
Current Rank Won........... 1999

Compiled by Anne Garfield

PACK MATTERS

ALPHA FEMALE:
ELLEN SARONG

Number.................................. O-C[H] 03AF
Inclusion .... Charter Member
Marital Status .... Widowed (1999)
Claimed Status 1979
Offspring............................Patricia Sarong
Address........................... 600 Sirius, Apt. P
 Hollows, KY 45202
Phone 513-555-7002

DESCRIPTION: In her late 50s, Ellen Sarong is the apex of female werewolves, being petite, elegant, and ruthlessly savage when necessary. She has been known to dye her hair blond, but it is naturally dark with wisps of gray. She wears copious amounts of jewelry and has a professional bearing that gets her into situations where she can take advantage of those who underestimate her political and physical strength. She markets a perfume that smells like ferns and moss (Everglade).

IDENTIFYING MARK(s): Her pack tattoo twines about her right shoulder and up her neck where a flower is visible on the back side of her ear.

HISTORY: Sarong was a minor member of the Broken Fence pack at its inception at the beginning of the Turn. Never a cur, Sarong worked her way up, marrying member Troy Sarong. After gaining monetary clout through the purchase of a fading baseball team, which they then built to the successful Howlers, they were able to further their alpha claim. Sarong and her husband, Troy, then took several years off to train for their ultimately successful bids for alpha while raising their daughter, Patricia.

Troy Sarong died of cancer in 1999, and

Ellen Sarong has had a string of alpha males since, all pulled from her batting lineup. Current alpha male Yale Vernon has had his position unchallenged for over three years. Beta male Allen Newell was handpicked by Troy before his death. It is thought that he is the unseen backbone of the Howlers' empire, and Ellen Sarong the brains and teeth.

CHALLENGES: Sarong has successfully beaten down five challengers. The last challenger died under suspicious circumstances while recovering, and there have been no claims since.

LEADERSHIP: Sarong is an excellent alpha female, taking on most of the alpha male duties since the death of her husband.

CONNECTIONS: Sarong is the owner of the Howlers, an all-Were baseball team.

OF NOTE: Sarong is known for keeping the rivalry between the Broken Fence pack and the Silver Koi pack alive and virulent. Simon Ray has recently accused her of trying to kill him, which might be true as Simon Ray has made no attempt to hide his wish that Ellen Sarong should join her first husband in death sooner as opposed to later.

Compiled by Anne Garfield

Pack:
CELTIC KNOT

Number..................................MI-D [SC] 153
Established .... October 31, 1968
Tattoo Registered .... October 31, 1968
Charter Pack...................... 1000+ members
Influence .... High

ALPHA MALE:
WALTER VINCENT

Number......................MI-D [SC] 153AM
Inclusion.................... Charter Member
Claimed Status............................1975
Address .... 775 Runway Dr.
Bois Blanc I.S., MI 49775

STATUS PENDING

ALPHA FEMALE:
PAM VINCENT
(AAROS)

Number.......... MI-D [CS] 153AF
Inclusion........ Charter Member
Claimed Status................. 1975

BETA FEMALE:
JULIE MAYFIELD

Number...........MI-D [CS] 153BF
Inclusion......................... 2001
Witnessed .... Walter Vincent
Pam Vincent
Brent Markson
Current Rank Won...........2002

BETA MALE:
BRETT MARKSON

Number..........MI-D [CS] 153BM
Inclusion............Inducted 2001
Witnessed .... Walter Vincent
Pam Vincent
Jeff Markson (Sr.)
Current Rank Won...........2001

Compiled by Anne Garfield

PACK MATTERS

ALPHA MALE:
WALTER VINCENT

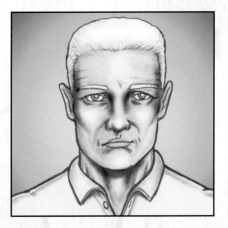

Number .... MI-D [SC] 153AM
Inclusion .... Charter Member
Marital Status .... Widower: Pam (Aaros)
Claimed Status 1975
Offspring .... Hanna (1970)
Elizabeth (1972)
Jamie (1974) deceased
Joshua (1981)
Prior Pack Affiliations .... None
Address .... 775 Runway Dr. Apt. A
Bois Blanc I.S., MI 49775
Phone 231-555-1103

DESCRIPTION: Small man, 5'8", about
average for a Were. Born 1942 before the
Turn. Has gray hair cut close to skull.
Gray eyebrows. Extremely physically fit
for his age. Dresses casually but well. Been
described as ruggedly attractive. Moves fast,
even in his human guise.

IDENTIFYING MARK(s): Has only one
tattoo on record—Celtic Knot on inner arch
of ear where it shows whether on two legs or
four.

HISTORY: Vincent was instrumental in the
development of the Celtic Knots shortly after
the Turn and has belonged to no other pack.
He met Pam Aaros after gaining beta male
status, and they married soon after. After
the miscarriage of their third child, Vincent
fought for and won the alpha male status.
Shortly thereafter, the pack resettled to Bois
Blanc Island at the straits of Mackinac, MI

where the entire pack is instrumental in
wolf research with a strong military-like
presence.

Vincent's wife, Pam (Aaros), recently
died in an alpha female contest under
extraordinary circumstances, taken down
not by her attacker, but the wolves she was
studying.

Vincent has since retreated into
depression, leaving his pack. It remains to
be seen if he emerges thirsty for revenge, or
retreats even further, demanding that the
pack take action and force a new leader.

CHALLENGES: Vincent has not had a
challenge to his alpha status since gaining it.

LEADERSHIP: Vincent is an excellent
alpha, delegating where appropriate and
maintaining utter control.

CONNECTIONS: Vincent's pack has a strong
military feel and has been known to work in
an adviser capacity overseas with the I.S.

OF NOTE: It is thought that Vincent lost his
wife in his bid for the focus.

Compiled by Anne Garfield

PACK MATTERS

ALPHA FEMALE:
PAM VINCENT (AAROS)

Number:.............................MI-D[CS] 153AF
Inclusion: ....Charter Member
Marital Status: .... Deceased 2007
Claimed Status: 1975
Offspring:........................... Hanna (1970)
Elizabeth (1972)
Jamie (1974) deceased
Joshua (1981)
Prior Pack Affiliations:........................ None
Address:................. 775 Runway Dr., Apt A.
Bois Blanc I.S., MI 49775
Phone:................................. 231-555-1103

DESCRIPTION: Small, diminutive, petite, and capable of meting out death, Pam was the perfect model for an effective alpha female. She was known for her delicate, china-doll features and straight black hair. As a wolf, she was smaller than most, closer to the ideal and therefore well suited for her chosen profession of wolf researcher.

IDENTIFYING MARK(s): Celtic Knot tattoo upon inner arch of her ear, and echoed upon her back. Pam did not have any other pack tattoo despite her associations at Oregon University.

HISTORY: Pam entered the pack fairly high up in the hierarchy, being loosely related to the first female alpha. It wasn't until the premature death of her third child that Pam and her husband made a successful bid for the alpha positions. Pam went on to successfully raise one more child while alpha female.

It's thought that it was Pam's idea to move the Celtic Knots from Detroit to Mackinac, allowing her husband the freedom to reshape the pack into a more military feel while she studied the wolves she loved so much.

CHALLENGES: Pam successfully beat down three challengers before her death. Her death during an alpha challenge by Rachel Morgan is still under investigation, hampered by a lack of willingness of the witnesses to cooperate. Witnesses claim that the contest was held too close to the indigenous wolf population, and the female alpha of the wolves Pam was studying took the opportunity to remove a rival. Morgan was not attacked, and several witnesses claim the female alpha wolf was coming to her aid.

LEADERSHIP: Vincent was an excellent alpha female, known for her ability to get to the root of a problem and rip it out.

CONNECTIONS: Pam graduated from Oregon State University, focusing on wolf studies.

OF NOTE: Pam maintained her alpha female status after death as it's claimed the contest she died in was not for pack control, but for the focus.

Compiled by Anne Garfield

PACK MATTERS

ALPHA MALE:
BRETT MARKSON

Number.............................MI-D[SC] 153BF
Inclusion 2001
Witnessed...........................Walter Vincent
                                Pam Vincent
                            Jeff Markson (Sr.)
Marital Status ....Divorced
Claimed Status 2001
Offspring................. J. Markson (Jr.) 2004
                            A. Markson 2005
Prior Pack Affiliations...Bent Grass (family)
                            Celtic Knot
                        Broken Arrow (Marine)
                        Diamond Chip (divorced)

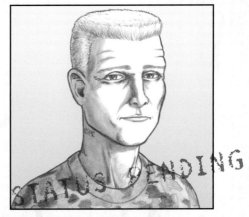

DESCRIPTION: Markson is 5'6", graying hair, narrow build, athletic, with a military bearing. Brown eyes, thin lips, short hair. As wolf: Markson is gray with white ears.

IDENTIFYING MARK(s): Previous pack tattoos: Marine anchor/globe—right bicep, Broken Arrow—left inner arm, Diamond Chip chain—left wrist. Celtic Knot on inner ear and was visible in both morphs.

HISTORY: Markson was inducted into the Celtic Knot pack in 2001, where he immediately challenged and won the beta male position. Though the challenge and subsequent win was a formality since pack leader Walter Vincent hired Markson to head up a new area of wolf studies, Markson quickly gained the respect of those under him with his calm, decisive reactions under stress.

CHALLENGES: Markson fought his way up to high male in the Broken Arrow, then bettered it when he became a member of the Celtic Knots, winning his beta male position in his entry.

LEADERSHIP: Skilled in both the sciences and military matters, Markson is an involved beta, maintaining discipline and carrying out the alpha's designs. He demanded and received a high level of respect.

CONNECTIONS: Markson had many contacts in the military before he became involved in the Celtic Knot pack. He maintained close connection to his ex-wife, who kept her position in the Diamond Chip pack after he left. He was devoted to his out-of-pack children when time permitted. His relationship with his first pack was strong enough to permit his children to be conceived after he left their mother's pack.

OTHER: Markson's current position in the Celtic Knots is in flux as alpha male Walter Vincent mourns the loss of his beta and wife, Pam. Markson is no longer active in the pack, and it's believed that he has been forcibly ousted from the Celtic Knots due to his inability to gain the focus.

Compiled by Anne Garfield

ADDITIONS OR CORRECTIONS: PO BOX WR66, 45702

The Hollows Gazette

Summer Fun on the River **C 2**
Obituaries **C 3**
The Week Ahead **C 4**
Almanac **C 4**

Monday, July 30, 2007

LOCAL / STATE

C

The Way I See It
Devin Crossman

WHOOPS, SHE DID IT AGAIN!

Though free from suspicion of the murder of master vampire Piscary, Rachel Morgan of Vampiric Charms has the motive. It was her lover found murdered twice, hours after Piscary's death, a blood gift from the master vampire to another.

Perhaps it's because Morgan is a suspect in her former lover's death that the FIB and I.S. are allowing the witch her freedom, hoping she'll make a mistake that links her to both deaths.

I hope this is the case as Morgan continues to wreak havoc on the city now bereft of one of its most powerful protectors. Who will keep us safe as minor camarillas vie for Piscary's place? Morgan herself? I think not.

Devin Crossman brings his uniquely human point of view to the Hollows. Comments will reach Mr. Crossman at: dcrossman@hollowsgazette.com

Emergency Plan in Action
By Winifred Gradenko
winniegrad@hollowsgazette.com

While preparations are made to put to rest one of Cincinnati's most beloved and influential citizens, another set of plans, one locked away for over a century, is being dusted off.

The three-month mourning for a master vampire isn't only out of respect, but need, as a nationwide search is on for a vampire of alternative descent willing, and having the clout, to take Piscary's place and prevent a potential bloodbath as minor local camarillas strive to exert

See Search **C 8**

CITY HOLDS BREATH AS VAMPS MOURN
By Gary Brown
gmbrown@hollowsgazette.com

Concerned vampires waiting for news.

Much of the Hollows and Greater Cincinnati area are in shock today as information concerning the brutal murder of beloved master vampire Ptah Piscary continue to surface.

Longtime Hollows resident Piscary's second-life was cut short yesterday when camarilla hopeful Dorothy Claymor decapitated Piscary shortly after his release from the Greater Cincinnati Area Inderlander retention facility. Claymor is currently in an undisclosed high-security facility for her own protection while waiting for her trial, and she has already entered a plea for self-defense.

The attack took place downtown at the FIB building during closed-door negotiations with City Council member Trent Kalamack, Ellen Sarong of the Howlers, local businessman Simon Ray, gambling boat owner Stanley Saladan, and Captain Edden of the FIB. Also present were Rachel Morgan and Ivy Tamwood of Vampiric Charms.

Little is being released pending further investigations, but it's surmised the attack is linked to the recent murder of Piscary's scion, Kisten Felps.

"The room was full of people who had a stake to grind with Piscary," Officer Rimer said when asked. "Captain Edden was in there, and we still don't know what happened."

Though no other arrests have been made, Saladan was questioned due to the unsolved arson of his gambling boat. Sarong and Ray have both been cleared of suspicion.

Members of Vampiric Charms are unavailable for comment, but have been asked to remain in the Greater Cincinnati area.

Piscary was a longtime Cincinnati area resident, best known for his highly successful eatery, Pizza Piscary's. He'll be missed as the city waits to learn who will keep the minor camarillas in line.

See Boat **C 2**

@ A Glance July 30, 2007 Average High/Low: 86° / 66°		
	Today	Tomorrow
Sunrise	5:36 AM	5:37 AM
Sunset	7:52 PM	7:51 PM
Moonrise	8:34 PM	9:02 PM
Moonset	6:02 AM	7:15 AM
Phase: Full		

SEE ALMANAC C 4

Kalamack Industries, Inc

Jonathan Davaros
Chief Personnel Officer
Kalamack Industries, Inc
Building A
15 Rolling Acres
Cincinnati, OH 45239

I N T E R O F F I C E   M E M O

To: Trenton Kalamack
From: Jonathan Davaros
CC:
Date: 7/31/07
Re: Property Acquisition

Sa'han,

I understand your wanting leverage over Morgan, but I can't realistically make the purchase of her church invisible, even with outright cash. Further ties between the two of you need to be avoided.

I'd like to reassure you again that I have put all resources into finding out how Crossman is getting through I.S. and FIB security to access your files. He knows your father and Morgan's worked together, and it's only a matter of time and initiative until he links your family with Morgan's. If you continue to refuse to allow Quen to remove your information from unsecured files, I would advise you—as I advised your father for so many years—to initiate a final solution to this problem immediately.

Also, did you have a preference as to where you'd like to meet with Rynn Cormel? He's flying in this next week to look over the arrangements of taking ownership of Piscary's camarilla, and his schedule is very flexible.

Yours,

Jonathan

Kalamack Industries, Inc

Trenton A. Kalamack
CEO Kalamack Industries
Kalamack Industries, Inc
Building A
15 Rolling Acres
Cincinnati, OH 45239

INTEROFFICE MEMO

TO: Quen Hansen
FROM: Trenton Kalamack
CC:
DATE: 7/31/07
RE: Plumbing Issue

Quen,

Will you please make arrangements to purchase Morgan's church outright from Piscary's estate? I'd like to use it as a bargaining chip to convince Jenks to work with you in removing the recent arrest warrants the FIB has acquired. I will not tolerate my fingerprints on file. And before you roll your eyes and sigh, I want you to work with Jenks specifically to evaluate a pixy's effectiveness in security. Morgan does extremely well despite her scattered working style, and I think the pixy is the difference.

The impetus behind all this is to find out how Crossman is getting through the FIB security to supposedly locked-down information. My concern is that if the FIB is vulnerable, we probably are too. I know you don't think pixies make effective backups, but Morgan seems to have had great success with Jenks, and there's always the chance Crossman managed to find one to work with him, especially if he has indeed gained access to Morgan's church again.

I know Jon advises a clean end to this, but I'm reluctant until there's no other recourse. I think Crossman might be amendable to persuasion if the price is right. Will you have a personality profile made up on him with significant detail given to how strong his feelings are between justice and truth? I do not want to become my father.

Trent

Kalamack Industries, Inc

Jonathan Davaros
Chief Personnel Officer
Kalamack Industries, Inc
Building A
15 Rolling Acres
Cincinnati, OH 45239

INTEROFFICE MEMO

To: Trenton Kalamack
From: Jonathan Davaros
CC:
Date: 11/1/07
Re: Crossman

Sa'han,

I would again beg to you to reconsider your lenient stance on Devin Crossman. As Quen has told you, Crossman has unearthed Morgan's birth father, and that will ultimately lead him to your father's involvement in her continued survival. I understand the reasonings behind your decision, yet I'm compelled to point out again that your decisions do, and will continue to, impact the survival of our entire species. I implore you to set aside your emotions and do what is best for all as your father did before you. He was a great man, and you carry his legacy well.

Give me leave, and I will settle the final arrangements for Morgan and Crossman myself without your involvement. Her true threat is clear, not only to your person, but to our entire way of life.

Yours,

Jonathan

Devin's
Journal
Entry

November 5, 2007

And the story just keeps getting weirder. Morgan wasn't raised by her birth father. I've seen her birth certificate. It's real enough, but they can only go by what the mother says, and Alice Morgan says that Monty Morgan is Rachel's father. There is NO WAY that can be true, even with wishful thinking. If Rachel had the Rosewood syndrome, then both her parents would have to be carriers. Monty Morgan was never tested for it. But Alice's college boyfriend, Takata, was. Takata has got to be Rachel's father. It would be too stupid, but it's true. And I can prove it.

Fact: Alice, Monty, and Takata went to the same college. Alice got pregnant about the time Takata left for the West Coast, and Monty made an honest woman of her. How, you might ask, do I know? I followed Rachel from the Kalamack estate after his Halloween party/fund-raiser. Morgan spent the night there. I don't get it. I thought she hated him. I said she had the hots for him in an article once to see what kind of a response I'd get, but maybe she has a thing for him after all. I never was good at figuring women out. Winnie is driving me nuts.

Anyway, Rachel made a run for her mom's house about daybreak in one of Trent's cars. I thought it might be because either Trent was really good in bed, or really bad in bed, but I followed her and tucked in under a window to overhear her mother having a mental breakdown. Half an hour later, I find out why when Takata shows up. He almost catches me in the bushes when he walks in like he owns the place. And then the shit hits the fan.

Takata, the rock star, admitted to Morgan that he is her dad, and Morgan didn't even know.

I went over some of Takata's lyrics from his hits, and you can see the man whining about the family he gave to his best friend in college. I thought they were all about vampires, but they're about Rachel, Robbie, and even their mom, Alice.

Maria at the paper won't let me print it without proof. "Liability," she says. "It's wrong to sensationalize a family's pain to sell papers," she says. Like ruining families isn't our bread and butter?

Morgan's medical records make a hell of a lot more sense now.

Both Takata and Alice are carriers for the Rosewood syndrome. She really did have it, making one more nail in the proverbial coffin that Kalamack has a genetic lab tucked away somewhere in his compound since Morgan is still alive.

So the question is why would Kalamack Senior risk life and reputation for a witch baby? I can't bring up charges of genetic tinkering against Kalamack without solid proof, but the thought of him working with a demon practitioner is enough to keep me awake at night. And Rachel is practicing. I can prove that. It's so obvious it makes me want to pull out my hair, now that it's grown back in again.

1.) She summoned a demon named Al into the courts to put Piscary away.

2.) She survived an I.S. death threat. I've seen the woman work. There's no way she could survive unless she's either really lucky, or extremely powerful. And she's not that lucky.

3.) Morgan has a playdate with Al the demon every week, and she comes back fine. She even left her fish in the ever-after with him.

4.) I know some of those books in with her cookbooks are demonic in origin. The pictures are somewhere on my hard drive. It's just a matter of time. I sent my hard drive off to a recovery firm in California. They got the photos of the normal spells and charms back for me, but none of the demon texts yet. I'm starting to think the pixies messed with my hard drive.

5.) That charm Morgan uses to Were into a red wolf is not witch magic. I've searched it on the Internet, and everything says that it's a demon curse. I've quit searching because every time I do, I get a virus.

6.) Who ever heard of a witch living with a vampire, and NOT getting bitten? Okay, she's been bitten, but not on a regular basis, and only when she wants it. Morgan is clearly in charge. She's got to be using a demon curse to do it.

7.) She survived a banshee attack. Enough said.

Maria is threatening to put me on probation if I don't stop investigating this, but as long as I don't put it into an article, what can she do? I honestly think she's more worried about me tarnishing

Kalamack's reputation than anything else. I'm not buying that altruistic overcoat he wears. If he's kind to orphans, it's only because he's keeping a couple locked in his basement.

I told that to Winnie on our date last week and she almost had a cow. It cost me a hundred bucks in roses before she'd talk to me again.

Spells

Noncontact
Extensions
Using Ley Lines

Compiled by:
CHARLES M. CHRISTIAN

ALLERGY RELIEF

APPLICATIONS

A medicinal ley line charm to alleviate most allergy symptoms associated with pets. Though tedious, once mastered, this charm is often preferred to earth magic as there are no physical changes, simply symptomatic, making it a safer charm and less likely to cause permanent damage if done incorrectly. The charm itself is lodged in the maker of the spell and is therefore very discreet and long-lived.

PROCEDURE

1. Sketch protective circle in which to perform the spell with salt or magnetic chalk. Making sure you have everything you need with you, tap a ley line and set the circle.

2. Draw a medium-size pentagram using magnetic chalk or salt.

YOU WILL NEED
- Magnetic chalk or salt
- White candle
- Ceremonial knife
- Feather (any species)
- Dandelion
- Blessed candle
- Crucible
- Hearth fire flame or suitable alternative

Table 8.1

3. Set white candle in #1 location with the word *adaequo*.[1]

4. Set ceremonial knife in #2 location using *me auctore*.[2]

5. Set feather in #3 location using *lenio*.[3]

6. Set dandelion in #4 location with word *iracundia*.[4]

7. Set unlit candle in #5 location, lighting it with a hearth fire flame using the word *evulgo*.[5]

8. Using the place-named ceremonial knife, prick finger to draw blood.

9. Move feather to crucible, and anoint it with three drops of blood to form a connection.

10. Invoke the charm with *non sum qualis eram*.[6]

11. Feather will ignite spontaneously if charm is performed correctly.

COMMON REASONS FOR FAILURE

- Poor grade or table salt used in making pentagram.
- Lack of concentration while place-naming symbolic articles will result in lack of connection and spell failure.
- Poor grade of candle, or blessed candle contaminated with smut.
- High amounts of pesticides on dandelion will weaken charm's effectiveness.

FIRST AID

Symptoms of an ill-spun charm include, but are not limited to, severe itching, uncontrolled sneezing, and eye watering. Spasms and heart attack are known to occur in severe misfires. Seek immediate medical help if you think you have improperly invoked this charm. Though working by covering up allergy symptoms, not removing them, there is still the potential for severe complications with this spell.

---

[1] To make equal. [2] At my suggestion. [3] Unknown. [4] anger. [5] to publish.
[6] I am not what I used to be.

DIVERTING OBJECTS IN MOTION

APPLICATIONS

An easily memorized ley line magic to divert objects in motion that has many applications in the film and law enforcement industries as well as in personal protection. The effectiveness of the charm is determined by the proficiency of the spell caster, but is also dependent upon the mass and velocity of the object being diverted. Can be performed using stored line energy, but large or quickly moving objects require a continual connection to a ley line.

YOU WILL NEED
• Focusing object (sponge, foam ball, marble, beachball, etc.)
• Gesture (see Table 2.1)
• Word of invocation
• Lab partner to throw object

PROCEDURE

1. Connect to ley line or, after mastering basic procedure, ensure that sufficient quantity of energy is stored in chi.

2. Hold focusing object in nondominant hand. The best focusing object is identical to the object being diverted, but sympathetic magic will work with enough practice and sufficient mental connection.

3. Have lab partner toss the object to be diverted. At the same time, perform gesture and allow line energy to flow through hand, saying word of invocation at finish of the hand upswing.

4. Object should be diverted.

- Gesture is performed with dominant hand.
- Thumb and pinkie touch at tips under gathered middle three fingers.
- Wrist circles in loose clockwise motion, ending with three middle fingers pointing at object to be diverted.
- Thumb and pinkie position vary to adjust amount of energy used.

Table 2.1

FURTHER PRACTICE

Try using different focusing objects to determine your level of sympathy.

Once charm is mastered using energy from the line, practice using stored energy from chi.

FIRST AID

Only known ill effect from performing this ley line charm incorrectly is a mild sensory burn caused from failure to use an appropriate focusing object.

MAINTAINING DOMINANCE OVER AN ATTACKED CIRCLE

APPLICATIONS

Though circles are often thought to be impenetrable, they are not. A set circle can be broken by another practitioner if they possess enough strength and skill. The following techniques are most often used by demons attempting to take a summoner's circle in order to escape, the skills here are also employed in both hospital and law enforcement settings.

> **YOU WILL NEED**
> - Access to two ley lines
> - Magnetic chalk or suitable substrate to scribe circle
> - Lab partner with a similar chi strength

They are presented here now only as a way to develop the skills to prevent circle breakage before moving on to higher-level manipulations.

It is recommended that people suffering from decreased aura performance should refrain from this practice until aura strength is within normal parameters.

PROCEDURE

1. Decide who is to be the aggressor, and scribe a blemish-free circle that is comfortable for the defender to hold.

2. While within the circle, the defender taps a line and sets his or her protective circle.

3. The attacker taps the second line, and using that energy, tries one of the techniques in Table 7.1 to break the circle, being careful to protect his thoughts against the backlash of power when the circle falls.

4. The defender strengthens his circle with increased concentration

or a heavier draw upon the ley line.

5. Use caution while both attacking or defending, and monitor energy levels closely to prevent a backlash of power when the circle falls.

6. After several attempts, trade places.

FURTHER PRACTICE

- Try drawing the protection circle with an intentional gap to see how circle continuality impacts circle strength.
- Try to have the defender break a forming circle to feel the difference in amount of energy needed to prevent a circle collapse.
- Change the line used to defend your circle to see how distance from the ley line impacts circle strength.
- Vary circle size to see how diameter relates to circle strength.

A. With your mind's eye, examine the aura flow over the circle, looking for thin or weak spots caused by a skip or jump in the circle's sketching. It will show as a wispy tear. Being careful not to physically burn your thoughts, try to force your aura through the hole with your hand or foot. If your aura passes the boundary of the circle, you will break it.

B. If no tears are present, try to burn a hole using your aura by forcing as much energy as you can safely channel into your aura, more specifically, the aura about your hand.

C. If you're equally matched, you can try to break the circle by tapping the same line as the defender, and absorbing the line's energy to a degree that the defender has nothing to work with. Find or create a weak spot and exploit it.

Table 7.1

FIRST AID

Mild burns from backlash will dissipate within 24 hours, heavier burns will take 48. Use caution in performing ley line manipulations in the interim.

Severe burns can cause pain while tapping a line. Seek medical help.

CALLING A FAMILIAR

APPLICATIONS

An easy method using ley lines to call your familiar to you. Though the compulsion placed upon an animal to return is guaranteed with this charm, it is advisable to reward with food to create a pleasant association between the summons and you.

PROCEDURE

YOU WILL NEED
- Access to ley line
- Food reward for the familiar

1. Connect to a ley line and allow the energy to flow through you while reciting the binding incantation: *polliceor hoc vobis bona fide*.[1]

2. Employ your inner sight and imagine your aura gathering into your chi, absorbing energy from it.

3. Mentally send the energy of your chi out with the incantation: *quam celerrime potest*.[2]

4. If your familiar is able to respond, he or she will find you. Reward with food.

HEARING THROUGH THE EARS OF YOUR FAMILIAR

APPLICATIONS

This ley line spell has its beginnings pre-Turn as a way for the witch in hiding to know when his or her security

YOU WILL NEED
- Access to ley line
- Scribing implement

[1] I promise in good faith. [2] As quickly as possible

was in danger of being compromised. In today's enlightened times, it's no longer necessary, but it's still useful upon occasion. It gives a variety of results from faint impressions to clear, understandable voices.

PROCEDURE

1. Connect to a ley line and allow the energy to flow through you while reciting the binding incantation: *polliceor hoc vobis bona fide*[1] to reaffirm bond.

2. When your familiar acknowledges your presence (signaled by an increase in pulse or a general feeling of anticipation), sketch a small, basic pentagram while imaging your aura gathering into your chi, absorbing energy from it and harnessing it with the word *rogo*.[2]

3. Hand fixed firmly upon completed pentagram, mentally send the energy of your chi you collected out with the incantation *audimus*.[3]

4. There will be a moment until the spell finds your familiar, the time dependent upon the distance he or she is from you. Successful completion of spell will be indicated by an increased amount of audible input.

5. You may now remove your hand from the pentagram, and the spell will hold. To break the spell, you simply need to touch your familiar, and the connection will break, much like touching your circle will invalidate it.

[1] I promise in good faith. [2] I am asking. [3] We hear.

SUMMONING A DEMON

APPLICATIONS

Though simple in design and implementation, this is a *highly dangerous* spell that requires a firm understanding of ley lines to be performed with any assurance of safety. Demons were often summoned before the Turn as a way to acquire knowledge, and with the advent of proper curriculums in accepted universities, it's no longer necessary, though admittedly not illegal. It's presented here only to be compared *in theory* to the various versions, and *should not be attempted.*

YOU WILL NEED

- Candles that were initially lit upon holy ground
- Hearth flame or suitable substitute
- Magnetic chalk or similar substrate to scribe circle
- Cremation dust
- Demon's summoning name

PROCEDURE:

1. Draw a holding circle using magnetic chalk.[1]

2. Set appropriate amount of cremation dust inside the circle to force the demon to materialize inside it.[2]

3. Light the candle with hearth fire or a flame given firm, symbolic meaning. Set it beside the cremation dust so the demon fixates on it instead of your stock of ash or the ash on your fingers.[3]

4. Tapping nearest ley line, set the holding circle with you outside it.[4]

5. Pronounce the following, inserting the demon's name you wish to summon: "*Facilis descensus Tartaros,*[A] DEMON NAME."

6. To banish the demon, say firmly and with meaning, "Demon, I banish you directly to the ever-after." If the demon is stubborn,

or you don't show enough determination, you may have to repeat using the demon's name.

7. Don't break your holding circle until the demon has vanished, taking the cremation dust with it.[5] It is advisable to maintain the circle's integrity until the sun rises.

FIRST AID

There's no first aid for doing this spell incorrectly. If the demon escapes, the practitioner will be abducted. Chances of survival slim to none, depending on the demon summoned.

COMMON REASONS FOR FAILURE

The reasons for failure are many, and can only be guessed at since failure means abduction.

[1] Chalk skipping while drawing circle allows a thin spot the demon can break. Many charms require the traditional salt, which can gap. Candles that were not lit on holy ground or inferior chalk can cause failure.

[2] Many summoning charms don't require cremation dust, relying on lit candles to focus demons within the circle. This practice is questionable at best.

[3] Demons improperly fixating on alternative cremation dust sources is the reason many summoning charms do not employ dust. Having a candle as backup alleviates that possibility.

[4] Inability to hold enough ley line energy is likely the cause for 90 percent of abductions and why no one should attempt it regardless of the reason. Your aura breaking the circle the demon is trapped behind is a common error. Never get too close.

[5] Never trust that a demon is truly gone once you have summoned it. Remain vigilant until past sunrise.

[A] Easy is the descent into hell (Tartaros).

PENTAGRAMS and Their Associated Uses

1.

2.

3.

4.

5.

1. PROTECTION: Standard pentagram with braided outer ring. Rings are shown in color for illustration purposes and shouldn't be drawn with colored chalk unless directed. Typical ingredients for bands include—but are not limited to—salt, ash, cinnamon, and sand.

2. DIVINATION: New moons at points and a Mobius strip in cave of pentagram. Not recommended to be hand drawn by novices.

3. SUMMONING (INTERNAL POWER): Used to summon, concentrate, and contain power within practitioner. Not recommended for hand-drawn use by novices.

4. SUMMONING (EXTERNAL POWER): Standard pentagram with Celtic chain binding the points. Hand drawing not recommended even for experienced practitioners.

5. BASIC PENTAGRAM: Drawn with a multitude of substrates, this is the beginning point of most pentagrams.

INCANTATION TO BIND A FAMILIAR

Binding a familiar is one of the earliest tasks undertaken by the serious ley line witch. It's often said that the familiar finds the witch, the witch does not find the familiar, and to a great extent this is true. Care should be taken that the intelligence of the familiar should be in line with the skill of the practitioner, meaning that a skilled witch should aspire to at least a cat or dog, though rats make excellent familiars to those who understand their needs.

Once the practitioner is content with the possibility of what has the potential for a lifelong connection, it's an easy task to create an auratic and emotional bond that will serve to protect the practitioner from psychic attack and greatly extend the life and health of the animal.

In a cool, quiet place free of distractions, settle yourself with your familiar and a morsel of food that you will both enjoy. Do not give your potential familiar anything to eat, but be sure he or she knows it's there. If your potential familiar shows a desire to leave at any time during the charm, the match isn't good. Disconnect from the line and try at a later date with a different animal.

While holding or touching your familiar begin by tapping a line and letting it run through both of you. Once your potential familiar begins to accept the energy, set a cutting of your hair, a cutting from your familiar's hair or nail, and the bite of food that you will later share within the center of an as-yet-undrawn pentagram of medium size.

Begin to draw the pentagram while saying the following, reserving one word per leg of the figure: *polliceor hoc vobis bona fide*.[1] This phrase is the foundation for all ley line communication between you and your familiar, and it's essential to form a strong bond at this time. There

---

[1] I promise in good faith.

will be a slow buildup of energy within you until the pentagram is complete, echoed by the sensation of prickles as your aura expands to encompass your potential familiar.

Your potential familiar will likely respond positively to the energy flow. When he or she settles down, share the bite of food as a symbolic gesture that you will provide for your familiar in exchange for his or her psychic protection. The sensation of prickles will fade as your aura eases back into its normal reach, leaving a trace of it upon your familiar.

If the animal accepts the food, then you may break your connection to the line and the bond is complete. If not, break your connection to the line and continue to be open to alternate possible familiars.

LAVIA ANDERSON

101 Earth Charms for Home and Office

Epidermis Irritation Relief

Class II: Medicinal

A relatively easy spell: has the potential to cause serious discomfort if done incorrectly.

Suitable for home use to aid in relief of mild itching. Not for use for internal irritation. Not recommended for potion application.

1. In small copper vat, combine 10 milliliters of springwater and 1 teaspoon of celandine syrup.[1][2]
2. Heat to a full boil, continue to boil for three minutes.
3. While water warms, crush 1 mullein leaf.[3]
4. Soak mullein mush in ½ cup of cream.[4]
5. Remove celandine and springwater from heat. Add three jewelweed flowers and one fully open dandelion head. Crush against side of pot to release juice, but do not masticate.
6. Stir.[5] Add zest of goldenseal root, 1–2 teaspoons, depending upon severity of discomfort needing to be addressed.[6]
7. Return to heat and boil until spell develops a camphor smell and yellow froth develops. Remove from heat.
8. In small crucible, stir 1 teaspoon of froth into 1 teaspoon of mullein-soaked cream. Discard leaves and boiled liquid.
9. Kindle froth/cream mixture with three drops of blood.

Springwater
Celandine syrup
Mullein
Cream
Jewelweed flower
Dandelion head
Goldenseal root
Redwood discs

- Makes seven charms.
- Good for six months to a year depending upon use.
- Must be in contact with skin to function.
- Broken by salt dip or extended contact with natural sweat.

Epidermis·Irritation Relief

10. Divide mixture into seven portions, allowing potion to soak into clean redwood discs for at least three minutes before wiping clean and using.

11. Amulets are invoked by second application of 3 drops of blood.

First Aid

Most complications arising from an improperly stirred Epidermis Relief charm include, but are not limited to, no relief discernible, an increase of irritation, and in rare cases, a lack of sensation, either localized or over entire body.

If removing the amulet does not provide relief, take charm with you and seek medical treatment.

Common Reasons for Failed Charm

[1] Using utensils other than copper or ceramic to measure celandine.

[2] Failure to get all syrup off measuring spoon.

[3] Mortar contaminated from previous charm.

[4] Using nonorganic cream containing preservatives.

[5] There have been claims that stirring counterclockwise has caused spell failure. Widdershins stirring is not recommended, and particularly not after midnight.

[6] Grating goldenrod with noncopper utensil.

Charm to Straighten Hair

Class II: Appearance Modification

Though hair straightening is one of today's most popular cosmetic charms, it's one of the most difficult earth charms to produce en masse since what straightens one person's hair often will not work upon another, even within the same charm. Ley line charms glamouring the hair are not as desirable, and it's often worth the effort to tweak a popular earth charm to find something that works with your particular chemistry.

With that in mind, amulet applications are far more desirable in case the results are not as expected.

It is advised to stir this spell while under a protection circle to prevent the introduction of undesirable elements.

> Coconut milk
> White vinegar
> Lime zest
> Redwood stirring rod
> Chamomile
> Springwater
> Rosemary leaves
> Cotton netting
> Burdock oil
> Rose geranium essences
> Practitioner's blood
> Potion ampoules or
> amulet discs
>
> • Makes seven charms.
> • Good for six months to a year depending upon purity.
> • Must be in contact with skin to function.
> • Broken by salt dip or removing amulet.

1. In a small, despelled glass container, mix 10 milliliters of coconut milk and 5 milliliters of white vinegar. Let stand until cream separates. Spoon off 10 milliliters of cream into a small copper spell pot. Discard vinegar.[1]

2. Add 7 shards of fresh lime zest to cream. Stir with redwood rod. Set aside.[2]

3. Prepare 1 cup of chamomile tea using springwater and loose tea.[3] Do not cover.

Charm to Straighten Hair

4. When proper color is achieved, strain tea through rosemary leaves and a cotton netting into a spelling bowl coated with burdock oil.[4]

5. Bring to boil and remove from heat.

6. Add 3 drops of rose geranium essence.

7. Add coconut cream and stir, being careful not to scrape sides.[5]

8. Kindle with 3 drops of blood. Stir, again being careful not to scrape sides.

9. Allow concoction to cool and solids to settle to the bottom.

10. Apply 2 milliliters of the amber-tinted liquid to each redwood disk. Allow to dry before use. (*Alternatively may be taken or stored as a potion. Not recommended as charm misfires are harder to remedy.*)

11. This charm is possible to "batch," making more than the usual seven charms at a time.

First Aid

Most complications arising from improperly stirred hair-straightening charms are mild, ranging from hair discoloration, snarling, and brittleness. Temporary hair loss has been observed upon occasion.

Rinsing in saltwater should alleviate adverse side effects, though it will not regrow hair that has been lost.

As with all charms, if physical discomfort is observed, take charm and seek medical help after breaking the spell.

Common Reasons for Failed Charm

[1] Using a spoon made of anything other than ceramic or copper will prevent charm from spelling properly.

[2] Organic limes seem to increase the chances of this charm working on multiple hair types.

Charm to Straighten Hair

[3] Microwaving a cup of springwater will give you no results. Use ceramic teacup and copper teapot to boil water.

[4] Using a sieve other than copper will negate spell.

[5] If burdock oil is introduced in too large a quantity (as by stirring), charm will not fix but remain "slippery."

Charm to Vanish Freckles

Class II: Appearance Modification

Most blemishes can be covered by simple complexion charms, but freckles pose a deeper problem. It often takes a "freckle specific" charm to hide them with any degree of success.

Not suitable for potion use.

This charm is unusually sensitive to contaminants. It is advisable to stir this spell while under a protection circle or in a "clean room" to prevent accidental introduction of adverse elements.

1. In spell-free crucible, mix ½ gram of cotton pollen with 1 ounce of raw sweet potato,[1] 1

Cotton pollen
Sweet potato or yam
Ivy roots (aerial)
Sunflower oil
Snowmelt
Cocoa
Dandelion sap
Kelp juice
8" by 8" square of undyed silk
Fairy dust
Amulet discs
Dandelion-tuft paintbrush
Practitioner's blood

• Makes seven charms.

• Good for six to twelve months once fixed, depending upon purity and storage conditions.

• Broken by salt dip or removing amulet.

Charm to Vanish Freckles

gram of aerial ivy roots,[2] and 2 ounces of sunflower oil.[3] Crush until a paste.

2. Add sweet potato paste to 20 milliliters of water from solstice-fallen snow. Stir while heating until water begins to boil.[4]

3. Remove from heat.

4. Reserve 10 milliliters of concoction, discard the rest or use within 30 minutes for additional charms.[5] Add to 10 milliliters of diluted sweet potato, 3 grams of cocoa, ½ gram of dandelion sap, and 1 gram of kelp juice. Stir until homogeneous.

5. Strain through undyed silk into small, test-tube size, spell-free glass container. Set aside to cool. [6]

6. While concoction is cooling, prepare receiving amulets by dusting the surface with fairy dust using a dandelion-tuft paintbrush.

7. Once concoction cools enough to be able to touch the glass comfortably, kindle with 3 drops of active witch blood. DO NOT STIR BY CONVENTIONAL MEANS. Mix liquid by flicking the side of the test tube to create a slow current. Introduction of any substances at this stage, even as an implement, will break the charm.

8. Divide entire amount of liquid between seven prepped amulets, taking care to not wash off the fairy dust.[7]

9. When amulets are dry, hang in the dark to preserve freckle-hiding qualities.

First Aid

Most complications arising from improperly stirred complexion charms are mild but annoying, ranging from skin discoloration, irritation, redness, swelling, and what has been called "being hit with an ugly stick."

Charm to Vanish Freckles

Removing the amulet will alleviate all adverse side effects.

If you consistently have difficulty with freckle charms prepped by a qualified technician, please contact your local health authority to take part in an ongoing, anonymous genetic study.

Common Reasons for Failed Charm

[1] Pesticide-free yams are essential for long-lasting results.

[2] Ivy roots must be aerial to prevent unwanted wrinkling.

[3] Olive oil will cause skin to feel greasy.

[4] Best results are gained when using snow that is fallen and gathered on the winter solstice.

[5] Delayed charm use of longer than 30 minutes after invocation will cause the kelp to react badly and smell, ruining the charm.

[6] Manufactured silk will not give desired result.

[7] Do not use eyedropper or other implement. It will contaminate the charm.

Sleep Charm

Class III: Medicinal

A complex spell with the potential to cause serious complications if administered incorrectly. Stir only under the protection of a circle.

Not suitable for home use, this charm is most often used in a hospital setting under the care of a physician.

Occasionally used in law enforcement.

Not recommended for amulet application.

> Springwater
> Spiderwort (powder)
> Valerian (powder)
> Monkshood (fresh leaves)
> Tutsan oil (St. John's wort)
> Hops (H. lupulus)
> Chamomile (M. chamomilla)
> Fir needles
> Empty, food-grade paintballs
> Organic cotton ball
>
> • Makes seven charms.
> • Good for six months to a year depending upon purity.
> • Must be in contact with skin to function.
> • Broken by salt dip or extended contact with natural sweat. (48 hours)

1. In small copper vat, combine 100 milliliters of springwater and 5 millileters of spiderwort and valerian, and 3 small monkshood leaves.[1]

2. Heat to a full boil, continue to boil for three minutes. Remove from heat and allow to cool.

3. While the preparation cools, coat the inside of a copper bowl with a thin film of tutsan oil using cotton.[2]

4. Bring 30 milliliters of water to a boil in tutsan-coated bowl.

5. Boil equal parts of hops and chamomile until a rich, golden color develops (5–10 minutes). Remove from heat.[3]

6. Strain 10 milliliters of hops and chamomile through a sieve lined with crushed fir needles into spiderwort and valerian.[4] Do not scrape bowl free of tutsan oil.

Sleep Charm

7. Remove monkshood leaves.[5]

8. Kindle with 3 drops of blood. Stir.

9. Divide stock potion into seven portions. Store in blue ampoule to prevent light damage. Alternatively, inject into empty, food-grade paintball pellets. [6]

FIRST AID

Most complications arising from an improperly stirred sleep potion include, but are not limited to, increased inability to sleep, dangerously low blood pressure, and in rare cases, coma.

A saltwater bath should alleviate adverse side effects.

This charm should only be crafted and administered by licensed practitioners and used only under professional supervision.

Common Reasons for Failed Charm

[1] Broken or dried leaves will increase danger of coma. Use whole, undamaged leaves only.

[2] Contaminated cotton can have damaging results as preservatives interfere with the body's natural ability to break charm.

[3] Boiling too little or too long may unbalance the charm and result in hyperactivity.

[4] Using a sieve other than copper will negate spell.

[5] Remove with ceramic utensil, not your finger.

[6] Non-food-grade pellets contain preservatives and will lower charm's effectiveness.

EARTH CHARMS:

Practical Applications

SHAUN VANDERSTONE

Recipes and theoretical explanations supporting the
manipulation of high-level earth charms

WWW

WARMTH AMULET

APPLICATIONS A high-level, amulet-based charm used "as needed" by workers in extremely low-temperature settings. This charm is NOT suitable for potion use and can cause death if administered as such. This is not a diet aid as repeated use will cause the body to lay on extra fat reserves.

DESIRED RESULTS A gentle, even warming throughout the body caused by an accelerated burning of stored energy.

COMPLICATIONS Extended use will cause a backlash of fat reserves being laid down at the expense of muscle.

NEEDED

Organic Materials:
- Gingerroot
- Chili pepper (whole)
- Tequila worm
- Olive oil (virgin)
- Whole milk
- Chamomile tea leaves
- Shredded cotton fibers
- Rosemary
- Bitter orange
- Practitioner's blood

Instruments:
- Mortar and pestle
- Copper teapot
- Ceramic brewing cup
- Spell pot
- Flame
- Finger stick
- Amulet redwood discs
- Glass stirring rod
- Graduated cylinder
- Small-weight balance

PROCEDURE

1. **Crush 1 gram of gingerroot, 1 gram of chili pepper, 1 tequila worm in 5 milliliters of olive oil. Set aside.** Do not use any part of the pepper's skin. Organic produce and a high grade of tequila results in a longer storage capacity. Olive oil should be first pressings to promote better uptake of the ginger's ability to burn fat.

2. **Steam 1 cup of whole milk in a copper teapot. Pour over 1 teaspoon of loose chamomile tea leaves in a spell-free ceramic brewing cup.** The chamomile will not brew to any significant color at this time. Cover to help retain chamomile's ability to slow the heart rate and counteract the metabolism uppers in the ginger and pepper. Use of any teapot other than copper will prevent the blood from kindling the charm.

3. **When the ceramic brewing cup has warmed through, add the crushed organics and olive oil. Heat over a live flame, stirring constantly until rich color develops. Do not boil.** This will take ten to fifteen minutes. Use of a hearth flame to warm the preparation adds to the stability. Electric heat tends to promote a faster breakdown of an invoked charm.

4. **Remove from heat and carefully strain 15 milliliters through a funnel of cotton fiber into a spell pot.** Discard remaining preparation or use to prepare more charms before solution reaches room temperature. The cotton fiber imparts a measure of binding, so do not reuse for prepping additional charms.

5. **To the 15 milliliters of preparation, add 3 drops of commercially prepared rosemary oil, 3 drops of bitter orange, and 3 drops of the spell caster's blood.** The preparation will give off a strong redwood scent if done properly. Rosemary and bitter orange aid in breakdown of fat without increasing the heart rate.

6. **Divide preparation among seven clean, dry amulets.** Each amulet will accept about 3 milliliters of solution. Amulets will not invoke until a second application of witch blood, after which, extreme care must be taken to keep them from touching skin until needed.

7. **Store prepared, uninvoked amulets in cool, dry place out of the sun.** Invoked amulets will remain active for six to twelve months depending upon quality of ingredients and skill of maker. Store invoked amulets out of reach of children in a cool, dry place.

CHARM TO SUMMON THE DEAD FROM PURGATORY

APPLICATIONS A high-level, temporary charm used occasionally in law enforcement and in treating severe psychoses. This charm has a low success rate as much from its high difficulty as from the fact that it can act only upon souls trapped in purgatory. This charm gives a spirit a temporary body with which to act on the physical realm and possibly free him- or herself.

DESIRED RESULTS A summoned spirit will have substance until the sun rises. Early confusion in the summoned is expected. This will quickly fade, whereupon the practitioner may ask needed questions and/or help set the soul to rest.

NEEDED

Organic Materials:

    Lemon juice

    Holy dust

    Yew pollen

    Holly leaf

    Local wine

    Ivy roots

    Identifying agent

    Practitioner's blood

Instruments:

    Spell pot

    Glass stirring rod

    Graduated cylinder

    Mortar and pestle

    Silver snips

    Small-weight balance

    Storage bottle (if not used directly)

    Finger stick

    Collective to kindle spell

PROCEDURE

1. **Measure out 4 milliliters of lemon juice into a small copper spell pot.** The need to use organic lemons has been debated since it was first found that residual pesticides often have an adverse effect upon many spells. It is hard to determine if this is the case here because of the difficulty of repeating the spell with any regularity. More importance should be placed on trying to find a locally grown lemon than one grown without pesticides. If you have trouble finding locally grown produce due to your climate, inquire at your closest university. Lemons are used to sympathetically "wake up" a drowsing spirit. Pulp is okay.

2. **Add ½ gram of holy dust and ½ gram of yew pollen to lemon mixture.** Yew is a potent ingredient in most charms that deal with communing with the dead. That this charm utilized pollen is thought to be because of the growthlike nature of the charm itself. It is believed that the yew pollen and holy dust act as a substrate for the soul to begin building a temporary body upon. Dust that is holy will precipitate out upon stirring clockwise. Dust that is not will dissolve.

3. **Grind fresh holly leaf with 5 milliliters of wine in a thoroughly despelled mortar and pestle.** Because of holly's thick leaf, it is permissible to cut the leaf into smaller portions prior to crushing. Use silver scissors to prevent any spell contamination. Maintaining a "clean hands" procedure with continual salt rinses is essential. Choose a wine that was grown and pressed within the area where the deceased lived to imbue the wine with its full soul-gathering potential. Wine and holy dust are invariably the building blocks of choice to give spirits substance.

4. **Add an approximately equal amount of aerial roots from an ivy, and continue to grind.** Be sure to snip the roots with silver snips. Aerial roots act as a binding agent to pull the lingering essence of a soul together. Ground roots will give no result. The mixture should have a pleasant wine and chlorophyll scent.

5. **Add a small amount of the identifying agent to the wine mixture.** Identifying agents can vary wildly, but success is more certain with familiar substrates such as hair, a snip of a favorite article of clothing, or a piece of jewelry. Leather from shoes or vinyl from a car seat has been known to bring results as well. As long as the deceased connects with the agent positively, there is a good chance of success.

6. **Combine the lemon and wine mixture, taking care to include all the undissolved ingredients.** Because of the need for a collective of witches to provide the required psychic energy to serve as a catalyst to kindle this charm to life, this charm is often stored for up to 24 hours. Use of a clean, glass container with a ground-glass stopper gives the best results.

7. **To invoke charm, pour mixture into a lingam-stone bowl. Add 3 drops of the practitioner's blood.** If the surrounding energy is great enough, the liquid in the bowl will spontaneously begin to steam, giving the soul something to condense upon.

PAIN AMULET

APPLICATIONS A moderately high-level earth charm used to provide symptomatic relief from pain. Used extensively in hospital, emergency, and first aid, this charm should only be crafted by a licensed practitioner and administered by amulet to better gauge its necessity. It does not function as an anesthetic and will not provide relief in surgical settings.

DESIRED RESULTS Temporary pain relief

COMPLICATIONS When administered as a potion, the body quickly becomes immune to its effects.

NEEDED

ORGANIC MATERIALS:
- Willow bark
- Hickory bark
- Dandelion seeds
- Feverfew
- Lilac wine
- Acorn meal
- Bittersweet pollen
- Fish oil
- Indian pipe root
- Springwater
- Practitioner's blood

INSTRUMENTS:
- Crucible
- Spell pot
- Live flame
- Glass stirring rod
- Graduated cylinder
- Mortar and pestle
- Small-weight balance
- Pipette
- Storage bottle (if not used directly)
- Finger stick

PROCEDURE

1. **Burn over live flame in a despelled, ceramic crucible, 10 grams of seasoned willow bark, 5 grams of hickory bark shavings, 1 gram of dried dandelion seed heads, and ½ gram of powdered feverfew root.** Allow the smoke to escape. Avoid breathing the fumes. Bark that has

been allowed to dry naturally makes a more stable preparation than bark that has been kiln dried.

2. **Into a small spell pot, combine 20 milliliters of commercially prepared, spell-quality lilac wine, 5 grams of the bark and root ash, 1 gram of acorn meal, and ½ gram bittersweet pollen**. Lilac wine is often used in forget charms, but here it's thought to impart a nerve-deadening quality as well as providing a substrate in which to dissolve the solid ingredients. Add power to the liquid, not the other way around.

3. **Heat to boiling over a flame.** Do not stir. Boil until the liquid turns a pale blue (ten to fifteen minutes).

4. **Remove from heat and allow to separate. Draw 10 milliliters of the clear liquid off using a pipette.** The heat has condensed the anti-inflammatory substances at the top. Avoid taking up the heavier ingredients. If there's no clear separation, discard and start again. Mixture will have a pleasant, woodsy scent.

5. **Move 10 milliliters of drawn-off liquid to clean spell pot and heat to boiling, adding 1 milliliter of fish oil and 1 gram of Indian pipe root.** It is thought that the oil helps move the spell's action deep within the tissues. Studies continue to try to identify what the Indian pipe is adding at this point, hoping to find a more readily available replacement for this hard-to-harvest ingredient. Most theories place it as a binder.

6. **When small bubbles form at bottom of spell pot, remove from heat and add 3 drops of active witch blood.** Spell is kindled, but not invoked. There should be a strong redwood scent. If not, discard and start again.

7. **Before kindled potion cools, divide potion among seven clean, dry amulets, being careful not to get any on your skin.** If you get any on your skin, wash immediately with salt water and seek professional help if there is a lack of sensation at the contact site.

8. **Store kindled amulets in a cool, dry place out of direct sun.** To invoke, apply 3 drops of witch blood.

HERITAGE
LOST

by

H. M. Pursaint

A CHARM TO FIND UNMARKED GRAVES

ONE OF MY FAVORITE PARTS of researching old ley line texts is finding gems such as this one, a spell once common among our ancestors, but falling out of favor after the Turn. Now, much as it was centuries ago, the dead are still a part of our lives, either when peacefully at rest, or demanding restitution. The skill to find them, once popular among Inderlanders, has declined until it's almost a forgotten art.

Because it doesn't necessitate a gesture or the ability to regulate line energy, it was the perfect charm for Victorian garden parties when the dead and frivolity went hand in hand.

Today, it can assist law enforcement, construction, and in the rare historical studies. It's also a good teaching tool as even novices to ley line studies and most magic-using humans are capable of engendering good results.

I've dated the ley line charm below to the early 1800s, but its roots are likely much older than that. It's elegant in its simplicity, and charming in its enactment.

Whilst outside in the dusk on a fine summer evening, one can discern the resting places of the unhappy dead by communing with a ley line and chanting the following:

Dead unto dead, shine as the moon.
Silence all but the restless.

Whereupon the dead will show themselves by their gravesites glowing when the entire party should shout favilla in goodwill and intent.

Be ready to assist the faint of heart, as unmarked graves of the murdered and slain will now be visible as a glowing apparition to all using their second sight.

I've found no record of, or experienced any, negative consequences of performing this particular ley line charm incorrectly, but if you should encounter any, seek professional help immediately.

Date: July 27, 2008
Working title: Dangerous Dance (Vamp track in parentheses)
© Copyright Takata

Footprints of the Ghost

The ghost is leaving footprints
In the sunshine
Past the gate

Choices made in ignorance
Lead to aberrant
Twists of fate

Pain looks for a vessel
Tracking footprints
for a mate

And she goes . . .
Dancing. . . .

Barometer is falling (Rain in the desert)
Sun rises red (Out of time, out of place)
Trouble is coming (Look at her dance)
Dancing to dangerous music (The footprints of a ghost)

Rain is falling (Rain in the desert) Sun rises red
Pain looks for a vessel (He will take you if he can)
Don't look forward (Don't stop dancing)
Don't look back (Or the worlds are damned)

Didn't know the burden
Didn't mean
To give you wings
Faultless soul will damn the world
morally wrong
Might not be sin

Barometer is falling (Rain in the desert)
Sun rises red (Out of time, out of place)
Pain's become your savior (Don't stop dancing)
Refuse to follow where you're led (Dancing)
The line begins to blur
When you look too far ahead

When you're the footprints of a ghost (No one told me)

Date Aug 15, 1988
Working title: Stupid SOB (Vamp track in parentheses)
© Copyright Takata

Red Ribbons

You are my secret.
You will lead to my fall.
But I want you to know,
Before truth's past recall.

Self-cursed to watch you,
By choice made in sin.
Didn't know the cost I'd paid,
Till I saw you again.

A thief in the spotlight,
Stealing motes of your life.
Lying that you gave me them.
A double-edged knife.

Hear you sing through the curtain.
        (You're mine, in some small fashion.)
See you smile through the glass.
        (You're mine, though you know it not.)

Wipe your tears in my thoughts.
    (You're mine, bond born of passion.)
No amends for the past. (You're mine, yet wholly you.)

Didn't know it would consume me. (By your will.)
No one said the hurt would last. (By your will.)
No one told me. (By your will.)
No one told me.

When desire's sold for freedom,
And need's exchanged for fame,
Those bargains made in ignorance,
Turn to bloodstained dreams of shame.

Red ribbons bind us,
Though no blood has been spilt.
No one told me they were wove of thorns.
No one told me of the guilt.
No one told me bonds of blood,
Were too poisonous to wilt.

Realized I was empty,
When a memory kept my place.
Left looking in the window.
Red ribbons hide my face.

Hear you sing through the curtain.
　　　(You're mine, in some small fashion.)
See you smile through the glass.
　　　(You're mine, though you know it not.)
Wipe your tears in my thoughts.
　　　(You're mine, bond born of passion.)
No amends for the past. (You're mine, yet wholly you.)

By way of my will. (By way of your will.)
By way of my will. (By way of your will.)
By way of my will. (By way of your will).

Date: June 2007
Working title: Tough Love　　No vamp track ??
© Copyright Takata

The Long Breath

I can't read the map that shows your salvation
Torn by your claim to a bloodless frustration
I stole it from you. It's smudged and it's burned
The roads don't connect, no matter how turned
And it don't lead to nowhere

Cause you live in hell
But it's all that I've got
So I'll keep turning

Turn, turn around
See me here, lost, forsworn
A fistful of roses
Long wilted and torn
Struck to the quick with a hope-bloodied thorn
While you wait for me
My mind's turning

The dust in your veins is an unseen ocean
Turned as the tide by the pull of emotion
Leaves lose their green to show their true hue
Fallen sun, risen moon, the same do to you
My passion, my fear
Shift to show what remains
Your shadows of truth
Keep me turning

The man with the smile, he says it's okay
We'll all live together, in kinship today
I see in your eye, the lie that remains
Half-truths unspoken. There's safety in chains

Loosing your passion
To live free of pain
Will twist you to madness
Am I turning?

Turn, turn around
God, why do I stay?
Blinded by rapture
Death's subtle decay
Sooner be dead, than your protégé

Turn, turn around
Spiral helix falls prey
To the taste of your soul
Consummate betray
Why is it wrong, to want you this way?
Turn, turn around
Turn around

See me . . .
Waiting for you.

Date: May 12, 1973
Working title: Stupid Son of a Bitch   No vamp track ??
© Copyright Takata

Shattered Sight

A spirit is chained when alone and apart
Though one graced with flesh, one with a heart
Can search. Can love
Can find. Can lose
But being without flesh, I only can choose

Grandfather reborn into his child's son
That is how it is usually done

We looked down through time, from God's mighty peak
Together we pondered, "To which life should we leap?"
Wanting to slip from the family line's woes
I jumped to a new one. You kept to the old

I learned too late what I lost with the rest
I loved you best
I loved you best

So I chose, and I leapt, and I promptly forgot
Amnesia, the blessing of angels was wrought

Left with a want that I couldn't explain
As I struggled to speak, and learn my new name

Is it no wonder the newborn cry?
The choice was real
The chance a lie

Fragments of you, splinters in dreams
Analysis tears them apart at the seams
For shattered sight clears only when in God's Keep
But you never will wait. My harsh words cut you deep

Spirits kept unknowing,
lifetimes left to fill
But I loved you then
And I love you still

Searching through the eons to make the wrong right
Scent triggers memory to mend shattered sight
Splinters weave together, pieces fall into place
We both would remember if I touched your face

Sift the clues from the dust, from my lives, of my will
I loved you then
I love you still

Date: April 2008
Working title: Folk Lullaby
© Copyright: Available?

Rachel sent this to me. She thought I'd be interested in
doing a remake. She heard it from her latest boyfriend.
Creepy little song from her creepy little man. It has a feel
of the South—200 years ago. If I can verify it's not under
copyright, I might set it to an uncomfortable harmony. Try
it out next Halloween, maybe.

Pierce's Lullaby

Go to sleep, baby.
Mama will sing
Of blue butterflies,
and dragonfly wings

Bathe in sweet water, on pollen you'll dine
Silver and gold, for baby of mine.

Go to sleep, baby.
Papa is here.
Or elves will steal baby,
To him you are dear.

Ice rims the river. Sunflowers that shine.
Silver and gold, for baby of mine.

Go to sleep, baby.
Sister will tell,
Of wolves and of lambs,
And demons who fell.

Moonlight and sun beams. Raiments so fine.
Silver and gold, for baby of mine.

The Hollows Gazette

Tuesday, November 6, 2007

LOCAL / STATE

C

TAKATA RAISES THOUSANDS

By Yevon Darling
ydarling@hollowsgazette.com

One of Cincinnati's hometown boys gave back this week and in a big way, when pop star Takata held an open-air concert at the commons the day before Halloween, all proceeds after expenses going to rebuild the city-run, fire-damaged homes.

"I remember what it's like to be down on your luck," Takata said with his trademark grin, looking embarrassed as he accepted the thanks of Ms. Carmen, head of Cincinnati's Public Provision Department. "Sometimes all you need is a clean place to sleep to get your thoughts in order. The rest takes care of itself."

And the rest is set to take care of itself, now that the repair coffers have been filled by enthusiastic fans eager to hear Takata's latest.

Cincinnati's fire-damaged buildings have been empty for months awaiting repairs, and Carmen's office is attempting to use the opportunity to coordinate with local tradesmen to refit the buildings and teach the willing entry-level skills to help them in a way a "clean place to sleep" can't.

Concertgoers enjoy the music, while helping the homeless

Takata was born and raised in the Hollows, and his tradition of using his hometown as a proving ground for unreleased tracks is well known, guaranteeing sold-out performances whenever he comes to the Greater Cincinnati area. It's also only in Cincy that nonvampire fans might get a chance to hear the fabled "vampire tracks," if his drummer Ripley can be persuaded to make a rare singing performance.

See Takata **C 8**

The Way I See It
Devin Crossman

BEDROOM POLITICS ALIVE AND WELL IN THE QUEEN CITY

Or perhaps I should title my column today AS THE WORLD TURNS, because the political climate is starting to sound more like a soap opera than an elected, governing body functioning fairly and aboveboard.

Many names in the news over the past year seem to be there as a publicity promotion rather than any true progress, or should I say a flamboyant, overly generous gesture of the right hand as the left reaches into our pocket and grabs something a little more sensitive than our wallet.

Naming names would be "slander and libelous," my editor tells me. So I will merely relate the simple truth my grandmother used to tell me. If a man comes to you with his hands full of roses, check your flowerbeds.

See Crossman **C 8**

Halloween Party a Howling Success

By Winifred Gradenko
winniegrad@hollowsgazette.com

Councilman Trent Kalamack again hosted his Halloween party to great success in his yearly, and unapologetic, bid for Cincinnati's well-to-do's dollars, aimed at refitting the city's orphanages and growing their college scholarships.

Kalamack was elusive at the party, making only one appearance before

slipping away, but his presence was hardly missed as visiting pop star Takata was on hand to provide entertainment, in town for a benefit concert the previous night.

Guests were treated to a rare look at the inside of the Kalamack compound, and the kids had fun in the pool. Previous parties have garnered

See Party **C 8**

@ A Glance Nov 6, 2007
Average High/Low: 55° / 41°

	Today	Tomorrow
Sunrise	7:11 AM	7:12 AM
Sunset	5:32 PM	5:31 PM
Moonrise	4:04 AM	5:04 AM
Moonset	3:46 PM	4:08 PM
Phase: Waning 4 days from now		

SEE ALMANAC C 8

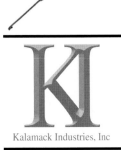

Kalamack Industries, Inc

Quen Hansen
Chief Security Officer
Kalamack Industries, Inc
Building A
15 Rolling Acres
Cincinnati, OH 45239

I N T E R O F F I C E   M E M O

To: Trenton Kalamack
From: Quen Hansen
CC:
Date: 11/7/07
Re: Crossman's Hard Drive

Sa'han,

You wished to be informed when and where Crossman sent his damaged hard drive out for repair. Unfortunately it has gone to a company west of the Mississippi, and my contacts there refuse to deal with us in response to your encroaching business dealings in that area. I will continue my efforts to find something they want. My advice is to wait out the interim and see if they're successful pulling the demon spell pictures off his drive. Ms. Gonzalez has been more than cooperative in screening Crossman's columns, though I'd be remiss in not pointing out that his personality makes it easy for him to quit the paper and inform the public by way of his original blog if he feels he can make a difference.

You've asked my opinion on the path you should follow numerous times, and I have always remained silent. I'd only ask now for you to consider that you would be a slave in the ever-after if Morgan had not risked her life for your freedom. She didn't even consider leaving you there, Sa'han, but instead lost a portion of her freedom in buying your own. Such a mind will not be swayed by lures of money, power, or status. She's ruled by her emotions, which is not a bad thing if you can successfully show her your goals are the same as hers. I still believe that Morgan is a good risk. Crossman, on the other hand . . .

I will continue to monitor and destroy any potentially damaging evidence as he continues.

Quen

Kalamack Industries, Inc

Trenton A. Kalamack
CEO Kalamack Industries
Kalamack Industries, Inc
Building A
15 Rolling Acres
Cincinnati, OH 45239

INTEROFFICE MEMO

To: Jonathan Davaros
From: Trenton Kalamack
CC:
Date: 12/18/07
Re: Pandora Charm

Jon,

Would you please give Sara Jane access to my father's spell library and instruct her to search for a Pandora charm? I believe these things do best when woven on solstices, so please make this a priority for her. I apologize for your having to pick up her normal duties until she finds it. Also, please clear your evening—I would appreciate your help in weaving this. You have a fine touch, and I want to get this right as it might help me foster a better relationship with Morgan.

TK

Kalamack Industries, Inc

Jonathan Davaros
Chief Personnel Officer
Kalamack Industries, Inc
Building A
15 Rolling Acres
Cincinnati, OH 45239

I N T E R O F F I C E   M E M O

To: Trenton Kalamack
From: Jonathan Davaros
CC:
Date: 12/19/07
Re: Pandora Charm

Sa'han,

I would be honored to help you weave such a complex charm and have already cleared your calendar for the entirety of the solstice and will assemble the properties needed for its successful completion.
I'm not entirely comfortable with your choice of searchers. There's a point where fostering a feeling of teamwork should take a backseat to preserving one's secrets.

Yours,

Jonathan

DEVIN'S
JOURNAL
ENTRY

JANUARY 1, 2008

My God, Maria is pissed, but I got my article about Rachel being
shunned into the paper with minimal editing. I heard her yelling at
Randy when I came in this morning. My piece went below
the fold, but it's there.

   Getting my article in helps ease the sting that I
couldn't link Morgan to Aston's roller rink burning down,
or the death of her old ley line instructor, Dr. Anders.
It ticks me off about the rink. I used to skate there. I
followed Morgan into the rink last Halloween, and it looked
exactly the same as I remember. They still have that stoner
at the shoe return. They still give out buttons if you hit the boards
hard, too. (ow) Seeing her and Kalamack skating together kind of
threw me. They looked like an old couple having an argument.

   My button is probably worth something now that the place is gone.

One more Cincy icon destroyed due to Morgan. They really need to leash her.

My money is on Morgan having something to do with Dr. Anders's car going over the bridge and into the Ohio River, too. Morgan and Anders go way back, and Morgan was investigating her at the time for the FIB. They even paid for a class so Morgan could go to school and spy on her. The FIB thinks Anders was the ley line witch murderer, but the I.S. wrote the woman's death off as a victim. I'm tending to agree with them.

My guess is that Morgan was out for revenge, and killed the woman herself, not the ley line witch murderer. Dr. Anders died the exact same way that Morgan tried to kill her ex-boyfriend, Sparagmos. Over the railing of a bridge, and into the water.

I'm not sure what's going on with Morgan's boyfriend situation. I think that Marshal dumped her after she got shunned by the coven of moral and ethical standards, but that doesn't seem to bother this new guy . . . Pierce.

Something is weird about this guy. He's like a ghost, slipping in and out without me seeing him. I've never been able to follow him, so I've no idea where he lives. The pixies call him Pierce, but when Morgan gets mad, she calls him Gordian Nathaniel Pierce.

I should probably do a work-up on both of them in case they stick around. That gargoyle Bis hasn't left yet, so I should do a profile on him as well, though I feel kind of weird about it. He's just a kid.

Subject: GORDIAN NATHANIEL PIERCE

Species/Sex: Witch/Male

Location: Hollows

Employer: None that I could find

Gets Around: Walks or bus

Home: Unknown

Height: 5'6"

Weight: ~145#

Build: Somewhat short, but doesn't look small

Age: Midtwenties, I think

DESCRIPTION: This guy is smaller than most of the men Rachel eyes, but he's well muscled and knows his magic. He has long, curly black hair that gets into his eyes. The first time I saw him, he had a small beard, but he's been clean shaven most other times. Blue eyes. He likes to wear hats and dresses in elegant, fancy clothes that remind me of the 1800s.

He has a watch with a gold fob he seems extraordinarily proud of. He walks fast and has an accent I can't place.

He uses magic a lot; some of it looks pretty strong. Maybe that's what Morgan is attracted to. Tamwood barely tolerates him. I think she's jealous. Jenks and Pierce get along okay.

I couldn't find any acquaintances or family other than Rachel Morgan, and the only Gordian Nathaniel Pierce I could find in any database was a witch that died in 1852. He's buried in Morgan's backyard, so maybe this is some lost relative.

Subject: MARSHAL

Species/Sex: Witch/Male
Location: Hollows
Employer: New hire at the university
Gets Around: Big-ass SUV
Home: Cincy
Height: 6'2"
Weight: ~170#
Build: Athlete. Swimmer
Age: Midthirties, but looks younger

DESCRIPTION: Tall. He didn't have any hair the first time I saw him. I'd say it was an accident, but I think he charmed it off so he could swim better since that's what he's teaching at the university. Now that it's grown in, it's dark and curly. Maybe some African American heritage?

Brown eyes, honey-toned skin, wide shoulders, well-defined abs, even white teeth when he smiles, and he smiles a lot.

He dresses in high-quality flannel and wool. Jeans. He's got a slight northern Michigan accent. Cracks his neck when he's nervous.

ACQUAINTANCES / FAMILY

Talked to a very angry ex-girlfriend named Debbie up in Mackinaw City. She burned his house down before he left.

He's got several buddies he hangs out with when he's not at work or with Rachel. He's a local boy come home.

RESEARCHED

EDUCATION: Highly educated. Originally from Cincinnati, he graduated from the university in 2001 with a bachelor's in business management. He's going for his master's right now. Sold his business to do it and works at the university to pay for classes.

He knows how to dive in a wet suit and is licensed to make and sell medicinal-level charms (warmth amulets for his business).

EMPLOYMENT: Self-employed until recently. Used to own and run Marshal's Mackinaw Wrecks, which ran diving excursions on some of the wrecks in the Mackinac Straits. I think that's where he and Rachel met. Now he works for the university, building their swim team while he gets his master's.

Subject: BIS (Gargoyle)

Species/Sex: Gargoyle/Male
Location: Hollows
Employer: N/A
Gets Around: Flies or crawls on ceiling
Home: Rents the belfry
Height: About a foot? Size of a big raccoon
Weight: ~25#?
Build: Looks like a mix of a rottweiler and a bat
Age: Over fifty, but he's basically an adolescent

DESCRIPTION: Adolescent gargoyle. He's still thin in places where an adult would be muscular. He has pebbly gray skin that shifts color to match his background, like a chameleon. His skin turns black when he's embarrassed. His teeth are black, and he's got some wicked canines. His ears are big and stand upright most of the time, with white hair tufting them. His ears are very expressive and give away his mood. Big red eyes. Horn nubs show occasionally. Long tail with tuft of white fur on the end. Huge, batlike wings. Dexterous hands with long fingers and clawed nails. Heavy haunches with clawed feet. He doesn't wear clothes, but everything retracts, I guess.

HAUNTS: He spends most of his time outside, even in the snow, and sleeps when the sun is up. He's usually on the church steeple or the eaves. Now that it's cold, he goes inside, but it's more for company than the warmth.

HABITS: He used to play a lot with the pixy kids when it was warmer and they were outside. I've seen him melt the snow off the church roof and suck in the water (increasing his size tremendously), then spit it into the garden, hitting the gravestones like it's artillery practice. He laughs a lot, sounding like a teapot, and he can squeeze into tiny holes to hide.

ACQUAINTANCES / FAMILY
His family lives on the Hollows basilica.

Rachel's ex-boyfriend isn't dead, by the way. Sparagmos, I mean. I'm 90% sure he's hiding right here in Cincy. Why the man is in Cincinnati when he's playing dead is beyond me. Maybe he's watching her, too. It wasn't until I found his address at the zoo while looking up Morgan's after-hours runner's pass that I figured out he was still alive. I looked up Morgan and found she had bought him a pass for his birthday. I made copies of them both just in case.

Get this—his apartment is empty, but I talked to the lady who owns the place and she said Sparagmos came in right before the lease expired and paid an entire year's rent. Cash. And this is after he supposedly went over the bridge in Mackinaw. I've got to track this guy down. He probably has the dirt on Morgan better than anyone.

That timeline I've been working on is almost done. If I can get a few more holes filled in, I might have a positive link with the Kalamacks other than they went to the same summer camp.

> Estimated migration from the ever-after: Elves: ~2000 years pre-Turn
> Witches: ~5000 years pre-Turn
> Birth of Weres: ~6000 years pre-Turn
> Birth of Vampires: Estimated 5000–2000 years pre-Turn

1943	Leon Bairn born October 27.
1948	Quen Hansen born.
1950	Rachel's parents born.
1953	Watson and Crick develop DNA helix model. Collaborating with Rosalind Franklin, they turned Cold War funding to them instead of space and unconventional weapons, greatly advancing the

understanding of genetic manipulation as the U.S. develops genetic weapons instead of nuclear. Space exploration fizzles out.

1958 Rosalind Franklin continues her research, helping to push genetic understanding up twenty years and giving us a wealth of genetically produced drugs in the '60s.

Edden born.

1962 Genetic insulin becomes readily available.

1965 Alice, Monty Morgan, and Donald (Takata) start high school.

1966–1969 Turn begins and ends, the T4 Angel virus transported by a tomato designed to feed the people of the third worlds.

1969 Alice, Monty, and Donald (Takata) meet in college. Takata's band starts to make it big locally.

1972 Takata goes to California, Alice and Monty are married.

1973 Robbie Morgan born, Takata writes "Shattered Sight."

1977 Stanley Saladan born in the spring.

1978 Glenn born.

1979 Ivy Tamwood born (January), Trent Kalamack born (October 21).

1980 Kisten Felps is born (January 29), Nick Sparagmos is born (April 1).

1981 Rachel Morgan is born (July 27). Personal computers become available.

1988 Takata writes "Red Ribbons."

1989 Stanley Saladan sets the ward on Trent's father's window. Trent's mother dies that same year.

1993 Last year at summer camp for Rachel. Ivy Tamwood goes to California to finish her last two years of high school to get away from Piscary.

1995 Trent's and Rachel's fathers die in the spring. Leon Bairn quits the I.S. and is "assassinated" to keep his findings quiet.

1997 Rachel graduates from high school and starts classes at two-year school.

1999 Rachel helps Gordian Pierce in December. Trent graduates from CA State.

2000–2004 Rachel interns with the I.S. hiring in mid-June.

2001	Ivy joins the I.S. as a full runner after graduating a six-year course of study.
2003–2004	Rachel and Ivy work together during Rachel's last year as an intern. She becomes a full runner in 2004; she's almost 22.
2006	Rachel quits the I.S. Ceri Dulciate moves in across from the church.
2007	The focus is unearthed. Kisten Felps and Piscary die. Ceri becomes pregnant. Takata writes "The Long Breath." Kalamack buys church and gives it to Jenks.
2008	Takata writes "Footprints of a Ghost."

It's getting harder to follow Morgan now that she's been shunned. The maps I made at Juniors while watching her are pretty much useless now that her old haunts won't let her in. She's been spending a lot of time up at Eden Park at Twin Lakes Bridge and the overlook. She never says much, just smiles at the kids and dogs in a sad way and drinks her coffee. Oh, Juniors banned her, by the way. Serves her right. She's going to have to get her grand latte, double espresso, Italian blend, light on the froth, heavy on the cinnamon with a splash of raspberry in it somewhere else.

Her shunning is starting to hit her mom, too. Other Earthlings, the spell shop her mom sells her hair-straightener charms to, won't buy them anymore. I'd feel sorry for the woman, but she's as flaky as her daughter. The woman swears like my old man when he's drunk.

I thought maybe that shunned witches couldn't hold property when I found out the church had been sold, but it turns out the pixy, Jenks, owns it. I didn't think pixies could own property, but apparently he got it from Kalamack. For a dollar.

The property was auctioned off when Piscary died, and Kalamack bought it. To evict her, I would have guessed, but no. He sold it to the pixy. Just one more weird link between Kalamack and Morgan. I swear, they either hate each other, or love each other. I can't figure it out. The man better watch himself. All her serious boyfriends end up dead.

Which brings me back to Felps. I thought we were done with that, but apparently Morgan found his murderer in the tunnels under the city while she was tracking down that banshee that started the fire at Fountain Square.

And then she cemented them behind a stone wall.

I wrote an article pointing out that this was black demon magic, and Maria e-mailed me the paper's fact sheet on the difference between black, white, and legal magic and dropped a copy of <u>Witch Weekly</u> on my desk, pointing to an article on "How to Tell If Your Roommate Is into the Dark Arts." They're laughing at me, but cementing people behind walls with magic is not funny. My source says they were dead at the time, but I bet they were alive. Or maybe undead.

I want to get down there with a jackhammer and see for myself, but they have the tunnels blocked off pretty good. The entrance at Walnut Street is out, but if I follow Central Parkway out of the city, I bet I can find an entrance they've not bricked up yet. From there, all I have to do is walk down to where Morgan sealed up the wall. I'll bring Winnie with me in case there's a hungry vampire behind the door. You don't have to outrun the vampire, just the girl with you. (Ha, ha)

Winnie has been acting weird the last couple of weeks. I think she wants to break up. I'm starting to think it might be a good idea. Winnie's sister, Sara Jane, works for Kalamack. I hear Kalamack is a generous employer. Maybe Winnie just wants a new job.

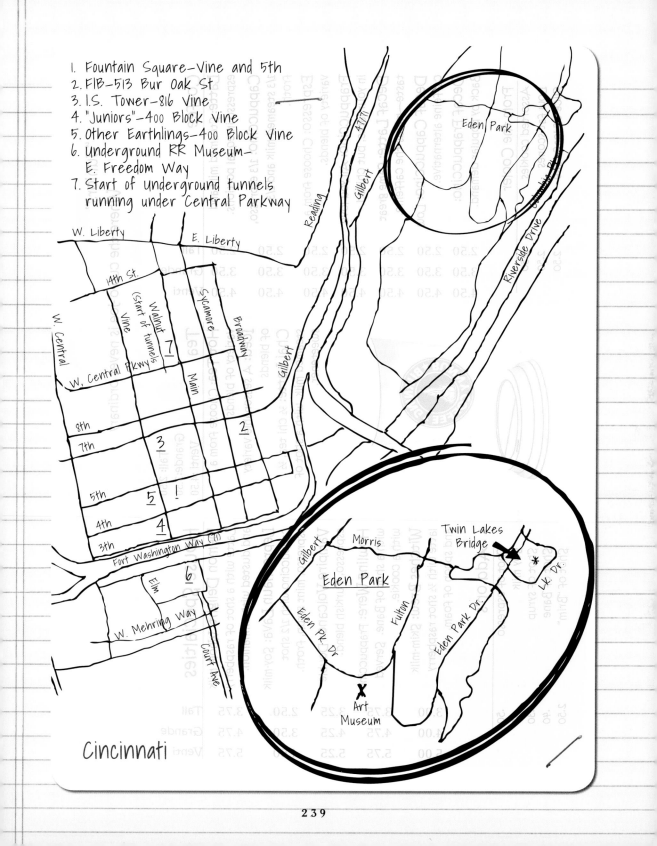

1. Fountain Square—Vine and 5th
2. FIB—513 Bur Oak St
3. I.S. Tower—816 Vine
4. "Juniors"—400 Block Vine
5. Other Earthlings—400 Block Vine
6. Underground RR Museum—
   E. Freedom Way
7. Start of underground tunnels
   running under Central Parkway

Cincinnati

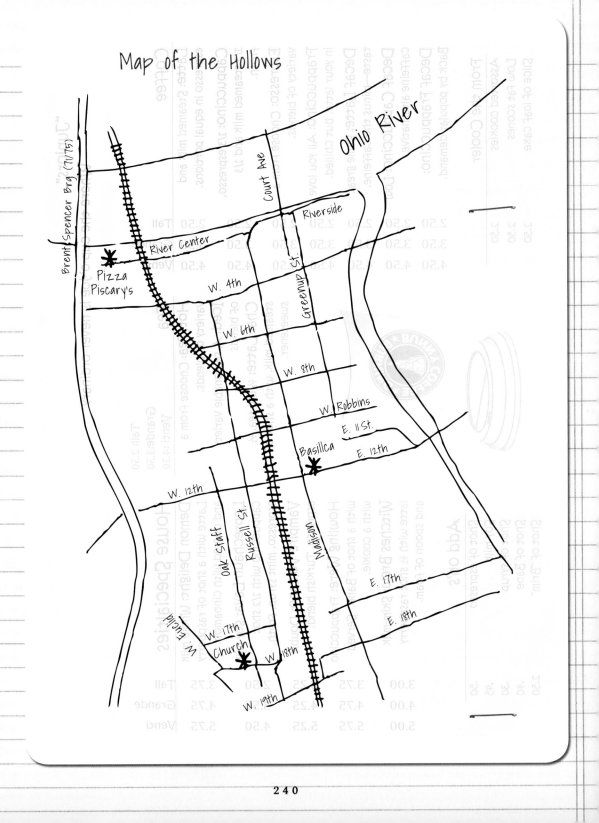

Map of the Hollows

Ohio River

Brent Spencer Brg (71/75)

Court Ave

Riverside

River Center

Pizza
Piscary's

Greenup St.

W. 4th

W. 6th

W. 8th

W. Robbins

E. 11 St.

Basillca

E. 12th

W. 12th

Oak Staff

Russell St.

Madison

E. 17th

E. 18th

W. Euclid

W. 17th

Church

W. 18th

W. 19th

Map Cincy Outskirts

Cincy Observatory

Observatory Ave

Herschel Ave

Delta Ave

Aston's Lookout Dr.

Linwood Ave

Rachel's Mom's House

Kroger Ave

Observatory Ave

Madison Rd.

Dr. Martin Luther King Dr.

University of Cincy

City of Hollows, County of Kenton

Quen Hansen

to

Jenks Pixy

}

I hereby certify that this deed has been filed in my office on the __10__ day of ___August___ in the year__2007__

Register of Deeds

This Deed, made on ___August tenth, two thousand and seven___ between ___Quen Hansen___ in the county of ___Hamilton___ in the state of ___Ohio___ in the first part, and ___Jenks Pixy___ in the county of ___Kenton___ in the state of ___Kentucky__, in the second part.

Witness that the said property located at ___1597 Oak Staff, Hollows, KY 41011___ ownership is now transferred from said first party to said second party and his heirs and assigns forever, to retain the rights and privileges therein belonging to said property in its entirety for the sum of ___One___ dollars.

Witnessed:

Quen Hansen
Quen Hansen

Trenton Kalamack
Trenton Kalamack

INTERNAL FACT SHEET

Document Shepherd: Cindy Strom (513) 555-7735 ext 7
Updated 8/07

White Magic Does Not Equate with Legal Magic

Magic, be it ley line, earth, or demon, is most often thought of as black being against the law, and white legal, but what most humans don't realize is that white does not necessarily equal legal. Many spells that are technically white are considered illegal by the coven of moral and ethical standards, the governing faction and "last word" on all witch magic.

Three facets of a spell are considered by the coven of moral and ethical standards before it is deemed legal. This three-prong system was in place even before the Turn and has served to keep the courts relatively clear of spell abuses.

First consideration is if the spell causes a layer of smut on the practitioner's soul. This is what makes demon charms flat-out illegal, even though many demon spells pass the other two criteria.

Second to be considered is if the spell requires the death or mutilation of animals, either in collecting the ingredients or in the actual performing of the spell. Many of these spells cause smut on the practitioner's soul, but not all.

Lastly considered before a charm is branded legal is whether the charm causes harm to the recipient. This last aspect is the most difficult to ascertain due to morality and intent being a strong factor, and it's here that the courts stay busy in bringing witches gone bad to justice.

It's easy to understand why ley line witches often are lured into using spells that fail the "legal litmus" in this third category, but it's also notable that one earth witch who continues to use black magic is harder to catch and does more damage than ten ley line witches dabbling in black magic put together.

Unfortunately, the ley line witch has the highest potential to slip from mild infractions to the really ugly spells. Much of this is probably because the damage black magic causes on the soul is

INTERNAL FACT SHEET

WHITE MAGIC DOES NOT EQUATE WITH LEGAL MAGIC

harder to see and quantify, unlike black earth witches who have to harvest unsavory ingredients such as the spleen from a goat.

There are currently no laws concerning demons and their magic due to the coven of moral and ethical standards deeming that demons are tools, not individuals. Their actions are currently answered for by the person summoning them. This definition of demons and their magic is currently under pressure to change to accommodate free-willed, day-walking demons.

AT A GLANCE

WHITE: Magic that falls within the limits of probable, nonlethal results and whose ingredients don't necessitate harming animals or people. Leaves no smut on the practitioner's soul.

BLACK: Magic that causes harm to another or requires the death or mutilation of an animal or person to obtain the ingredients to create it. Leaves varying degrees of smut on practitioner's soul.

DEMON: Magic requiring a mixing of earth and ley line magic and is generally not reproducible by anyone but demons. Creates smut.

LEGAL: All black magic is illegal by definition, but many white charms are illegal due to their adverse effects on people.

For more information, contact:
Dr. Pandorn
Professor of Human Studies
University of Cincinnati
Cincinnati, OH 45221
513-555-2440 (ext 77)

December 2008

Witch Weekly

Happy Solstice Issue

Holiday Contest Winners

10 signs
your roommate
is into the
black arts

You know you're in the Hollows when...

Exclusive Interview with Rynn Cormel
"Why I wrote the Vampire Dating Guide"

Three Toss-The-Diet
Drinks to Die For

10 SIGNS YOUR ROOMMATE IS INTO THE DARK ARTS

We've all had it happen before. We come home unexpectedly and find our roommate in a compromising situation. If it's your boyfriend she's fooling around with, kicking them both out of your life is your best bet.

But what if it's not your boyfriend that your roommate is experimenting with, but something else? Something that leaves a scent of sulfur and a burn hole in the rug?

Should you leave and come back in an hour, or sit down with your closest friends for an intervention?

It's a serious question, and one that, if you leave it unanswered, could land your roommate and you in jail under the suspicion of black magic, possibly even leading to shunning.

We at *Witch Weekly* have come up with ten of the biggest telltales that you or someone you know might be sliding to the dark side.

Give yourself one point for every yes answer. If you score too high, don't beat yourself up. Black magic is seductive, and once forewarned, you can make better choices.

4.

THE APARTMENT IS TRASHED WHEN YOU COME HOME, AND SHE DOESN'T WANT TO CALL THE I.S.

- ❏ Unusual scent of brimstone. (Doesn't count if your roommate dates a vampire.)
- ❏ Unidentifiable chunks of "meat" in the freezer she won't let you put on the grill.
- ❏ An abundance of scented candles lit when you come home, and she's not had company over.
- ❏ The apartment is trashed, and she won't let you call the I.S.
- ❏ Graveyard dirt on the soles of her new "to-die-for" shoes.
- ❏ Unexplained welt or old burn marks on her wrist or behind her ear.
- ❏ You've found old books with no titles, written in Latin.
- ❏ She's going through her magnetic chalk faster than normal.
- ❏ She won't go out in the sun.
- ❏ She's undergone a short, drastic change in behavior, and she doesn't have a new boyfriend or girlfriend to account for it.

Score

10   You have a problem. Get out and call DAA. (Dark Arts Anonymous) 1-666-555-6666

9–7   There's a good chance your roommate is deep into the dark arts. Call DAA for a more detailed checklist of signs.

6-4   Your roommate might be experimenting, but before you stir up trouble, find out if she has a new significant other she doesn't want to share.

3-1   Chances are you're overreacting. Take a chill pill and relax.

3 Wicked & Wonderful BREWS For The New Year

It's the winter solstice, and nothing celebrates the promise of a rebirth of life like a party! We at *Witch Weekly* worked hard to find the latest drinks, both alcoholic and non for you designated spellcasters, to wow you and your guests this year as you illuminate the beginning of the new year with the flame that burns the old year out.

Tested and rated during our preholiday parties, here are three of our favorites.

DEAD MAN'S FLOAT

This was given to us by Louise Faberdine of Cincinnati, OH. Louise says she found this delightful concoction of Baileys Irish Cream and ice cream at one of Cincinnati's famed gambling boats. We at Witch Weekly *like the nonalcoholic version just as well.*

INGREDIENTS:
1 scoop of vanilla ice cream
4 ounces of milk (skim or whole)
1 shot of Baileys Irish Cream

In a lowball glass, place a generous scoop of vanilla ice cream. Pour 4 ounces of milk over it. Add shot of Baileys Irish Cream. Serve with a spoon and a sprig of mint.

For a nonalcoholic drink, substitute Baileys/Irish Cream flavoring and serve with a cherry.

DEMON COFFEE/TEA

We're not sure if this caffeine buzz drink submitted by Mark Henders refers to who likes to drink it, or what you'll feel like after you get hooked on it, but this coffee/ tea drink is a great alternative for the designated driver or for keeping you awake while cramming for finals. What we at WW like is that you can get your dessert-drink fix without having to leave the house.

COFFEE INGREDIENTS:
Brewed or prepared instant
coffee from Italian beans
Milk (skim or whole)
Shot of raspberry syrup
Powdered cinnamon
Cinnamon sticks

To a 12-ounce cup, add $2/3$ cup prepared coffee, $1/3$ cup steamed milk, $1/3$ cup boiling water, and a shot of raspberry syrup.
Sprinkle with cinnamon.
Serve piping hot with a cinnamon stick.

Tasty Tea Alternative

INGREDIENTS:
Prepared chai tea syrup
Skim milk
Raspberry syrup
Powdered cinnamon
Cinnamon sticks

For a 12-ounce cup, pour $1/3$ cup prepared chai tea syrup into a microwave-safe mug. Add $2/3$ cup steamed skim milk (skim milk allows the chai flavor to blossom) and $1/3$ cup water.
Add raspberry syrup to taste ($1/4$ to 1 teaspoon).
Sprinkle with cinnamon.
Garnish with cinnamon stick.
Serve.

More recipes on page 87

This summer, we asked for your best homemade holiday songs and poems, and you came through. Our offices were inundated, making us feel as if it was the winter solstice in July.

TUNES TO GET YOUR
TOES TAPPING

The grand prize winner received an all-expense-paid vacation to New York and our home offices to see how we put their creativity into print.

RUNNER-UP:
THE 12 DAYS OF PIXY CHRISTMAS
by Jenks Pixy

On the 12th day of Christmas, my true love gave to me . . .

12 Humans Hiding
11 Tinks a Tinkling
10 Porno Flicks
9 Pole Dancers
8 Pixies Partying
7 Karma Sutras
6 Fairies Farting
5 Trolls in Drag
4 Purple Condoms
3 French Ticklers
2 Horny Vamps
And a Succubus in the snow

All entries can be seen at the Witch Weekly *website.*

This Year's Holiday Poetry Contest Winner:

'TWAS THE NIGHT OF THE SOLSTICE
Anonymous

'Twas the week before Christmas, and up
  in the Hollows,
Solstice bonfires were burning, to toast
  the marshmallows.

The pixies were snug in their stump,
  even Jenks,
Who claimed he was tired, and needed
  some winks.

So I in my parka, and Ivy in her boots,
Were toasting the season, with
  thirty-year hooch.

When out in the street, there came such
  a crash,
I thought that it had to be 'coons in our trash.

Away to the gate, I trudged through the snow,
While Ivy just said, "If it's Kist, say hello."

I lifted the latch, and peered to the street,
My face went quite cold. We were in it
  thigh deep.

'Twas a demon, who stood in the headlamps
  quite bright,
With his coat of green velvet, and his
  uncommon height.

His eyes, how they glittered, his teeth
  how they gnashed,
His voice, how he bellowed, his tongue,
  how it lashed.

The street wasn't holy, so on Big Al came,
As he bellowed, and shouted, and called
  me by name.

"Morgan, you witch. You're a pain in
  my side.
"Get out of your church. There's no
  place to hide!"

Like hell's fury unleashed, he strode
  to my door,
Where he hammered and cursed, like a
  cheap jilted whore.

But Ivy and I, we circled round back,
To stand in the street and prepare for attack.

"You loser," I shouted. "I'm waiting for you."
And the demon, he spun, taking on a red hue.

Ivy stood ready, and I whispered, "Okay . . .
"If he wants to get rough, I'm ready to play."

With nary a word, us two girls got to work,
Putting foot into gut, of the soul-sucking jerk.

I circled him quick, with a few words of Latin,
While Ivy distracted him with lots of good
  wackin'

"Get back!" I yelled out when my trap was
  complete,
And Ivy somersaulted right over the creep.

My circle sprang up, entrapping him surely,
Al fussed and he fumed, like a demonic fury.

The neighbors all cheered, and came out of
  their houses,
Where they'd watched the whole thing, like
  little house mouses.

So Ivy and I, we both bowed real low,
Then banished Big Al, in an overdone show.

But I heard Al exclaim, 'ere he poofed
  from our sight
"You won this time, witch, but I'll get
  you one night!"

All entrants can be seen at the Witch Weekly *website.*

THE BOOK CORNER

This month's reading:

The Book Corner
with
Ms. Eloise Kinder

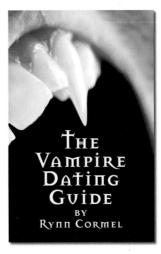

*R*ynn Cormel. He's best known as our unofficial president during the Turn, fighting to regain rights for Inderlanders, both living and undead, even after the successful assassination attempt took his life. His efforts in Washington and abroad kept the United States intact through the nightmarish four years the Turn encompassed. He will always be remembered as the man who announced to the world that the varied Inderland species existed. But we at Witch Weekly *think that perhaps his true legacy is his* Vampire Dating Guide.

I had a wonderful chance to spend the day with Rynn Cormel at his Washington hideaway as he took a break from his new duties as Cincinnati's head vampire. What I found was an amazing man of hidden talents and a sex appeal that didn't quit. Here now is a rare look into the thoughts behind the writing of his bestselling Vampire Dating Guide.

EK: *The Vampire Dating Guide* is unquestionably a marvelous collection of do's and don'ts, not to mention the graphic how-to section. All and all, it was a wonderful, titillating read that also sometimes scared me. My first question is, Why? Why did you take the time out of your busy political schedule to write such a complete guide for the undead and the soon-to-be undead?

RC: It was, as I saw it, a necessity. The world was falling apart. Humans were scared, not only because of the plague that was decimating their numbers, but because the people who were surviving were, in their eyes, "monsters." There was also a lot of confusion from the vampire public as well. A huge amount of freedom had fallen before them, and there was a real danger that, drunk on the new acceptance of who and what they were, individuals might turn into the monsters that humanity imagined us to be.

Information, I thought, had to be the key to finding our new balance. Knowledge crushes fear, promotes understanding. Then, when one of my nieces came to me, frustrated that her

VAMPIRE TURN-OFFS

Smell of old blood.

Indifference.

THE BOOK CORNER

VAMPIRE TURN-ONS

Showing interest in my family history.

Eating crunchy things with me.

Mingling our scents by wearing my clothes, or laundering them together.

Following me to continue an argument when I leave the room.

The smell of your fear.

The smell of your adrenaline.

The smell of your blood.

new boyfriend kept sending her the wrong signals and was creating havoc in her, the idea to write down a list of do's and don'ts took shape. From there, the rest followed, slowly evolving into what you see today on the shelf.

EK: Have you gotten fan letters?

RC: I do, mostly from living vampires who don't have the decades that the undead have to hone their skills at controlling their instincts. Many of them thank me for helping them create peace in their household. Humans have a huge capacity to push a living vampire's buttons, most of the time not even realizing it, and the information in the guide helps prevent accidents and bruised feelings. What I think is amazing is that the same information used to prevent trouble can also be used lovingly and in a responsible manner to heighten the sexual aptitude of a human to where he or she can satisfy their living vampire

partner in ways that they otherwise couldn't. Like all knowledge, what's in the book is a two-edged sword.

EK: Along those same lines, has there been any backlash from rivals for you telling humans their secrets? As you say, vampires have clear and obvious turn-ons that cross gender lines and encompass your entire species. They can be made to be used against you in the wrong hands.

RC: Making sensitive information such as this public is, of course, a risk, and at first there were quite a few lawsuits that were then dropped when it was realized there was far more good being accomplished than bad. The book was actually banned for a time, relegated to brown packaging and underground distributions. Many of the older vampires complained that it was too one-sided, until I worked with several of their scions to include more detailed and ex-

TO HELP ME CONTROL MY INSTINCTS

Citrus, which blocks my ability to smell you.

Fresh air, to get rid of the pheromones.

Calm attitude, especially when arguing.

Awareness of what pushes my hunger, and avoiding it.

If you are afraid, meet my eyes as if you are not.

Trust me.

THE BOOK CORNER

plicit listings of how to keep the more frail humans alive through the most exquisitely erotic bloodletting deemed legal, and still have them begging for more.

EK: I understand you have come under some fire for these more graphic chapters by more conservative groups. What can you tell us about that?

RC: I've had no complaints directed at me, personally.

EK: I'd like to take the time to say thank you, Mr. Cormel, for this lovely insight into your thoughts, but before I leave, I'd like to ask what's next for you? Can we expect another book in your future?

RC: It has been my pleasure chatting with you, as well, Eloise. I have no plans to write anything more right now. I've recently taken on a dear friend's camarilla when he passed unexpectedly, and I find, very surprisingly, that the intricacies of helping run a city are far more complex than running an entire nation. But perhaps if there's another evolutionary jump of vampire ahead, where we learn how to keep our souls after our first death, I could be persuaded to pick up pen and ink again.

Excerpts from The Vampire Dating Guide *are used here with permission and may not be reproduced or distributed without a formal agreement from Vampiric Awareness Manuscript Publishing (VAMP).*

TOP TEN SIGNS
YOU'RE IN THE HOLLOWS

1 A witch, a living vampire, and a pixy live in the church down the street.

2 No need to hide your tomato fetish.

3 The higher up you are in the company, the lower the floor. (It's not the corner office, but the corner crypt.)

4 Your pizza delivery guy gets hazard pay.

5 Cookies aren't just baked goods, and brimstone is a recreational drug, not a religious punishment.

6 Bank hours run past midnight, and magic books are in the self-help section.

7 Songs have more than one track to listen to, depending on your species.

8 The local pest control specializes in exorcisms.

9 The stray dog wandering the neighborhood has a cell phone strapped to his paw and is probably playing hooky.

10 Flowers are arranged in anti-black-magic hexes, basketball hoops are a third taller than NBA regulation, and basement windows are often bricked over.

The Hollows Gazette

Ice Rink Open Again **C 2**
Hospital Workers Could Strike **C 3**
Start April's Taxes Now **C 7**
Almanac **C 8**

Wednesday, January 2, 2008

LOCAL / STATE

C

The Way I See It
Devin Crossman

JUSTICE! MORGAN SHUNNED

Though not in custody, city trouble-maker Rachel Morgan has been served notice, and in a big way. The witch has been shunned by the coven of moral and ethical standards. No longer able to purchase the materials to create her spells and mischief, Morgan is slowly losing the privileges of society, ranging from riding the bus to getting a cup of coffee at her favorite coffeehouse. If she continues her ways, she will be sentenced to Alcatraz. And I say it's about time.

Before you think me harsh, let me illuminate. I've watched this woman for over a year, beginning when her "spell-gone-awry" denuded me of my hair while on the bus.

Her actions in the last 19 months are astounding, ranging from her involvement in the death of master vampire Piscary to a tragic car accident in Mackinaw City that left an ex-boyfriend dead. She was questioned in the death of another boyfriend, who was murdered twice in quick succession just last year. Neither the FIB nor the I.S. filed charges.

Morgan has wrongly accused Kalamack of murder twice, arrested him once, and was on the boat that blew up under him December 07. I say beware, Mr. Kalamack, of the Morgan Black Widow. Her history speaks for itself.

@ A Glance Jan 2, 2008		
Average High/Low: 40° / 25°		
	Today	Tomorrow
Sunrise	7:57 AM	7:58 AM
Sunset	5:27 PM	5:27 PM
Moonrise	2:47 AM	3:48 AM
Moonset	1:03 PM	1:32 PM
Phase: waning half		
SEE ALMANAC C 8		

FIRE AT FOUNTAIN SQUARE

By Gary Brown
gmbrown@hollowsgazette.com

Cincinnati's traditional closing of Fountain Square circle turned tragic this year when a fire broke out on the stage during the event.

Fire trucks quickly arrived, and no one was injured, but investigations are under way to determine the cause of the incident.

Foul play is expected, and rumors that a rare species of Inderland, the banshee, is to blame, have the I.S. concerned.

"We have a very small, stable population of banshees in the city," Officer Denon Gradey said when questioned. "They are all good girls, and we have nothing to fear from them. It's when a young banshee tries to move in on another's territory that problems like this happen."

It's believed that the encroaching banshee was at the festival soaking up the ambient emotions when a local banshee attacked, starting the fire to cover her actions.

See Blaze **C 8**

Little remains to show last night's damage thanks to work crews

Carew Tower Party Tops Them All

By Winifred Gradenko
winniegrad@hollowsgazette.com

Cincinnati's university elite partied in the new year with style at the top of Carew Tower to the sounds of big band music and the clinking of champagne glasses. Among those on the invite list were university benefactor Trent Kalamack, who recently donated funds to overhaul the floundering nuclear transplant wing at UC.

Also present was Rachel Morgan from Vampiric Charms—though not in an official capacity—adding fuel to the question everyone's been asking: Did Kalamack leave Seattle socialite Ellasbeth Withon at the altar for childhood sweetheart Rachel Morgan?

Though the two shared no more than a cursory conversation, Kalamack was seen leaving shortly after Morgan left—both missing the year's beginning countdown—perhaps seeking privacy for a New Year's kiss?

See Party **C 8**

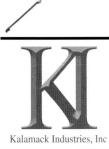

Kalamack Industries, Inc

Trenton A. Kalamack
CEO Kalamack Industries
Kalamack Industries, Inc
Building A
15 Rolling Acres
Cincinnati, OH 45239

I N T E R O F F I C E   M E M O

To: Quen Hansen
From: Trenton Kalamack
CC:
Date: 1/4/08
Re: Devin Crossman

Quen, I have a meeting with Jon tonight after hours. Will you please listen in? I'm concerned that he's harboring an agenda of his own that runs contrary to mine. His attitude, though always bad, has changed since he helped me prep the Pandora charm for Morgan. He thinks I'm falling for her, as ridiculous at that sounds, and he might be tempted to take matters into his hands.

Also, is there any more information concerning Crossman's hard drive? His article attacking Morgan is thankfully free of my name, apart from a cautionary warning, but Maria at the paper is giving him free rein as long as he keeps it free of outright slander. I'm concerned that adding the proof of demon texts in Morgan's kitchen will be Crossman's tipping point. Perhaps we can arrange a face-to-face, or would that, in your opinion, only force a complete breakdown of the status quo?

Regards,

Trent

Kalamack Industries, Inc

Quen Hansen
Chief Security Officer
Kalamack Industries, Inc.
Building A
15 Rolling Acres
Cincinnati, OH 45239

I N T E R O F F I C E   M E M O

To: Trenton Kalamack
From: Quen Hansen
CC:
Date: 04/11/08
Re: Hard Drive Information

Sa'han,

Crossman's hard drive has shipped. My sources say that there was a full recovery of data. I'll do my best to intercept, but I'd like to schedule a time to discuss what steps you wish to be taken under various scenarios. Unfortunately, after watching this man for over two years, I'm of the belief that Crossman cannot be bought or scared, and will feel it's his responsibility to make the public aware of his findings at all costs.

You are not your father, Trent, and your decisions, though possibly having a similar result, do not spring from the same place.

Quen

Kalamack Industries, Inc

April 11, 2008

Ms. Maria Gonzalez
Senior Editor
Hollows Gazette
Hollows, KY, 41011

Dear Maria,

Has it really been a year since we discussed a possible scholarship program for the families of your employees over lunch? Are you free this week? I'm embarrassed to say this, but I'm looking for a tax break, and I need a decision fairly quickly.

I'm thinking Carew Tower restaurant, unless you have an aversion to heights.

All the best,

Trent Kalamack

Trent Kalamack

4/13/2008

Trenton A. Kalamack
CEO Kalamack Industries
Kalamack Industries, Inc.
15 Rolling Acres
Cincinnati, OH 45239

Dear Trent,

It's wonderful to hear from you, and of course I'm available to discuss a scholarship for my employees' children and immediate family. Carew Tower is fine. I will bring the paper's lawyer and one of my best reporters in the hopes I can lure you into another interview. The one you gave last year was a welcome boost to our circulation. I look forward to getting everything finalized by dessert.

All my very best regards,

Maria

Ms. Maria Gonzalez • Senior Editor • Hollows Gazette • Hollows, KY 41011

Devin's
Journal
Entry

April 16, 2008

And so my faith in the system fails. Am I the only one seeing what's going on here? Morgan finally gets herself shunned, and then, because she begs for clemency with some bogus claim of being tricked into making black magic, they pat her on her head and forgive her? Maybe it's because she showed off her goodies on national TV. It sure in hell is something.

What do I get when I try to inform the public? My original story cut and told it's slanderous. It's a disgrace. I'm keeping my original article, and by God, I'm going to get it published if I have to cram the evidence down their throat.

Yesterday, I packed up everything I've collected the last two years and went to the I.S. with it. I waited three hours before I got in to see some creepy vampire guy. He kicked me out after twenty minutes and told me they were aware of the situation and to leave it in their hands. They were "handling" it.

Handling it?! Right. More like shoving it under the rug because they're afraid of her. Or Kalamack, maybe.

Morgan has them all in her back pocket. Every last one of them. And that coven guy . . . Oliver. When I saw him at Fountain Square, he was ready to take her to Alcatraz. An hour later, he's on TV granting her a stay of shunning. Bull crap. It's all bull crap. They want Morgan put away, and put away now. They're just scared.

The _Gazette_ fact sheet that I picked up on the coven wasn't any help beyond a who's-who playbook, but these six witches are supposed to be the best we've got. Why can't they take Morgan down?!

It's not like they haven't tried. Their fairy hit-squad failed to touch her, so they simply snatched her. Dumped her in Alcatraz where she belongs. She was out in 24 hours and gone, laughing at them. No one has escaped Alcatraz since the Turn. She's got to be using the help of a demon. Has to.

What ticks me off is that I've been collecting criminal evidence on her for over two years, and no one will listen to me. Not Maria, not the FIB, not the I.S. And it isn't as if I'm not trying!

That Detective Glenn I talked to at the FIB last week just kept yammering on about how it wasn't gathered legally, and therefore was inadmissible as evidence, and to get out of his office. I'd go over his head, but his captain is the one who gave Morgan the car she smashed up when the coven summoned her to Alcatraz.

And that's another thing. How can you summon a witch? I'm starting to think she's a demon, not a witch at all. Maybe Kalamack senior tinkered with her DNA to make her more powerful, not just survive. Now, he's dead, and his son is trying to get control? Just take her out and be done with it!

I finally tracked down the e-mail of her ex-boyfriend, Nick Sparagmos—the one that supposedly went over the Mackinac Bridge. He goes by the name 753INS when online. He refused to talk to me when I contacted him by e-mail. I think it's because he's scared of Morgan. He's so scared that he turned down TWICE my usual payment for information—then drops out of cyberspace. I'll never find him again. I got lucky with the runner's pass from the zoo. I don't blame him for wanting to disappear if his ex-girlfriend is dabbling in demon magic.

Though I'm usually not this paranoid, I printed out our correspondence in case I lose everything again.

From: 7531NS
Subject: Re: **Upcoming Hollows Gazette Article**
Date: December, 11, 2007; 1:17 a.m.
To: Devin Crossman

Are you really that stupid? Rachel Morgan is dangerous. She has dangerous friends. She has even more dangerous enemies, and they are the ones who will take offense and give you a plot in Spring Grove, not a Pulitzer. Don't get me involved.
--NS

In a message dated December 10, 2007; dcrossman@hollowsgazette.com
mailto:devin@hollowsgazette.com **writes:**

Dear Mr. Sparagmos.
My apologies again. I didn't mean to insult you. Obviously you still care about the woman, and I'm sorry. If we could talk, I'm sure you could impress me with the good in her. Can we meet at Fountain Square during lunch hour tomorrow? The water will cover any chance of our conversation being overheard. My standard payment for information is 1,000.00 dollars for an hour of your time, and I'm prepared to double it in this case.
Best regards,
Devin

In a message dated December 10, 2007; 7531NS@B0L.com **writes:**

You've got the wrong man, Mr. Crossman. I find your Inderlander slurs disturbing and what you're doing to Rachel reprehensible. Stop emailing me. It's not that I can't help you, but I won't.

In a message dated December 9, 2007; dcrossman@hollowsgazette.com **writes:**

Dear Mr. Sparagmos.
My apologies. I should have been more forthright with someone smart enough to play dead with the I.S. and FIB. I'd still appreciate your help in this matter, and I'm prepared to pay handsomely for your time. Your choice of time and location. I have never given up a source before, and I don't intend to start now. We humans have to stick together.
Best regards,
Devin

Speaking about losing things, I finally got all the pictures of Morgan's "cookbooks" back from the data recovery place. Those old books under her counter in the middle of her kitchen are demon. I printed them out. All of them. And as soon as I compare them to the legal definition of demon magic I got from the paper, I'm going to shove them down Detective Glenn's throat. And if that doesn't do it, I've got the list of Latin words in Morgan's handwriting.

The paper's fact sheet on demon magic says that if you mix earth and ley line magic, you've got demon. I'm no expert, but that's what these books look like they're doing. As if the need for demon blood isn't enough of a clue.

I'm so close on this, I can taste it! I'm going to get a damned Pulitzer! I just need to get someone to listen to me.

Words I've Used to Set Candles

Al used: _Salax_—lust, _Aemulatio_—jealous rivalry, _Adflictatio_—suffering, _Cupidus_—greedy, _Inscitia_—stupidity.

I've used:

In fidem recipere—protection	_Septiens_—seven times
Traiectio—transference	_Libertas_—status of a free man
Obsignare—seals the curse	_Fidelitas_—loyalty
Adaequo—to make equal	_Probitas_—honesty
Me auctore—at my suggestion	_Diligentia_—diligence
Lenio—to soften	_Fides_—trust
Iracundia—quick anger	_Necare_—murder
Evulgo—to publish	_Animi motus_—passion
Alius—another	_Sempiternus_—unending
Ipse—myself	_Explicatio_—unfolding
Rogo—I am asking	
Mutatis mutandis—things to be changed	
Ex cathedra—from the office of authority	

Three Phrases I've Used to Unlock Doors

Quod est ante pedes nemo spectat—No one sees what's before them.
Quis custodiet ipsos custodes?—Who guards the guards?
Nil tam difficile est quin quaerendo investigari possit—Nothing is so difficult it can't be found by looking.

<u>Abrie</u>–Brooke used this to get rid of Al. Means depart or go.
<u>Finire</u>–Ceri used this on Quen and it knocked him out. To finish or die.

<u>Rhombus</u>–magician's circle. My trigger word for a circle.
<u>Omnia mutantur</u>–part of a transfer curse. All things change.

<u>Sunt qui discessum animi a corpore putent esse mortem. Sunt erras</u>–There are those who think the departure of the soul from the body is death. They are wrong. Used this in Al's soul curse, the bastard. I'm still mad at him about that.

<u>Dilatare</u>–I heard Vivian use this. It's white. It makes an explosive bubble of air. It means to expand.
<u>Celero dilatare</u>–to quicken, to expand.
<u>Interrumpere</u>–break up or sever. Black magic. Pierce used this to break a circle.
<u>Animam agere efflare</u>–black magic. Pierce used this. Breathe one's last?
<u>Accendere</u>–Ceri used this. It's black magic. It burns living things. It's not a curse, but it's black. Means to set on fire.

<u>Adaperire</u>–Al used this to unstick a drawer. It unzipped my pants, too. Means to throw open.
<u>Glomerare</u>–conglomerate.
<u>Flagro</u>–to be on fire.
<u>Esse</u>–to be.
<u>Corpus</u>–body.
<u>Negare</u>–no.
<u>In eo est</u>–It has come to this.
<u>Lenio cinis</u>–light charm. Burn softly.

Qui dicitur—so called.

Doleo—Lee used this on me. Caused a lot of pain.

Si qua bella inciderint, vobis auxilium feram—I finally looked this up. It means something like, If any wars befall you, I will bring help. Cool...

Si peccabas, poenam meres—If you did wrong, you should be punished.

Facilis descensus tartaros—The descent to hell is easy.

Quid me fiet—demon doppelganger curse. Means what will become of me. It's a glamour, not real.

Adsimulo calefacio—Al used this to warm a silver knife. To compare, to heat.

Detrudo—Al used this on David. Knocked him for a loop. Means push down.

Vacuefacio—Singed David's fur. Curse? Means to empty or clear.

Celero inanio—Breaks bone with heat. Auras block it. To make empty.

Celero fervefacio—Heats water. Watch the control. To quicken and boil.

Corrumpo—Newt used this to take down Ceri's circle. Break up, ruin.

Non sum qualis eram—I am not who I used to be. I've seen this/used this a lot.

Infelix—Lee used it to bring me bad luck. Unhappy or infertile. Black charm.

Animum recipere—Transfer curse.

Malum—Not sure. I've heard Newt say it. I think it's a swear word.

Ita prorsus—Think this means, "just so." Used to make a circle.

Leviter—Pretty sure this means newbie.

Abyssus abyssum invocat—Used this to invoke a public spell from the collective when making a demon mark. Translates to Hell calls Hell. Nice.

The Hollows Gazette

SUBMISSION SHEET

For salaried employees only.
Freelance, please use submission
form FL16008B.

SUBMITTED BY:	Devin Crossman
TITLE OF ARTICLE:	Courts Corrupted
PROPOSED RUN DATE:	Wednesday, April 16
CHARACTER COUNT:	1040 w/spaces

Much to my shame, it seems that the corruption haunting the halls of the I.S. tower has taken root in my own beloved FIB as both factions of our judicial system are now kowtowing to the demands of one Rachel Morgan, demon practitioner and black magic user.

Hours after appearing naked in Fountain Square sobbing a story of manipulation and "I'm a good girl," Rachel Morgan has forced not only the FIB and the I.S. to drop their joint claims of criminal activity, but also blackmailed the coven of moral and ethical standards to "rethink" their decision of shunning the wrongdoing witch on the claim she was "testing the security system of Trent Kalamack." Testing it, no less under the auspices of the very coven who shunned her.

And yes, this is the same Council-man Trent Kalamack whose life keeps tangling with Morgan with claims of wrongdoing, misappropriation of public funds, and murder trailing along behind them like happy puppies.

Corruption in our public service systems indeed, or possibly black magic twisting the thoughts and memories of those pledged to protect us?

We may never know, now that her shunning is scheduled to be permanently revoked at the next yearly witches' meeting in San Francisco.

I was as shocked as you when Morgan leapt upon the stage in Fountain Square, flaunting her nakedness before the entire TV-watching nation. Her cry of "spare me" rang clear—and false in my mind. Perhaps the politics are too deep for me to fathom, but the more likely cause is that it's not politics, but blackmail.

Checked By: __Randy Traxton__ Date __4/15/08__

Comments _Trim it. Also, I'm not okaying this until you take out or substantiate every hint of slander. On a more personal note, you need to stop grinding this ax. You're pissing off the wrong people. Kalamack does a lot of good for the city. You seem bent on destroying it. —RT_

Hollows Gazette Fact Sheets

INTERNAL FACT SHEET

Document Shepherd: Cindy Strom (513) 555-7735 ext 7
Updated 8/07

The Coven of Moral and Ethical Standards

WHO THEY ARE

MADAM BROOKE: Eldest member. Currently missing. Ley line master.

SIR OLIVER: Expert in earth magic. Single-handedly held the West Coast together during the Turn.

SIR WYATT: Middle ley line user. Solved the Syerans knot and prevented the deaths of thousands in the early '80s.

MADAM AMANDA: Middle earth witch whose expertise is in transformations.

MADAM VIVIAN: Junior ley line user, said to be able to use white magic to kill, making her a plumber of note.

SIR LEON: Junior earth magic user. Newest member of the coven.

It's important to remember that Inderland politics have been interwoven with humanities for almost all of our joined history, and only recently has there been a "them and us" mentality.
—RYNN CORMEL, WINTER 1968

There's a long tradition for the varied Inderland species to police themselves, a policy began before the Turn as a way to keep troublemakers from revealing their joint existence. It would be foolish to think that there are no secrets kept from humanity, even today, but for the most part, Inderland politics and police procedures are out in the open for scrutiny.

One of the largest bodies of decision makers in Inderland society is the coven of moral and ethical standards. This small group of six people is elected by the witch community. It's generally a lifetime post, changes to the membership being made at the witches' annual meeting in San Francisco. The highly coveted positions are part judge and part enforcer, carefully chosen to balance sex, age, and skills.

Most coven members train for the position from birth, much as an Olympic athlete. Entry to the coven is usually accomplished at the junior

INTERNAL FACT SHEET

THE COVEN OF MORAL AND ETHICAL STANDARDS

position, but oral history claims that during the dark period of the American and European witch trials, older, less experienced witches stepped into top vacant positions to maintain a balance of age and skills.

The coven of moral and ethical standards comprises two senior positions (100–160 years old), two middle (60–100), and two junior (20–60), each composed of a male/female pair, one earth magic, the other ley line.

The senior witches are the primary decision makers, though everyone has an equal say when matters require a vote. The middle two members are responsible for the clerical, day-to-day business of handling complaints. They're also responsible for deciding where to send the youngest set of coven members. It's the newest members who are responsible for investigating claims and enforcing decisions. Often called plumbers, they can spend up to several decades traveling the U.S., developing their already considerable skills and meeting their constituents.

The coven as a whole is responsible for taking in and reporting information to the general body of witches, who will then request changes in the laws to better serve the needs of a constantly evolving society.

There have recently been serious charges that this system of six "ruling" members is outdated and should be abolished for a more conventional system based upon the current U.S. democracy system of two houses and joint decision making on a regional level. Much of the complaints come from humans. Most witches are content with the present system and see no reason to change something that has worked for thousands of years, claiming that it's easier to watch six people than three dozen.

Though the coven holds sway over only a fraction of Inderland society, its decisions reach far wider, since it's witch magic that protects, enables, and keeps much of Inderland functioning.

When addressed, coven members are correctly referred to by the honorific of "Madam Coven Member" or "Sir Coven Member." If an identifying name must be used, it's traditional to use given names. Surnames are generally abandoned when taking on a coven position to symbolize the cutting of family loyalties and taking on those of society.

For more information, contact:
Dr. Pandorn
Professor of Human Studies
University of Cincinnati
Cincinnati, OH 45221
513-555-2440 (ext 77)

INTERNAL FACT SHEET

Document Shepherd: Cindy Strom (513) 555-7735 ext 7
Updated 8/06

Demons: What They Can and Can't Do

AT A GLANCE

WHO THEY ARE: Long-lived beings who use a mix of ley line and earth magic to perform extraordinary deeds. They can be summoned to perform tasks or impart knowledge. The summoner has a good chance of being abducted or killed.

WHERE THEY LIVE: Banished to the ever-after when a curse aimed at destroying the elves twisted wrong and marooned them. They are pulled back there when the sun rises.

IS IT LEGAL? Though it is not illegal to summon demons, it should be. Demons willingly come to reality to perform tasks with the blatant intent to trick or outright snatch people into serving as slaves in the ever-after.

Demons are one of the most feared and mysterious species of Inderland, if indeed this powerful species is Inderland in origin. There has never been a consensus on what demons actually look like since the same individual has been known to appear in different guises, tailored to cause the most fear in their summoner. Large dogs, shrouded images of death, mythical dragons, and even British noblemen are popular images.

It's not known how many demons exist since only those whose names have been recorded through the ages are ever summoned. It's believed that the population is slowly declining, and maybe as few as several thousand exist.

Demons originally created the ever-after as a bubble of time to capture and destroy the elven population. The creation of the curse required the participation of the entire demon population and resulted in the depletion of the ley lines that existed at that time. The remnants of these ancient ley lines can still be sensed in the American desert.

Fortunately, the demons scribed new ley lines into existence when

INTERNAL FACT SHEET

DEMONS: WHAT THEY CAN AND CAN'T DO

they abandoned the elves to the ever-after, but in doing so, they accidently bound themselves to the reality they created; and they are therefore pulled back into it when the sun rises and the tide of energy flows from reality to the ever-after.

Though the elves were not bound to this ever-after reality, they remained, continuing to fight demons until finally abandoning the ever-after about two thousand years ago.

It's now believed that the demons who exist today are the same who created the ever-after. No new demons have been born to replace them, because the entire species was cursed with infertility by the elves shortly before the demons tried to kill them. It's surmised that demons are not naturally long-lived, but that they continually reset their biological clock with magic.

There are many recorded instances of people summoning demons in the hopes of gaining knowledge. The practice still goes on today, though it's usually in the realm of black magic practitioners.

Both the I.S. and FIB ignore most instances of demon summoning because eventually the summoner grows careless and is abducted into the ever-after to serve as a demon's familiar. There's no recorded instance of a demon's familiar ever escaping or being granted release.

For more information, contact:
Dr. Anders
Professor of Ley Line Studies
University of Cincinnati
Cincinnati, OH 45221
513-555-2440 (ext 71)

Demon Curses

Curse to Run as the Wolf
Suitable for use upon oneself or another

Hearth flame
Transformation pentacle
Lock of hair from victim or self to show agreement
Wolfsbane
Blessed candle
Small vessel
Ceremonial knife
Scribing substrate, human ash (for nonself use), salt, chalk
Water
Demon blood
Word of invocation: <u>Lupis</u>
Word to break curse: <u>Non sum qualis eram</u>

This is a standard morphing curse. Average prep time is 30 minutes. Yield is one potion, but it may be safely batched for personal use. Smut is minimal.

Implantation: Take internally as potion. Splash or amulet implementation has a high probability of disturbing results.

Implementation

Weave lock of hair into braided loop designed to connect donor to curse.

Sketch a pentacle of transformation with human ash.

Burn the ring of hair within the pentacle using standard burn curse.

Move ash to small ceremonial pot using ceremonial knife.

Mix ash with crushed wolfsbane and roughly 10 cc of water. Warm over blessed candle lit from a hearth fire until scent of brimstone arises. Mix will be lukewarm and have a red sheen.

Add three drops of demon blood to kindle curse.

Take internally. Imperative for safety if self-administered.

Create connection to ley line before invoking with phrase Lupus

Curse is broken by counterphrase, Non sum qualis eram.

Notes

1st note: Victims retain their intelligence, heightening the degradation you can put them through. Changes go to genetic level so any offspring engendered while transformed will be Weres, extending the shame of the victim. Nice benefit.

2nd note: Need new stock of candles. Archimedes' weren't really blessed, the fucking bastard. The bitches died before I had a chance to torment them properly.

3rd note: Ceri can prep ten of these before breakfast.

4th note: Salt can be substituted for ash if you're not going to rape them, but making them dig up their dead is s-o-o-o-o much more satisfying. It's the DNA ash that is utilized for creating a second genome for a viable offspring. Brats from sex with victim will not have demon DNA, but a mix of victim's and the person they got the ash from.

5th note: Seriously, don't use amulets for this one. The one time I tried, the amulet slipped in a most delicate place of our arrangement, and the bitch died of shock before I could properly finish.

6th note: The hardest part is getting the blessed candles.

Transference Curse

Suitable for use shifting sentient curses from
one situation to another.

Storage item: bone works best, living bodies better
Lock of practitioner's hair, knotted
to show intent and joining of will
Four candles: white, black, gray, and one
to represent practitioner's aura
Drop of demon blood

Substrate to sketch circles: salt, chalk, or ash
Invocations to set candles
Invocation to transfer curse

This curse is used to sentient curses from their original container to a living body. Average prep time is 20 minutes. Yield is one curse.

Implantation: Use immediately.

Smut is minimal.

Implementation

Scribe three interlocking circles to create seven individual spaces using salt, chalk, or preferably ash.

Within first space, place the item that presently contains the curse.

Within the second space, place the item that will contain the curse. If the item is too large, such as a person, and space is at a premium, set a knotted and looped bit of hair or other body part to create a connection.

Within the third space, place a knotted and looped bit of hair of the practitioner as a symbol of his will within the curse.

Place and light a white candle into the fourth space with the words *In fidem recipere* (protection).

Set and light a black candle in the fifth space with the word _Traiectio_ (transference).

Place and light a candle in the sixth place with the word _Obsignare_ (binds or seals). The candle color should represent the practitioner's aura.

Place an unlit gray candle within the seventh place. It will spontaneously light at end of the curse if done correctly.

Scribe the symbol for transference within the seventh space using your blood, and anoint the gray candle with the excess.

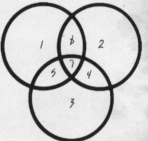

Close the circles with ley line energy.

Move the curse with the words _Animum recipere_.

Notes

I've found through trial and error that the white candle goes out when the curse is pulled from the original container. The black candle goes out when you refuse to let the curse settle within yourself. The final candle goes out when the curse is within its new owner. The gray candle lights when the curse is sealed within its new prison. If it doesn't go out, there's a problem, and you need to prepare to capture the sentient curse before it tries to take you over.

Scribing a Calling Circle

Suitable for repeated use in connecting
to the demon collective.

Scrying mirror
Stylus of yew, preferably from over a grave
Ceremonial knife
Silver snips (to cut lock of hair)
Sea salt
Local wine
Connecting glyphs

This curse allows a greater and easier access to the
demon collective at the cost of being eavesdropped
upon while doing it. It also allows the user to tap into
communal curses upon dire need.

Average prep time is 20 minutes. Yield is one curse.
Smut is minimal.

Implantation: Use immediately.

Implementation

Set a protective circle about yourself and your working
area to prevent loss of aura or introduction of
nefarious sources while vulnerable.

Prepare wine with at least three drops of blood, pricked

from yourself using a ceremonial knife. A glass of wine is sufficient for a small mirror, a pint for a larger one.

Scribe a basic pentagram within a circle using a yew stylus upon a clean and spell-free scrying mirror. For a more anonymous connection, scribe the outer circle around the pentagram with a second circle for a second spell layered upon this one.

Beginning in the lower left point and rising clockwise, scribe the symbols of communication, one at each point, again using the yew stylus.

Power should rise with each glyph, and you will feel your aura spill into the mirror.

Once glyphs are scribed, salt the mirror to balance the energies and remove your excess intent. Wash the unused salt from the mirror with wine and blood mix.

Set the glyphs into the mirror using *Ita prorsus.*

Finish invoking by touching wine-wet finger to lip to show connection and intents. For a more private connection, scribe nuisance symbols between the two outer circles. It is advisable to wait a period of no less than 24 hours before modifying a newly scribed calling circle.

Notes

1st note: The glyphs are actually pictorial representations of the hand gestures used to connect to the collective without the mirror. I've used the symbolic hand gestures to connect to the collective, and it's a damn nuisance. Thank God Newt figured this one out, though it gives me a headache when everyone's in there yammering.

2nd note: Also, I take the time to scribe some anonymity into the circle if I ever have to make a new one again. The outer ring is the ever-after, the inner ring is reality, and the space between is where you put your anonymity symbols. Yammer, yammer, yammer . . .

3rd note: I had Ceri make a basic one of these keyed to me to field my calls. She didn't lose nearly the amount of aura demons do. But maybe that's because she was chickenshit and scribed the glyphs with chalk upon the mirror first, then went over them with the yew.

4th note: And for the Turn's sake, don't forget the protective circle again. Last time I lost half my aura and burned synapses before I realized it and tried to tap a line. It doesn't hurt to slack off the curses for 24 hours, either. God, we're such wusses.

Curse of Illumination

Suitable in the task of exciting ley line energy to a higher
sphere to create light.

Ring of metal
Grapeseed oil
Invocation words
Strand of practitioner's hair
String (optional)
Drop of blood
Ceremonial knife (optional)

This curse allows the practitioner to harness ley line
energy to create a glowing sphere of light.

Average prep time is 10 minutes. Yield is one curse.
Smut is nonexistent.

Excellent for memorization and fast implementation
without curse paraphernalia.

Implementation

Suspend a ring of metal into the air where you want
your light, or let it sit in the floor or through a table.

Coat a strand of hair with grapeseed oil to help reduce
chance of ignition while reciting _In fidem recipere_ to

create a connection between your will and your hair and allow energy to continually flow.

Place strand of hair on metal ring.

Anoint ring with drop of blood to further connection.

Imbue the circle of metal with ley line energy. (Set a circle.)

To invoke the curse, simultaneously say <u>Leno cinis</u> and make the "illuminate" gesture.

This curse requires a continual connection to a ley line, and breaking it will extinguish the light.

Notes

I've found that the light being emitted while using this curse has decreased steadily over the decades, and I've finally attributed it to the slow accumulation of smut on my aura. Simply drawing heavier upon the ley line will adjust for it, but by God, it's depressing, especially since this curse exacts no smut at all.

It used to impress the hell out of potential familiars. Not so much anymore.

Curse to Exchange Summoning Names

Suitable to give an associate the chance to dabble in reality
without damaging the anonymity of his summoning name.
(Make them pay through the ass for it.)

Hearth fire
Ceremonial knife to draw blood
Scribing substrate: salt or ash
Four-sided copper pyramid
Flat stick of redwood, short
Candles: Two needed, representing
the auras of those involved.
Words to set candles: _Alius, Ipse_
Invocation _evulgo_, _Omnia mutantur_

Average prep time is 10 minutes. Yield is one curse.
Smut is moderate.

Implantation: Immediate results.

Cannot be broken and requires duplication of curse
to reverse it.

This curse needs to be registered in the collective to
work.

Implementation

Set a standard protection circle around work area to prevent introduction of unsavories while auras are compromised.

Sketch a Mobius strip as basis for spell structure using ash or salt.

Set copper pyramid where Mobius crosses, and balance redwood stick on top, the length of it running parallel to Mobius figure.

Place-set the candle representing demon taking your name in the loop farthest from you using the word _Alius_. Place-set the candle again by sifting a portion of the substrate used to set outer circle, again using the word _Alius_. Place-set the same candle a third time while lighting it from your hearth fire using the same word a third time.

Repeat the above procedure for the candle representing you, place-setting it three times in the loop closest to yourself using the word _Ipse_.

Anoint the end of the redwood stick with three drops of blood from the demon receiving your name.

Smear excess upon his candle.

Anoint the end of the redwood stick closest to you with three drops of your blood.

Smear excess upon your candle.

Prepare to register the curse in the collective using _Evulgo_. Auras will begin to separate at this time.

Invoke curse by turning redwood stick 180° to show intent, and trigger with words _Omnia mutantur_.

Registered names will be exchanged. Auras will return undiminished.

Notes

Note: I've made a lot from this curse, allowing a jerk-off, pantywaist of an associate the chance to scare the hell out of some poor flop of a human using my name. I've not done this since Pokkflickerange borrowed my name and got circled by some coven member who thought he had the balls to force him to save some lame village. His mistake gave me a bad reputation.

God save me from amateurs.

Curse to Layer Souls Atop Your Own

Suitable for use upon oneself in matters of protection from soul-sucking banshees.

Soul to be layered upon yours, either fresh or bottled
Soul's name in owner's handwriting
Word-transfer bowl
Parchment
Quill
Practitioner's blood
Hearth fire
Water
Ceremonial knife
Words of invocation: <u>Sunt qui discessum animi</u>
<u>a corpora patient esse mortem. Sunt erras.</u>

This is a potentially dangerous curse. Care should be taken to ensure that the donor soul is significantly beaten down before implementation to prevent it from taking over.

Average prep time depends upon skill of practitioner, 30 minutes to several hours.

Yield is one curse. Smut can be substantial depending upon donor soul.

Implantation: Immediate.

Implementation

Scribe the name of the donor soul onto parchment using your blood as ink. The handwriting must match the soul's exactly, or the soul will not be correctly harnessed.

Scribe the name of the donor soul into the inside of the word-transfer bowl, and fill with water to allow liquid to absorb the name.

Set a protection circle to maintain purity of soul while in transfer.

Free the soul by harnessing with the phrase <u>Sunt qui discessum</u> animi a corpora patient esse mortem. <u>Sunt erras.</u>

Harness and control the soul by burning the soul's name with the flame from your hearth fire, and take in the soul's name by water.

Notes

QED. Nice spell. I use it all the time.

The Hollows Gazette

New Fire Regulations **C 2**
Recycling on Upswing **C 3**
Howlers' Howl-Out! **C 3**
Almanac **C 6**

Wednesday, April 16, 2008

LOCAL / STATE

C

The Way I See It
Devin Crossman
dcrossman@hollowsgazette.com

THE DEMONS AMONG US

The FIB knows it. The I.S. knows it. The press hides it because it might impact the reputation of a prominent city official and ruin the career of a popular music artist. And if you think you know who I'm talking about, you're probably right. No one wants to admit it, but demons are among us.

The evidence is clear: a demon called for testimony, another walking Cincy streets at midnight, a third possessing black witches so he can do the same by day. Demons so bold they attack master vampires while in our own FIB buildings.

But there's a worse demon than the ones summoned from the ever-after to torment us, one that's here already, walking the streets unnoticed, one having all the credentials of our society and perhaps still ignorant of what they are, but capable of evil regardless.

I'm talking about day-walking demons, demons born in reality to human or Inderland parents who then raised them as their own, demons only now starting to learn their dark trade.

You might laugh. Until last month, I'd have laughed too. But though I'm blocked from sharing the evidence with you, the evidence is there. Cincy is sitting on a powder keg. The only question now is what are we going to do about it?

@ A Glance April 16, 2008
Average High/Low: 66° / 41°

	Today	Tomorrow
Sunrise	5:59 AM	5:58 AM
Sunset	7:17 PM	7:18 PM
Moonrise	3:54 PM	4:56 PM
Moonset	4:05 AM	4:28 AM
Phase: 3 days to full		

SEE ALMANAC C 6

Kalamack supporters prepare for tomorrow's rally

COUNCILMAN KALAMACK TO RUN FOR MAYOR

By Gary Brown
gmbrown@hollowsgazette.com

Cincinnati councilman Trent Kalamack is following in his late father's footsteps by throwing his hat in the ring for the mayoral seat. The decision to run comes as no surprise to many of Cincinnati's movers and shakers, least of all to the city's current mayor, Marjorie Martson.

"He is welcome to try," Martson said when asked how she felt about the charismatic businessman making a bid for her position. "Managing a city requires a different skill set than running a business. Though we do seem to be invited to all the same parties," she added, laughing as she subtly acknowledged that multibillionaire Kalamack could be a threat.

Supporters of Martson have already begun a grassroots uprising by getting the word out in an attempt to boost the Were voting demographic. Voter reg-

istration for this traditionally quiet but highly political Inderland species has already begun to rise, but inquiries at the

See Voting **C 6**

Pixy Broods Up, Jobless Rate Down

By Winifred Gradenko
winniegrad@hollowsgazette.com

Any kindergartner can tell you, the more black on the fuzzy caterpillar, the colder the winter will be. Unknown to most, pixy newling populations follow a similar pattern.

Truth is stranger than fiction, and as odd as it sounds, three independent studies have been launched at the university

See Pixy Broods **C 6**

Kalamack Industries, Inc

Trenton A. Kalamack
CEO Kalamack Industries
Kalamack Industries, Inc
Building A
15 Rolling Acres
Cincinnati, OH 45239

I N T E R O F F I C E   M E M O

To: Quen Hansen
From: Trenton Kalamack
cc:
Date: 4/16/08
Re: Lunch at Paper

Quen,

Thank you for arranging the final preparations for my lunch with Maria at the *Hollows Gazette*. My new chief personnel officer is not working out as well as I'd hoped, and I appreciate your filling in for the more sensitive duties. Can we arrange about two hours to go over the results of our conversation? I would like your opinion on a few items before I move forward.

Also, arranging for Sara Jane to accompany me in her secretarial capacity was inspired. Seeing Sara Jane with her sister cemented my willingness to seek more employees from the outlying farms. Both women are smart, intelligent, tight-lipped, and loyal to a fault to those who get them out of the misery the farms represent. They are true assets.

Trent

Kalamack Industries, Inc

Quen Hansen
Chief Security Officer
Kalamack Industries, Inc.
Building A
15 Rolling Acres
Cincinnati, OH 45239

INTEROFFICE MEMO

To: Trenton Kalamack
From: Quen Hansen
CC:
Date: 4/18/08
Re: Demon Descriptions

Sa'han,

Here are the demon descriptions that you asked for in regards to your thoughts concerning Morgan's ultimate resolution. I'd like to be able to tell you that there's another way to accomplish this, but the coven's stubbornness and the I.S.'s lack of response leaves you little choice.

Quen

Algaliarept *(AKA Al, Big Al, Gally)*

- This is the demon that Piscary sent to kill you and Rachel two years ago. He's also Ceri's past master, which likely won't work well for us, as Ceri loathes him.

- Most often appears as a tidy British nobleman in a green, crushed velvet coat with tails. Lots of frills and buckles. His appearance is all about show. He has red, goat-slitted eyes and often wears round, blue-smoked glasses. He has dark hair, slightly wavy. Strong facial features, thick, blocky hands, usually covered

I N T E R O F F I C E M E M O

in white gloves. Thick blocky teeth that he shows when he smiles. He speaks in a noble, British accent and is wickedly fast with his curses. He moves with sharp motions and is very unpredictable.

- He has been known to appear as a dog the size of a horse, the Egyptian god of the dead, and upon occasion, Rachel herself.

- I'd advise against trying to deal with Algaliarept, first from the standpoint that he's currently suffering a decrease in resources due to acquiring Rachel. She cost him nearly everything. I feel he's still invested in her, but also that he won't work with you, even to save her. Also, Algaliarept makes his living abducting people to serve as other demons' familiars, and you, Sa'han, have already slipped him twice. He needs the money your sale would put into his coffers.

Newt *(no summoning name, but still able to contact her)*

- Newt is the last female demon in known existence besides Rachel. She is certifiably insane for having been tricked into killing all her sisters and Minias, her caretaker, dosing her into forgetfulness as a way to keep her from killing everyone. Even so, she's in the position of making policy that the other demons will respect out of fear. Newt is the most skilled demon in existence, knowing everything, and remembering little.

- She most often appears as an androgynous female, barefoot, and wearing a tunic that hides any curves or softness. It almost looks like a cross between a monk's robes and an ancient samurai uniform. She usually has no hair, but when she does, it's in a page boy cut. She carries a staff of black wood as tall as her. Her voice is soft and gender neutral. Her chin is pointed, and her eyes are entirely black instead of the red, goat-slitted monstrosities they all have. She's quick to anger and is unpredictable.

I N T E R O F F I C E   M E M O

■ Though she is the "Wendy of the lost boys" in the ever-after, commands respect, and can get things done, Newt is not my first choice. She seems to be fixated on Rachel and knows that the woman is the first demon able to breed true in 5,000 years. She might try to kill Rachel as soon as help her. Though admittedly becoming more lucid lately since killing Minias, I feel the risk of dealing with Newt is too great. I also haven't been able to divulge her summoning name, so you would never, ever, have control of her.

Dallkarackint *(AKA Dali)*

■ Dali is one of the oldest demons in existence. He has marginal influence with Newt, which puts him high up in the demon hierarchy. He's also Algaliarept's parole officer. He's in the position to make policy and has a voice in the courts.

■ Dali has not made an appearance in reality for over two thousand years, but the texts that I've found always have him appearing as a balding, middle-aged, marginally overweight man, confident, domineering, comfortable with himself, and taking no backtalk from those he considers beneath him, which is everyone but Newt. He has the usual red, goat-slitted eyes and seems down to earth in his dealings. He has considerable skill both politically and magically. Dali is the keeper of all the demons' spacial tulpas, showcasing the memories of sundry times and epochs into a "restaurant" that changes scenes as demons purchase the chance to live in them for a time. He's very intelligent and will play dumb to get the better of a situation.

■ On paper, Dali looks ideal as a candidate to work with, but his lack of dealing with people that makes him attractive also makes him less inclined to care. He doesn't need anything you can afford to give him, and I will not let you risk your soul again, Sa'han. Dali might be persuaded to work with you for the

I N T E R O F F I C E   M E M O

good of his race, but I doubt he knows they're in danger yet, and any agree-ment to work with you will be with the sole intent to better his situation to your detriment.

Ku'Sox Sha-Ku'ru *(AKA Ku'Sox, The Eater)*

■ This is a demon that I found in several ancient texts of the American desert. He's currently trapped in our reality under the St. Louis arch (unknowingly built over his prison where the demons in the ever-after placed him). He's said to take the shape of a huge bird that eats people to absorb their souls, but since the information has been handed down verbally through the generations, it's questionable. He also is known to appear as a somewhat tall man wear-ing sophisticated gray clothes, his slate-gray hair straight and cut short. His voice is said to be like razors, cold, sharp, and shiny, with an odd accent. He also has goat-slitted eyes, though they are said to be blue, not red. Thin lips, narrow chin, thick, blocky teeth. He was created by the demons with magic and science in their attempt to break the elven curse that prevents them from procreating, and apparently they were not happy with the results, seeing as they bricked him into the ground in an alternate reality. He's said to have the strength of a female demon, which is daunting, and might explain why they imprisoned him.

■ Ku'Sox might be the best alternative, as it is said that he, unlike other demons, can freely move from the ever-after to reality, even during the day. He clearly has no loyalty to his kin and might be willing to work with you if you free him. I would advise finding either a charm or a piece of blackmail to protect you before trying to contact him, even knowing his summoning name. He has been imprisoned with a curse, and finding the countermagic should be our first step.

Devin's
Journal
Entry

June 16, 2008

Oh. My. God! It was there all the time, and too horrible to consider as being a truth, but she admitted it on TV during her trial on the West Coast.

Morgan is a demon, not a witch.

No one is asking the question yet as to how, but I already know the answer to that one. It has to be the Rosewood syndrome she had. Everyone else who is born with it dies, which is why no one ever noticed it before, but Morgan survived. She is a demon, born not from demons, but witches.

It's almost too scary to believe. I think it was all Kalamack Senior's fault. He saved her through illegal genetic manipulation. But why? He had to know what he was doing. Or was he as oblivious as the rest of us and he was simply helping a friend?

Regardless, that weird relationship Morgan and Trent have makes a lot more sense. She has to know that the Kalamack family dabbles in genetic research, but if she says anything, he tells everyone she's a demon. Genetic manipulation, like murder, stays on the books. And if it gets out, Trent will fry for his father's sins.

I guess Morgan didn't like being blackmailed, because she came out with the truth at the coven's meeting to permanently shun her. Not only did they shun her, but Kalamack—rightfully concerned Morgan might nark on him for his dad's genetic manipulation—banished her with a curse to stay in the ever-after forever with the rest of the demons.

God! I wish I could have been there to see that, but they don't let anyone but witches into the coven meetings. Winnie went. I can't wait to see her face when she reads my article about her beloved

Kalamack family, a family who has dabbled in illegal genetic research to the extent of creating a day-walking, reality-living demon this side of the ley lines. No wonder the coven couldn't catch Morgan. She's a freaking demon!

I've got my evidence all in order and a copy made of my hard drive in case those damned pixies get into it again. I'm mailing everything off to a publisher after lunch today with Winnie. She's finally talking to me again, and we're going to go out tonight. Somewhere nice.

I'm going to put Kalamack into the ground, and a Pulitzer is going to come up, smelling like a rose!

Everyone is going to know my name. I'm like a hero, bringing the last of the perpetrators of the Turn to justice!

Donation Centers Set Up **A 2**
Obituaries **B 4**
Weekend Ahead **E 1**
Almanac **8 C**

Monday, June 20, 2008
Sunrise: 5:12
Sunset: 8:07
High/Low: 85°/62° Sunny

The Hollows Gazette

SERVING THE GREATER CINCINNATI AREA SINCE THE TURN

LOCAL WOMAN SAVES WEST COAST FROM DAY-WALKING DEMON

By Winifred Gradenko
winniegrad@hollowsgazette.com

It's when things are at their worst that our actions show who we truly are: good, bad, the best and worst of the human spirit.

Rachel Morgan—shunned, imprisoned without a trial, and lured to the West Coast with a false hope to redeem herself—has risen above the abuse to save the very people who reviled her in a stunning act of selfless bravery.

The news coming out of the recently demon-devastated San Francisco is still sketchy, but one thing is clear. Rachel Morgan succeeded in a task that claimed the lives of coven member Madam Amanda and Sir Wyatt.

For three days and nights, an unprecedented, day-walking demon has wreaked havoc upon San Francisco, destroying churches and sinking ships. The body count is estimated at several hundred, rising as people emerge from hiding to search the rubble for survivors.

The coven of moral and ethical standards found themselves outclassed earlier this week, unable to stop the day-walking demon from ranging freely, abducting and eating people's bodies and souls as he demanded Morgan to show herself.

Morgan was unable to respond, as she'd been ousted from reality in a rare demonstration of coven-sanctioned elven magic, ending a long-standing controversy that elves exist post-Turn, though greatly reduced in numbers.

When summoned from the ever-after by the coven early Wednesday, Morgan agreed to banish the day-walking demon in exchange for the right to be allowed to return to the sun herself.

The effort nearly cost Morgan her life, but saved thousands as she successfully cursed the demon to remain in the ever-after forever.

Sources at the private hospital who received her broken body say that Morgan was comatose for nearly three days, watched over by her vampire associate Ivy Tamwood and pixy associate Jenks Pixy.

"I guess you [deleted] lunkers ought [deleted] rethink shunning her, huh, you [deleted] backside of a [deleted] idiots," Jenks was quoted when questioned.

Morgan is scheduled to return to Cincy after some much needed R&R and is spending the interim recovering within the West Coast's prominent Saladan family at their resort, accompanied by Cincinnati's councilman Trent Kalamack.

Kalamack had been instrumental in banishing Morgan to the ever-after, an action he publicly apologized for later at a citywide press conference, quickly followed by a tongue-in-cheek offer for Morgan to come work for him.

Morgan was on the West Coast to deny her black witch status and petition for reinstatement as a white witch. She has since withdrawn her petition and filed for white-demon status.

See Demon **A 2**

The Way I See It
Devin Crossman

By Maria Gonzalez
mgonzalez@hollowsgazette.com

FAREWELL TO ONE OF OUR OWN

It's with great regret that I'm writing in Devin Crossman's column today for the last time. Devin recently lost his battle with depression, ending his life before it began. We will miss you, Devin.

See Obituaries **B 6**

San Francisco skate rink damaged by demon

WG

June 20, 2008

Dear Mr. Kalamack,

I'd like to take the opportunity to thank you again for your help the past two years in securing my first job outside of the farm. My sister told me you were a generous man, but I never imagined the satisfaction I could find working a job that allows me the chance to correct injustices, and all with the soft-spoken art of the pen.

This last week has been a trial by fire for me, but I survived—no—prospered with being awarded a column of my own and a place at the paper until I wish to leave it. Security is a wonderful thing, but knowing I have the respect of my colleagues and a chance to better not only my life but those around me as well is truly the prize.

If you ever need anything again—anything, Mr. Kalamack—please don't hesitate to ask.

Forever yours,

Winifred Gradenko

Kalamack Industries, Inc

Quen Hansen
Chief Security Officer
Kalamack Industries, Inc.
Building A
15 Rolling Acres
Cincinnati, OH 45239

I N T E R O F F I C E   M E M O

To: Trenton Kalamack
From: Quen Hansen
CC:
Date: 6/20/08
Re: Miscommunication

Sa'han,

Please accept my deepest apologies over my mishandling of the Crossman affair. I was not clear in my communication, and Ms. Sara Jane went beyond your original intentions and took matters into her own hands when confronted with his plans to go public with sensitive information. Though extreme, her actions did have a positive outcome, and I still feel that your decision to utilize the Gradenko sisters was a good one. Those women are shockingly levelheaded. If I wasn't already deeply committed, I'd be sorely tempted to break with tradition, the genetic pool be damned.

It is not always what we do, Sa'han, but who we love that makes us who we are.

Quen

The End